CHANTRESS FURY

ALSO BY
AMY BUTLER GREENFIELD

Chantress

Chantress Alchemy

A Perfect Red

Virginia Bound

CHANTRESS FURY

A **CHANTRESS** NOVEL

AMY BUTLER GREENFIELD

MARGARET K. McELDERRY BOOKS
NEW YORK LONDON
TORONTO SYDNEY NEW DELHI

MARGARET K. McELDERRY BOOKS † An imprint of Simon & Schuster Children's Publishing Division † 1230 Avenue of the Americas, New York, New York 10020 † This book is a work of fiction. Any references to historical events, real people, or real places are used fictitiously. Other names, characters, places, and events are products of the author's imagination, and any resemblance to actual events or places or persons, living or dead, is entirely coincidental. † † The text for this book is set in Granjon LT. † Manufactured in the United States of America † 10 9 8 7 6 5 4 3 2 1 † Library of Congress Cataloging-in-Publication Data † Greenfield, Amy Butler, 1968– † Chantress fury / Amy Butler Greenfield.—1st edition. † p. cm. † Sequel to: Chantress alchemy. † Summary: "Lucy faces her deadliest enemy yet as mysterious forces flood London"—Provided by publisher. † ISBN 978-1-4424-5711-9 (hardcover) † ISBN 978-1-4424-5714-0 (eBook) † [1. Supernatural—Fiction. 2. Magic—Fiction. 3. Singing—Fiction. 4. London (England)—History—17th century—Fiction. 5. Great Britain—History—Stuarts, 1603–1714—Fiction.] I. Title. † PZ7.G8445Chh 2015 † [Fic]—dc23 † 2014034041

FOR RUTH AND GRACE

Many waters cannot quench love,
neither can the floods drown it. . . .

—Song of Solomon 8:7

† † †

Heav'n has no rage like love to hatred turn'd,
Nor hell a fury like a woman scorn'd.

—William Congreve, *The Mourning Bride*

CHANTRESS FURY

CHAPTER ONE
SHE-DEVIL

I heard the mist before I saw it, a shimmering tune that crept in with the dawn. Rising, I wrapped my mud-stained cloak around me and went to the cracked window. Sure enough, the mid-September sunrise was veiled by wreaths of fog. From the sound of it, it would burn off within the hour—which was just as well, given what we needed to do today.

I turned back to the room. Though it was tiny and dilapidated, its roof hadn't leaked in last night's hard rain, and its mattress had been softer than most. I'd slept well—perhaps too well, for I'd been dreaming when the mist song had woken me, dreaming of Nat. Awake now in this shabby room, I suffered the loss of him all over again.

A gruff call came from the other side of the door. "Chantress?"

I was always called Chantress these days, never Lucy. But if the greeting was formal, the grizzled voice was nevertheless one I knew well. It belonged to Rowan Knollys, former leader of the King's guard, now the trustworthy captain of my own men. I shook my head free of troublesome dreams and lifted the latch.

As always, Knollys's ruddy face gave little away. Only his voice betrayed any sign of strain. "Time we were off."

"I'll meet you outside." I shoved my belongings into my bag, swallowed a quick breakfast of cheese and day-old bread, then made my way down the rickety inn staircase to the stable yard outside.

Most of my men were already there, checking their muskets and saddling their mounts. After more than a year in their company, I knew their moods almost as well as my own. As I strode over to my horse, I could feel tension in the air, as real and thick as the mist. Everyone was all too aware of what lay before us.

Our newest recruit, Barrington, waved at the mist, wide-eyed. "Did you sing that up, Chantress?"

"No," I said. "It came on its own."

Barrington nodded, but I could tell he was disappointed. This was his first journey with us. Unwilling to miss anything, he kept hopeful eyes on me always, even if I was only eating my dinner. Evidently he'd been expecting more magic than he'd gotten so far.

Knollys clapped him on the back. "Never mind, boy. If Lord Charlton doesn't surrender, I warrant you'll hear plenty of Chantress singing before the day's out. Now get on your horse."

That morning's ride pushed me to my limits. Constant practice had made me a skilled horsewoman, but today we were driving ourselves hard. As the mist rose and the footing became clearer, we raced through fields and woods alike.

I had just begun to worry that perhaps we'd lost our way, when Knollys swerved right, going uphill through the woods. Moments later we saw what had brought us here: the wall.

Higher than a man's head, it ran as far as the eye could see, a line of tight-packed gray stone imprisoning a forest of ash and oak. It had been built to intimidate, and even viewed from horseback it was a daunting sight.

I sidled my mare next to it, listening for what I could get, which wasn't much. Stones never wanted to sing to me. But there had been heavy rains this week, so the wall was damp, and water was something I understood. I could hear it humming in the gaps and on the wet surface of the stones themselves.

"So this is Charlton's new park," one of the soldiers said behind me.

"Part of it, anyway," Knollys said. "He's taken the best pasture and meadowlands, too, and a long stretch of the river. The village is in a dire state."

It was an old story, repeated time and again in England: Powerful lords fenced in common lands and called them their own, depriving villagers of their time-honored rights. No longer able to graze a cow or catch eels or cull deadwood for fires, poor villagers starved and froze.

Determined to put an end to these landgrabs, King Henry had outlawed the practice of enclosure a year and a half ago. But Lord Charlton was a great power in this county. He'd continued to build his wall regardless—partly in stone, partly in timber—and he'd repeatedly refused to take it down.

Our assignment was to demolish the wall, by whatever means necessary. First, however, we were supposed to give Charlton one last chance to take it down himself. The King had no desire to appear a tyrant. He had impressed upon us that Charlton must be given every possible opportunity to set matters right.

In most cases, my arrival would have ensured compliance; usually the mere sight of me made rebellious lords crumble. Yet my men and I had doubts about Charlton. Hot-tempered and arrogant, he was reputed to have scoffed at my magic, saying the stories about me were exaggerated. He'd threatened to shoot the next royal messenger on sight.

"Let's approach the castle and see what kind of reception we get," Knollys said. "If you're ready, Chantress?"

I nodded, and we moved off.

Soon we reached the half-abandoned village of Upper Charlton, which lay within sight of the new wall. Nervous faces appeared at the windows as we marched, and a subdued cheer went up when they saw the royal colors, and again when they saw me at the center of a score of soldiers in tight formation. The cheers grew louder as we passed through the village and started up the hill that led to Charlton Castle.

I'd seen the maps and read the reports. Charlton was a redoubtable castle, well-positioned and well-fortified, with a particularly massive gatehouse. The walls of the enclosure led right up to this gatehouse, so that the gate controlled access not only to the castle but to all the land that Charlton had claimed. The front of the gatehouse was further guarded by a half-moat, fed by the local river. Inside, the castle was blessed again by water. A deep well in its keep had allowed it to withstand many a siege. Listening hard as we approached, I could hear both the moat's vigilant melody and the faint, sulky song of the well water.

"Halt!" Knollys cried out. We were only halfway up the hill, still out of musket range, but the gray walls of the gatehouse seemed to tower over us. The gates remained shut, the drawbridge up. There was no sign of welcome.

Knollys picked one of the men to serve as emissary—young Barrington, eager for action—and sent him toward the castle on foot, bearing a white flag to show he was there to parley, not attack.

As soon as Barrington came into range, Lord Charlton's men fired from the gatehouse. A bullet caught the boy just below his helmet; he fell to the ground. Even back where we were, we could see the blood.

"Chantress?" Knollys said, but there was no need. Still in the saddle, I was already singing, honing my anger to a fine edge that worked for me and not against me.

Unrestrained emotion could make a song-spell veer in dangerous ways, yet I needed to maintain a certain flexibility. I didn't command the elements so much as charm and persuade them, and I had to work with the melodies I could hear in the world around me. These changed with the day and the season and the weather and a hundred other factors, so my magic was always a matter of improvisation. I never sang the same song twice.

What suited my purposes now was the sulky tune I'd heard

coming from the bottom of the castle well. There was restlessness there, and resentment. I had only to play on these for a few moments before the water shot up, splintering the well cover and spouting into the sky. As it jetted upward, I felt a fierce pleasure—partly an echo of the water's own relief at being set free, and partly the intoxication of the singing itself, and the power in it.

Yet pleasure too could be a distraction. I needed to focus on the job at hand. Working quickly, I sang some of the fine spray into the castle weaponry and gunpowder, wetting them so they could not fire.

If Charlton's men had put up a flag of truce, that would have been the end of it. But when I finished my song, arrows flew from the windows, landing within a foot of Barrington and the men who had gone to his rescue.

"Get back," I shouted to them. "All of you, get as far back as you can!"

Clamping down on my anger, I turned my attention to the water in the moat. Vigilant it might be, but it was frustrated as well—always on the edge of things, forever locked out. I harped on those notes in my own music, until the moat water rose up as vapor, drenching the walls of the gatehouse. Feeling again a fierce thrill in the singing, I worked the vapor deep into the mortar. Within moments, the mortar softened, and the gatehouse suddenly took on the appearance of a sandcastle in the rain. The foundations bulged. Walls sagged. The parapet collapsed.

I held on just long enough to give Charlton's men a decent chance to flee. Then, with another burst of song, I turned the mortar to liquid. The entire gatehouse peeled away from the castle and rumbled down the hill, a roaring landslide of slick stones and mud. When it stopped, all you could smell was earth, and all you could hear was silence. And then, in the silence, moaning.

Was that Barrington? Or had my landslide taken some of Charlton's men with it? My throat tightened, and the brief pleasure I'd found in the singing disappeared. Even after more than a year of this work, I found some of its consequences hard to handle.

They wanted to kill you, I reminded myself. *And your men*.

With the gatehouse fallen, the castle was wide open to the world. Moving closer to it, Knollys bellowed, "Surrender now, or the Chantress will sing again."

Men appeared at the wide gap in the castle wall, hands over their heads. They watched me as rabbits watch a snake. After divesting them of any remaining weapons, my men tied them up.

"It's treason to shoot at the King's forces," Knollys told them. "But if you cause no more trouble, and if you tell us where to find Lord Charlton, your lives may be spared."

This was our usual policy—if we were overly harsh, it might provoke more rebellion—but most of our current captives were too petrified to speak. A few, however, were eager to take Knollys up on his bargain and told us where we might find Charlton. As the hunt began, my men moved into the castle, leaving only a handful of us outside, including the guard by Barrington. At my request, Knollys set some of Charlton's men to checking for survivors in the landslide.

"I think you can take care of the rest of the wall now," Knollys said to me as we both dismounted. "We've waited long enough for it to come down. I'll go inside and take charge of the castle."

I nodded offhandedly, not wanting to let on what a challenge the rest of the wall presented. But a challenge it most certainly was. As we'd seen for ourselves, Charlton's enclosure went on for miles. It was by far the biggest wall I'd ever had to bring down.

At least there was no one shooting arrows now. I could take what time I needed. Listening to the world around me, I chose my songs carefully. First, a song to draw water up from the ground and into the wall, and then another to call a wind down from the chilly sky.

Wind was something I was still learning to work with. No matter how sweetly or imperiously I sang, it would not always do my bidding; sometimes it ignored me completely. But today my luck was in. If anything, the wind responded rather too strongly. I had to weave a tight net of song around it as I soaked the wall, then froze and melted it again and again. Only at the very end did I set the wind free. With a burst of explosive joy, it drove the stones and timbers apart, demolishing the wall all down the line.

A kindred spark of joy lit up in me. I'd done it. I'd taken the wall down.

"Chantress!" A call from my men.

As I turned, a wave of weariness hit me. Great magic was always draining. Yet if I'd learned anything as a Chantress, it was that I couldn't afford to show any weakness. Certainly I'd have been a fool to betray any vulnerability now, when my men were dragging Charlton out to me, his velvet-clad arms tied behind his back. Above his cravat, his face was apoplectic, and he was cursing the men with every step.

"Save your breath, Charlton!" I called out. "You're my prisoner now, and the King's, and you're bound for the Tower. And it will go better for you if you show some remorse."

If there was any remorse in Charlton, he hid it well. As the men shoved him forward, he spat at my feet. "You hellhound!"

I blinked. Was he too furious to care what I might do to him? Or was he deliberately trying to goad me into doing something rash?

"She-devil!" From the crazed look of his eyes, it was fury alone that drove him. "The King will rue the day he allied himself with you. You suck men dry, you harpy! Even the ones on your own side."

"Take him away," I said to four of my men.

Charlton kept spouting filth as they grabbed him. "But they're growing wise to you, aren't they? You're a witch, they say. You're a freak. No man will touch you. Even Nat Walbrook's abandoned you—"

"And shut him up," I ordered, more harshly this time.

Words, I told myself. *Just words. They can't hurt me*. But even after Charlton had been hauled off, I found myself shaking with anger. How dare he speak that way to me? How dare he mention Nat?

I looked up at my men. Not all of them met my eyes. Although I thought of us as a unit, the truth was that they always kept a certain distance from me. I was a woman and a Chantress; like it or not, that set me apart. When all was said and done, what did they think of me? Had Charlton's words struck some kind of chord in them?

You're a freak. No man will touch you. Even Nat Walbrook's abandoned you—

What could I say in my own defense? I couldn't tell anyone the truth about Nat. Indeed, after all this time, I was no longer sure what the truth really was. And to address any of the rest of Charlton's accusations was to give them more credence than they deserved.

Never mind, I told myself. *You are strong enough to handle this*. And I was. But as I stood looking at my men in the shadow of our victory, my loneliness went bone deep.

CHAPTER TWO
THE ROYAL BARGE

Six weeks later, cushioned on the red velvet seats of the royal barge, I watched London slip by in the late October twilight. Keeping the peace in the far reaches of the kingdom meant I rarely saw the city, and I was grateful for this chance to savor its sounds. Some were audible only to a Chantress—the gossamer-fine melody of the gathering haze, the rollicking music of the river itself. Yet as the sunset faded and the glowing sky turned a melancholy hue, it was the ordinary sounds I appreciated the most—the pipes and drums of street musicians, the last cries of the seagulls, the roar of a raucous theater crowd, the bass chime of the great bell at St. Paul's.

Across from me, King Henry watched the city, his blue eyes bright as ever under his copper hair.

Nodding at him, I pointed to a wall where people stood waving in the last of the light. "Listen! They're cheering for you."

His sober, freckled face broke into a smile. "They could equally well be cheering for you, you know."

"No." I could just hear the words drifting across the river. "They're cheering for you and the Queen."

It was almost six months since the King had married my friend Sybil Dashwood. I counted myself lucky that I'd been able to come to London—however briefly—for the ceremony. Their wedding had been an occasion to remember, the first time in centuries that a monarch had married a commoner. Although some at Court had objected to the marriage, many ordinary Londoners had been only too happy to celebrate the union.

The city's buoyant mood still had not dissipated. After many dark years, we'd finally reached a season of peace and plenty. The tyrannies of Scargrave were ended, and so was the year of famine and unrest that had followed his rule. We'd had a good harvest last summer, and a record one this year, thanks to Nat's brilliant work—

No, stop. I mustn't think about Nat.

Pushing back a wave of sadness, I said quickly, "Your Majesty, has Dr. Penebrygg told you about the fireworks he's designed for the opening of Parliament?"

"Not yet, but that reminds me . . ." The King reached for a box at his side. "I believe there are a few more items on today's docket. Shall we go over them now?"

I stifled a sigh. When the King had called me back to London to help with the opening, I'd been delighted. I couldn't wait to spend time with Sybil and Norrie, my childhood guardian. Both women were very dear to me. But ever since my arrival, the King had kept me so busy that I might as well have been in farthest Cornwall.

Of course the opening was important. I couldn't deny that.

This would be the first Parliament in a generation, and one elected on more democratic lines than ever before. It was critical that it be a success.

To that end, my days had been filled with endless worries about schedules, protocol, and security. This morning, with the help of Captain Knollys and my men, I had searched the Parliamentary rooms at Westminster Palace for potential threats. In the afternoon I'd gone up and down the river for a series of meetings with the King and some of his chief supporters. Now I was returning to Whitehall Palace, the main royal residence, after which the King would proceed to Greenwich for a supper engagement with the Lord High Admiral.

I knew there would be more matters for me to attend to once I was back at Whitehall. There always were. And we still had a week to go before Parliament opened. Was it really so much to ask, to have a brief moment of peace here on the Thames?

One look at the King's conscientious face, and I knew the answer. Henry never rested, so how could I? After all, this was what I had signed up for a year and a half ago, when he'd asked for my help in governing the kingdom.

"Let's see." Henry paged through the papers. "Here's a letter from the Earl of Staffordshire, who enthusiastically supports our Parliamentary reforms."

"Enthusiastically?" I reached for the letter in surprise. "Are you sure?"

The King grinned. "It seems your visit was most persuasive. He says quite complimentary things about you."

I raised my eyebrows as I scanned the florid words. "He did not say them at the time. Indeed, I had the distinct impression that he was horrified to see me." And no wonder, for I'd made that visit shortly after bringing down Charlton Castle.

The King flipped to the next document. "Viscount Hatton writes in a similar vein." He turned a few more pages. "Oh."

"Is something wrong, Your Majesty?"

"No, no. It's just a note from Sybil." He smiled as he pored over it, though there was a slightly worried look in his eyes. "Er . . . a private note."

I was surprised by the worry, but not by the smile. He and Sybil were a wonderful match—the King so steady, and Sybil so lighthearted, and each of them adoring the other. It made me happy to think of them together. Yet I felt wistful, too. Twenty months had passed—twenty months and two days—since I had last seen Nat. And what a painful parting it had been . . .

Don't think about it, I told myself for the ten thousandth time.

After all, there was no chance our paths would cross anytime soon. Although Nat was often at Court, he'd departed for the Continent two weeks ago, just before I'd arrived at Whitehall. Certain delicate negotiations were said to require his presence in Paris and Amsterdam, and he would have to miss the opening. I didn't know if this was true, but I had been relieved to hear it, for if Nat had planned to be at the opening, I would've had to find some excuse to miss it myself. Those were the rules. And I was grateful to be spared such difficulties. Nothing could take away the pain of our separation, but at least this way I didn't have to deal with the additional humiliation of rearranging my plans, while everyone at Court gossiped about my leaving and speculated as to why.

Don't think about it. . . .

"There." The King was rifling through the papers again. "I think that's everything of note."

We were nearing Whitehall Palace. Already the oarsmen were slowing, the better to maneuver themselves close to the ornate landing.

"There should be more dispatches waiting for us in the State Rooms," the King said. "And if there are any ambassadors waiting to see me, perhaps you could have a quick word with them in my absence?"

"Of course, Your Majesty."

With great precision and a little splashing, the oarsmen brought the barge toward the landing. It was tricky work, as they had to take care that the barge's gilded frieze of growling lions didn't scrape against the pilings. I heard an impish note in the river's music and made sure I had a good hold on my seat. If we bobbled about, I didn't want to go flying.

"And there are some more papers on my desk you may wish to see," the King said. "One is from Walbrook."

From Nat? My fingers tightened on the seat.

"He's found a way to get the seeds we need much sooner than he expected," the King went on. "He'll be back for the opening of Parliament after all."

Nat? Here? My heart slammed into my shoes.

It was an effort to speak. "When does he expect to arrive?"

"As soon as possible. If his luck has held, he'll be sailing over right now."

Worse and worse.

"He made quick work of those negotiations, I must say," the King mused. "But it's possible there's more to the story, something he needs to tell me in person." The barge swayed and rocked. The King looked round. "Ah! We've docked."

The master of the barge rapped on the glass door. "Lady Chantress, if you wish to disembark?"

Numbly I rose and bowed to the King. Nat could be at Whitehall any day now.

He must not find me here. That was one of the cardinal rules of the game, and so far I had never broken it. *But what possible excuse can I find to leave just before the opening?*

I went up the gangplank and stood between the great torches on the dock as the barge pulled away. As I waved good-bye to the King, it took all my self-control to present a cheery face.

"We'll meet when I return?" he called out as the oarsmen sculled.

"Yes, Your Majesty." He might not be back till midnight, but it was not unusual for us to work into the small hours as we prepared for the opening. "I'll be waiting." *Unless I find some perfect way to vanish before then*.

Once the barge was out of sight, I turned toward the looming bulk of Whitehall Palace. Built in a motley mixture of brick and timber and stone, it was almost a city within a city, boasting more than fifteen hundred rooms, all of them encircled by a high embankment that had been put up in Scargrave's reign and never taken down. It was the King's favorite of all the royal residences in London, a place that I usually returned to with pleasure.

But not now.

What on earth am I going to do?

The palace doors opened. I couldn't ask for time to think; I was about to be swept up in my duties again.

As I went forward, however, I heard a flurry of female voices above and to the left of me. Caught by the note of fear in them, I looked up. The disturbance was coming from one of the Queen's windows. As I listened, the babble of voices grew louder, and a terrible cry rent the air.

Was it Sybil? Was she in danger?

Forgetting my own problems, I broke into a run.

CHAPTER THREE
SYBIL

If Whitehall was the largest palace in Europe, it was also Europe's biggest warren, with innumerable passageways and cul-de-sacs. Thankfully, I knew a shortcut to the Queen's chambers, and I wound my way there as fast as I could. With me were two of the men in my command. They had been awaiting my arrival, had seen me rush into the palace, and had come to my aid.

There were no guards at the entrance to the Queen's chambers—another sign that something was wrong. I sped up and flew through the doors.

On the other side, everything was in an uproar. The guards who should have been in front of the doors were standing awkwardly beside them. The ladies-in-waiting and maids-of-honor were buzzing around the room, some of them crying out in distress. Servants were frantically dragging all the curtains shut. One lady lay half-prostrate on the floor. And Sybil, with her exquisite face and blush-pink gown, stood like an avenging angel in the middle of the room.

"That's quite enough," she was saying to the lady on the floor. "Enough, I tell you. Get up."

The lady moaned, and the sweet-faced girl beside her—whom I recognized as the King's young cousin, Lady Clemence Grey—said, "Oh, I wish Lord Walbrook were here. He would know what to do."

"What's wrong?" I called out.

In all the commotion, they hadn't noticed me before. Now they all turned and stared, even Sybil, until I started to feel quite out of place. Which in truth I was. Because of my magic, I occupied a strange position in the world. I sat in Council; I commanded my own men; I was almost an honorary man myself. In this domain, however, womanly grace and beauty were what mattered. And for that, I had the wrong manners, the wrong posture, the wrong everything.

Even my dress was unsuitable. Though well-cut and made of the finest wool, it was meant for the practicalities of a Chantress's life. It had no bows, no jewels, no soft silken folds to flatter my neckline. I cut a sober figure next to these ornaments of the Court. I didn't belong, and they knew it.

Still staring at me, a few of the ladies-in-waiting tittered behind their fans. Doing my best to ignore them, I looked at Sybil, who had gone very pale.

"I heard screaming," I said. "What happened?"

"Nothing," said Sybil. "A . . . silly game gone wrong, that's all."

The lady on the floor protested, "But I saw—"

"Nothing," Sybil said more loudly this time, cutting her off.

"Guards, if you will please resume your places outside?" As they shuffled out, she turned to me. "It was kind of you to come, Chantress, but as you can see, we have no need of you. Or your men."

So I was "Chantress" now? What had happened to "Lucy"? True, I hadn't had a moment to see Sybil on her own since I'd arrived in London. Not a moment, really, since her wedding.

"You may go," I said to my men, but I did not follow them. Looking directly at Sybil, I said, "But I shall stay, if I may?"

Her beautiful face froze. Had I been too informal? Perhaps she'd expected me to offer her the courtesies due a queen. But as I started to sink into a deep curtsy, something in her face changed, and she stopped me.

"Never mind that, Lucy. If you truly wish to stay—"

"I do," I said quickly. "I'd like to talk to you—"

"Not here," she cut in. "In my private chamber." Propelling me toward a grand door at the back of the room, she waved away the ladies who tried to follow us. "I will be gone only a short while, and I expect all of you to be calm when I return. There will be no more silly talk. Do you understand?" To an older lady-in-waiting, the most sensible-looking of the lot, she said, "I leave you in charge. Send Lady Gillian to her room if need be—and keep the curtains closed."

Frowning, she ushered me into her bedchamber. The room was so enormous and so laden with luxuries that it took me a moment to realize we weren't alone. Over by a mahogany cabinet, two gray-haired women were sorting through scores of apothecary bottles. The spry, thin one—Joan, Sybil's longtime maidservant—came right over to us. "Does Lady Gillian need more smelling salts, Your Highness? Or a calming tisane?"

"Both. Neither." Looking strained, Sybil threw up her hands. "Oh, I don't know, Joan. What do you think she should have?"

As they discussed the matter, I went up to the other woman, a steadfast, stocky figure clad in serviceable wool—my old guardian, Norrie.

"Lucy, dear, what a nice surprise," she said as we hugged. "I thought you'd be out all night again." She shook her head. "It doesn't seem right, the way they keep you so busy—"

"The King works just as hard, Norrie. But I'm sorry; I don't mean to leave you alone here."

"Oh, I'm not alone at Whitehall, child. It's you I'm thinking about." She let me go. "Of course, it's true that it's quiet over in our rooms right now, what with Margery visiting her mother this month. But the Queen said I should come over here and keep Joan company. And it seems it's just as well I did."

Cheerful and capable, Margery looked after Norrie when I was away. I'd forgotten she was leaving today. Thank goodness Sybil had stepped in. I looked for her, to show her my gratitude, but she and Joan were still speaking in quiet tones. The door opened again, and Joan slipped out.

"So don't worry about me," Norrie went on. "If there's anyone who needs looking after, it's you. Too thin by half, you are—"

Sybil advanced on us. "You're right, Norrie. She's much too thin."

"I'm fine," I said firmly. As they started to disagree, I held up my hand. "No, really, I am. But what's happening here?" As Sybil hesitated, I shook my head at her. "And don't tell me it was just a game, because I don't believe it was. That was quite a scream I heard. And the lady on the floor said she saw something."

"Jenny Greenteeth," Norrie said.

I stared at her. Jenny Greenteeth was a mythical figure said to lurk in rivers, where she lured the unwary into the depths and ate them. "You're not serious?"

"Norrie, please," Sybil said at the same time. "We agreed we would keep this to ourselves." And then, to me, "It's nonsense, Lucy. Absolute nonsense. Lady Gillian just wanted to cause a sensation. She was looking out at the river, and then suddenly she's calling half my ladies over and shouting that she's seen Jenny Greenteeth. What twaddle!"

Twaddle was what it sounded like, but why hadn't Sybil simply laughed at it? There must have been more going on, to upset her so.

"What exactly did she see?" I asked.

"A greenish face, and hands wriggling under the water," Sybil said dismissively. "Over by the landing, if you can believe her."

I hadn't seen any such thing when I'd been down there, but then, I'd been preoccupied. "Perhaps I'd better check, just to be sure there's no mischief afoot." It was possible, I supposed, that Lady Gillian really had seen something—a drowning, or a swimmer under the water. And the landing was where the King would come in later that night. "I'll ask my men to help me. And if need be, I can send word to the King—"

"To Henry? Absolutely not!" Sybil looked like an avenging angel again. "You're not to tell anyone, do you hear me? Not one word."

Her vehemence startled me. "Why ever not?"

"Because I won't have Henry thinking I can't control my own court," Sybil said. "And I won't have the broadsides saying it either. This is just the sort of gossip they'd love. And the next thing you know, some horrible ditty about the Mad Queen and her hysterical court will be all over London. It will embarrass Henry, and it will embarrass me. My reputation will be in ruins again. I won't have it."

I stood, speechless. I hadn't seen much of Sybil in the past twenty months, but I knew she'd been unhappy before the wedding. Small wonder, since so many powerful people had opposed and delayed the match between her and the King. Some had insisted he must marry a foreign princess; others had wanted him to marry their own highborn daughters. Almost no one had wanted him to marry a girl who'd spent years wandering around on the Continent with her eccentric mother.

Nor had the broadsides been kind. Ever since the King had lifted the censorship imposed by Lord Scargrave, chapmen had sold the sheets by the thousands—copies of popular ballads sung in the taverns and on the streets, complete with illustrations. I'd seen some about me, most of them rousing songs celebrating my defense of England, my defeat of the hated Shadowgrims, and my general fearsomeness. The ones about Sybil were different. While they noted her good looks, they claimed she was as crazy as her mother. In the weeks leading up to the wedding, her every gaffe had sparked another broadside declaring her flighty and stupid and common—an unworthy Queen of England.

I'd assumed that the situation was better now that they were married. She and Henry loved each other; I had no doubts about that.

Yet there was no mistaking the tension I saw in her now.

"Promise me you won't say anything." No longer giving orders, Sybil was pleading with me. "There's no reason to. Lady Gillian is always seeing things, isn't she, Norrie?"

"Loves a fuss, she does," Norrie agreed.

"Last week it was ghosts in the music room," Sybil said. "And before that it was a falling star portending doom for us all. So this latest scare means nothing."

"Lady Clemence took it seriously," I pointed out. "She wanted to report it to Nat. I heard her say so."

Sybil rolled her eyes. "That's only because Clemence wants to tell *everything* to Nat. She's a good-hearted girl, one of my favorites, but she's been besotted with him for months. Hadn't you heard?"

I hadn't.

"It's very tiresome," Sybil went on. "Her father—the Earl of Tunbridge, you know—hasn't done anything to discourage the infatuation, which just adds fuel to the fire. Clemence talks about Nat all day long. I wish she would stop." She gave me a crooked smile. "Not that I would mind if *you* talked about Nat. But you never do."

I shrugged. "There's nothing to say. We just had a parting of ways."

"That's what you keep telling me," Sybil said skeptically, "but I don't believe it. You've warned me off every time I've dared to ask any questions—"

"And me," Norrie put in.

"—But I have eyes," Sybil continued, "and this doesn't look like an amicable parting to me. You come to Court only when Nat's gone, and you leave before he returns, every single time. And it's been more than a year. You can't even look him in the face, can you?"

I wanted to deny it, but I couldn't, not when Sybil was right there in front of me.

Tiny earrings bobbing, Sybil took my arm. "Lucy, whatever it was that happened, you can tell me. We're friends." As I kept silent, her arm stilled on mine. "At least . . . I thought we were."

"Of course we are," I said quickly, but her arm had slipped away.

"If we are, then tell me what went wrong between you and Nat."

"It doesn't matter," I insisted.

"It *does* matter." Her voice was strained. "But you're like Henry. You both think you can hide things from me. If I ask any questions, you pat me on the head and turn away. You both think you're being kind, I suppose. But I'm not a lapdog, Lucy. I'm not an idiot. I know when someone's keeping the truth from me."

Was that how she really felt about Henry? About me?

"My dear," Norrie began, reaching out to Sybil. "It's not just you. She won't tell me, either."

Norrie's sadness made me ache, just as Sybil's desperation did. This was the cost of walling out the people I loved—a cost as heavy to them as it was to me. And yet how could I have told them the truth?

I looked up to find Sybil's eyes fixed on me. "You don't trust me, do you, Lucy?" she said. "It's been like this ever since you started working for Henry. I know you have state secrets to keep, but these days everything's a secret with you. For all I know, you hate Nat with a passion—"

I flinched. Only the tiniest bit, but Sybil noticed, and I didn't avert my eyes quickly enough. I'd forgotten the way she had of seeing straight into me.

"Oh, Lucy." Her frustration melted into sympathy. "You still care about him, don't you? Whatever you say, you still care."

How to recover from this? I should have kept her at arm's length, just as I had for the past twenty months.

As I scrambled for words, Sybil said triumphantly, "So there's hope after all."

"No." I didn't like where this was going.

"You two were made for each other," said Sybil, cheerfully ignoring me. "And if you care about him, it can't be as hopeless as all that. There must be some way we can get you back together again." She stopped, struck by a new idea. "I could be your go-between."

I looked at her, horrified. "No."

"But I would be happy to help." She skipped a little in her

bright slippers, like the Sybil I'd known in happier days, and gave me a delighted smile. "Please let me."

"No." My voice cracked. "You mustn't go to him, Sybil. Leave him alone, I tell you. *Leave him alone*."

Sybil and Norrie stared at me.

It was Norrie who spoke first, her voice rough with worry—Norrie, who had always thought Nat could do no wrong. "Child, I have to know. What did Nat do, to make you look like that?"

My throat burned. What could I say?

Sybil became fierce in my defense. "Should I tell Henry he's not to be trusted? He'll listen to me about that, you can be sure. I'll *make* him listen."

"No!" Never that. "Sybil, please . . ."

But I had only to look at her to see she wasn't backing down. And if she broke the King's confidence in Nat, then everything I'd worked toward would be ruined once and for all.

The game was up. I would have to tell them the truth.

CHAPTER FOUR
TRUTH OUTS

Behind me, I heard the fire crackle. Coal fell through the grate. When I looked up, Sybil and Norrie were still staring at me.

"Nat didn't do anything dreadful," I told them. "That's the truth, I promise you. But it was his idea that we part ways, not mine. He told me not to write to him, and he asked me to keep away when he came to Court."

Sybil looked taken aback. "I don't understand."

Norrie looked as flummoxed as Sybil. "Why would Nat do that?"

It would all have to come out now, I thought wearily. There was no getting around it. "Because he thought he didn't have the standing to court me. To do that, he said he needed to prove he could stand on his own two feet, and he couldn't do that while I was around. People would think I was propping him up."

"He wants to court you?" Sybil squeaked.

"He did a year and a half ago," I said carefully. "Of course, I don't know how he feels now—"

"He wants to court you," Sybil repeated, eyes shining.

Norrie was more circumspect, but I saw the tension ease out of her wrinkled face. "So that's what happened between you." She shook her head. "But where Nat got the idea he couldn't stand on his own two feet already, I don't know. A more capable young man I've never met."

I kept quiet. Twenty months ago, I'd argued the same point with Nat myself and had gotten nowhere. And I saw no need to expose to anyone—even someone as close as Norrie—how desperate Nat had felt, or to remind them of just how low his standing had been at Court back then.

But Sybil, wise in the ways of Court politics, hadn't forgotten. "Capable he certainly is," she agreed. "But that isn't the point, Norrie dear. It's true. He didn't have much standing at Court back then, or any real power. And you know how people here can be. They would've called him the Chantress's lackey—or worse."

Just hearing her say the words made me realize how bad it would've been. For myself, I could have endured it, for the sake of being with Nat. But his sacrifice would have been much greater. No one would have respected him. Small wonder he'd balked.

"Yes, I can see his dilemma." Sybil's eyes were full of concern as she turned to me. "But I still think he asked a lot, expecting you to pretend that you'd gone your separate ways."

"He didn't ask that in so many words," I admitted. "He said only that he needed to do everything on his own. But once I had time to think, I realized what I had to do. It wasn't enough for me not to interfere on his behalf, you see. I had to make it clear that

I didn't *want* to interfere, that I had no interest whatsoever in his affairs, that he meant nothing to me."

"Was that really necessary, child?" Norrie asked.

"Yes." I was sure of it. "Otherwise half the Court would think I was pulling strings for him behind the scenes."

"I hate to say it, but you're right," Sybil said. "They probably *would* think that, the toads. You ought to have told us, though. We could have helped you."

I shook my head. As much as I loved them both, it had been too great a secret to share, especially since discretion was not Sybil's strongest suit. Perhaps that was changing, now that she was Queen, but I'd thought it too risky to tell her—or anyone in her circle, including Norrie.

"It was simplest just to tell everyone we'd argued and there was nothing between us anymore," I said. "That way no one could accuse Nat of prospering because he was in my favor."

"And no one would give him assistance merely to get close to you," Sybil said, working it all out. "So Nat is standing on his own two feet, just as he wanted to." She looked at me admiringly. "What a clever plan."

"Not clever." It had cost me too dearly for that. "Merely desperate. But it seems to have worked. And Nat never objected to it."

At first I'd been afraid that I wouldn't be able to maintain the masquerade in his presence—that some unguarded look of mine would give us away to everyone. Yet it had never come to that. On the rare occasions when I'd been called to Court, I'd inevitably found that Nat had left before I'd arrived. I, in turn, had been careful to be gone before he came back. Only once had I been caught out, and then I'd pretended to be ill, staying in my room until he was gone again.

Although we never saw each other, it seemed we were in silent agreement. We were playing the same game, by the same rules.

At least I hoped we were. The problem with a game like this, however, was that you couldn't be absolutely certain what the other player was thinking. And there was always the chance that the game would finish in stalemate, with everyone walking away from the board.

Norrie's look of quiet sympathy almost undid me. She patted my hand. "Why, you're as cold as anything, child."

Sybil put her arm around me. "Cold? We can't have that."

While Norrie poked some life into the fire, Sybil sat me down in one of the high-backed chairs arranged before the hearth. Silk sleeves rustling, she picked up a fat silver pot that had been swaddled to keep it warm. "Chocolate. That's what you need."

After frothing up the drink, she passed the rich brew to me. Warming my hands around the cup, I felt obscurely comforted.

Sybil sat and sipped at her own chocolate. "What I don't understand," she said meditatively, "is why you and Nat are still apart."

I set my cup down with a clatter. "But I've just told you—"

"You've told us that you kept away from Nat so he could prove himself," Sybil said. "And very noble it was of you too. But he *has* proven himself, Lucy. The two of you never cross paths, so maybe you don't know, but you should see what it's like when he comes to Court now. Everyone in London shows him honor and respect."

Norrie nodded. "They know he's the man who saved us from famine—first with potatoes and then with that new strain of wheat last year."

"And he has a reputation as an excellent negotiator," Sybil said. "Henry says he can be trusted with anything. 'My right-hand man,' he calls him."

"But that's just the King," I objected.

"'Just the King,'" Sybil repeated, dimples showing. "Lucy, do you have any idea how many people yearn for Henry's favor? And how much prestige there is in having it? You should see how people fawn over Nat now."

I'd noticed that people said his name differently, but Sybil was right. I hadn't grasped quite how much his position had changed. "They fawn? Really?"

"Yes. You can see he doesn't care for it, so the sensible ones don't. But the rest do. Everyone at Court knows his worth now." Sybil gave me a sideways look over her cup of chocolate. "Including the ladies."

"The ladies?"

"Clemence isn't the only one who swoons at the sight of him," Sybil said. "Though she's probably the nicest."

This didn't exactly comfort me.

"He's considered one of the most eligible men in the kingdom." Sybil spoke dispassionately, as if she were assessing the prospects of a stranger. "He doesn't come from great wealth, of course, but because of his position at Court, people are certain he'll rise. And now that he's become Lord Walbrook—even if Henry did have to twist his arm to accept the title—many families are willing to overlook the facts of his birth."

"Oh, they are, are they?" How very magnanimous, after all the times they'd sneered at him for not knowing who his parents were. "The beasts."

Sybil's dimples showed again. "My point is that Nat's done what he set out to do: He's made a place for himself. There's nothing to stand between you anymore."

"And no earthly reason at all," said Norrie, "that the pair of you should keep avoiding each other."

Sybil nodded. "I couldn't have put it better myself. You've both waited long enough. You just need a chance to talk to each other, and it will all come right."

I traced the rim of my cup. I dearly wanted to walk into the picture they were painting, where the waiting and the longing and the anguish were over. But so much still seemed to stand in the way.

"He's coming back to London now," I told them. "For the opening. The King told me today."

Sybil looked ready to cheer. "Wonderful! This time you must stay and wait for him. Promise me you will."

"He hasn't said he wants to see me," I pointed out. "He hasn't written."

"Maybe he thinks you've changed your mind," Sybil said.

My worst fear raised its ugly head. "What if he's changed *his* mind?"

"Then you'll find out." It was Norrie who spoke this time, in her briskest voice. "Best you know now, rather than sit around for years waiting."

"Yes," said Sybil. "You really must speak to him. I think—"

A cry from beyond the door interrupted us. "The Chantress! I need the Chantress!"

I rose from my chair, Sybil and Norrie close behind me. But before I could reach the door, Lord Gabriel raced through it.

His breath came in great gasps, as if he had been running hard, and his polished boots and immaculately tailored coat and breeches were spattered with rain. "The King needs you, Chantress. You must come at once."

"The King?" Sybil's hand flew to her heart. "Is he hurt?"

"No, no. Nothing of the sort," Gabriel assured her, bowing to her with all his hallmark charm. "He just needs the Chantress. I can't say more, I'm afraid. Chantress, will you come? His message asks that you sail to Greenwich Palace to meet him."

"Of course." Greenwich was where he'd planned to see the Lord High Admiral; it was a good five miles downriver from Whitehall. I turned to Norrie and Sybil. "I'm sorry, but I must go."

Norrie was used to quick good-byes. She let me go with a word of caution and a hug. Sybil's leave-taking was more restrained. She wanted to come with us; I saw it in her face. But it was all too plain that the summons hadn't included her.

Instead of protesting, she became quiet and remote. As Gabriel and I left, she took her place again among her ladies-in-waiting. When I glanced back, her beautiful face had become a tense mask, and the distance between us yawned.

CHAPTER FIVE

DARK DEEDS

An hour later, I still hadn't reached the King's side, though not for want of trying. Instead I stood on the dimly lit deck of a small pinnace, knees braced against the dark slap of the waves, listening hard to the music of the river and the patchy mist around me.

Now and again, I'd used magic to speed the journey, singing us through the rapids at London Bridge and urging the currents to flow in our favor. Whenever the mist grew too thick, I cleared it so that the rising moon could light our way. So far, however, I hadn't resorted to the more powerful music that would send us hurtling toward Greenwich at a truly miraculous rate. That was a demanding magic, and since I didn't know what I would face at the end of our journey, I wanted to conserve my energies.

Behind me, voices rose and broke my concentration. I glanced back and saw that Gabriel was talking with Sir Barnaby Gadding.

"I tell you, I know no more about it than you do." It was Gabriel speaking, with a slight edge to his suave voice. "The summons reached Whitehall as I was coming in, and it was in the King's own hand. He wanted the Chantress and his chief councilors to meet him at Greenwich, to aid him in a matter of great urgency. He said nothing more."

"Chief councilors, eh?" Sir Barnaby tapped his fine ivory cane against the deck. Head of the King's Council, he had been at death's door not all that long ago, and he was continually plagued by gout. But you would never have guessed that from the dapper figure he cut on deck. "And yet you came too?"

"I wanted to be of help, Sir Barnaby." Gabriel's reply was mild, but the edge was still there. "And the Chantress asked me to come."

That wasn't how I remembered it. Instead it had been Gabriel who'd suggested he escort me onto the waiting pinnace. But I wasn't going to correct his version of events. The newest member of the Council, he already had problems enough with old-timers like Sir Barnaby. They couldn't forgive him for either his present liberties or his past mistakes.

As far as I was concerned, however, liberties were just part of Gabriel's nature. Take the habit he used to have of proposing every time he saw me. Whenever I refused him, he'd merely laugh and kiss my hand, then try again next time. It was a habit he had with other women as well, I suspected, for no one enjoyed flirtation more than Gabriel did. When his courtship had finally ended, just as amiably as it had begun, I'd been relieved but also surprised.

When he wasn't playing the suitor, Gabriel could be quite

good company. Not that Sir Barnaby saw it that way. As he and Gabriel continued to wrangle, I moved up to the bow and trained my attention on the river again. Nothing had changed, except that the mist was dissipating; all was just as it should be.

I found my thoughts returning to Nat. *He'll be here soon*, I told myself. *You need to decide what to do*. Perhaps Sybil and Norrie were right. Perhaps it was time I stood my ground and learned what Nat truly thought of me. Yet I loathed the thought of having to play out our drama while the entire Court watched. Because they would be watching, of that I could be sure.

"Ah, there you are." Holding fast to his floppy cap, Cornelius Penebrygg came up beside me. The mist had given a sheen to his spectacles and his thick silver beard. "You look worried, my dear. Is everything all right?"

"Yes. Quite all right." The oldest of the King's councilors, Penebrygg was also my good friend. Nat was like a son to him, and I knew that our seeming estrangement worried him. That was reason enough not to bother him with my troubles. "I just wish I knew what was in store for us at Greenwich."

Penebrygg nodded, still clutching his cap. "As do I. But we will be there before long. This is the last bend."

He was right. The breeze picked up, clearing away all but a last few threads of mist. Soon the brick turrets of Greenwich Palace, lit up by smoldering torches, came into sight. It took me a few seconds longer to notice the ship that was anchored just beyond the palace landing.

"What's that?" Sir Barnaby demanded, coming up behind me

and pointing at the vessel. Only a few glimmers of light punctuated its long, dark lines.

As Penebrygg fumbled with his spectacles, Gabriel said with assurance, "A frigate, by the looks of it. Twenty guns, I'd say—and one of ours. But odd that it's anchored here, right by the palace."

As our pinnace came up to the landing, a detachment of guards emerged from the palace to meet us. Instead of allowing us to disembark, their leader asked who we were, then gestured toward the shadowy ship. "The King is waiting for you on the *Dorset*."

"What's all this about, then?" Sir Barnaby barked at him.

"Couldn't say," the guard replied. "The *Dorset*'s just come over from Holland. That's all I know. But whatever it is, His Majesty wants to see you right away."

As we came alongside the *Dorset*, the glimmers of light were revealed as lanterns, with more being lit as we approached. Beneath one of them we saw men huddled on the deck. The crew, I supposed. But when Gabriel hailed them, the first man to break away from the circle turned out to be the King himself.

He came striding over to the rail. "You're here at last!"

We greeted him in turn, but my voice almost failed me. The other men in the circle were now coming over to us—and one of them was Nat.

For more than a year, I'd pretended that he meant nothing to me. Now, in the half dark of this moonlit night, I stopped acting a part. I was simply myself, hungry for the sight of him.

The King's right-hand man, Sybil had called him, and he

looked it. He'd always had a quiet strength about him, but now that strength was in the open. Tall and sure and capable, he came toward me, and what I saw in his face made my heart hammer like a drum . . .

But then I caught sight of what had been at the center of the men's circle, and my heart nearly stopped altogether. It was an enormous barrel, stood on its end. Just visible inside it was a woman, and she was gagged.

Seeing her, I felt sick. Gags and muzzles and scold's bridles—until the King had come to the throne, these had all been common ways of stopping a woman's tongue. Especially a Chantress's tongue. My own godmother had been gagged before she'd been killed, and the memory filled me with horror.

"What's going on here?" My voice was shaking with anger. "You're gagging women and putting them in barrels?"

I could've asked the question of any of them. But it was Nat I was looking at.

Even in the dim light I saw his face change. When he answered, his voice was guarded, almost steely. "She isn't a woman, Chantress. She's a mermaid. And she's gagged because she tried to kill us."

CHAPTER SIX
ONDINE

I stared at Nat, my anger spent, but the pinnace shifted, and we were forced apart. By the time we came alongside the *Dorset* again, there was no going back to that hopeful moment when he and I had first laid eyes on each other. Nat was no longer near the rail but stood some distance away, speaking with a member of the crew. He didn't look in my direction at all.

A wave of sorrow, almost of grief, went through me. *You really must speak to him*, Sybil had said. And now we'd met, and it had all gone horribly wrong.

Giving in to my emotions would accomplish nothing, however. Instead I concentrated on getting us all over onto the *Dorset*—especially Sir Barnaby, whose gouty leg proved troublesome.

Once everyone was on board, the King made introductions. I was already acquainted with the Lord High Admiral, a bluff man of forty or so, with skin like leather. Standing next to him was my old friend Sir Samuel Deeps—King's councilor, dandy-about-town, and current Secretary of the Navy. This was the first time, however, that I'd met bull-necked Captain Ellis and frail Dr. Verney, both of the *Dorset*.

Once courtesies had been exchanged, we gathered around the barrel, which was sloshing with seawater.

Seeing herself surrounded, the creature submerged, retreating in the only way left to her. Her long silvery-green hair floated on the surface, partially obscuring our view. Still, you could see that she had a woman's head and a fish's tail, and that tight ropes bound her arms and torso. In the light of the lantern, her skin was luminous; the scales near the surface glowed.

She wasn't human. But when I saw the rope cutting into her skin, I bit my lip.

She's dangerous, I reminded myself. A killer, from what Nat had said. And the rope and the gag didn't seem to bother anyone else. They were watching the mermaid with dispassionate eyes—all except Penebrygg, who looked upon her with something close to reverence.

"Miraculous," he breathed. "A true ondine."

Ondine? I looked up at Nat, who was standing across from me. "I thought you said she was a mermaid?"

"That's the layman's term," Gabriel cut in. "Those of us who have read the great Paracelsus would more properly term her a water elemental—that is, an ondine."

"Or undine," Sir Barnaby said.

"Or nymph." Sir Samuel flourished his cape. "My edition translates the term that way."

Captain Ellis and the ship's doctor looked confused. So did the King and the Lord High Admiral.

"Or we might just use the old English term 'mermaid,'" Nat said calmly, "whether or not we've read our Paracelsus. Then everyone will understand what we mean."

"There's much to be said for that," Penebrygg agreed, but even in the dim light I could see Gabriel looked a little annoyed. There had never been any love lost between him and Nat.

"I prefer the terminology of Paracelsus," Gabriel said in his best aristocratic manner. "After all, he was the first one to look at the matter scientifically, to understand that each of the four great elements has its own associated spirits—"

"Ondines for water, salamanders for fire, gnomes for earth, and sylphs for air," Nat said.

Gabriel raised an eyebrow in surprise. "So you *have* read him."

"Yes. An interesting theory," Nat said. "But short on evidence."

Gabriel looked as if he were about to argue some more, but Sir Barnaby cut in with a question for the ship's doctor. "Tell me, how long can she stay down like that?"

"Much longer than a human can." A slight man with a scholar's stoop, Dr. Verney consulted his memorandum book. "We've clocked her at a maximum of seventeen minutes and twenty seconds. But that was earlier in the day. The periods are noticeably shorter now."

"Yes." Deeps had his own timepiece in hand. "The last one was only four minutes and thirty-six seconds."

"Interesting." Sir Barnaby leaned forward on his cane to get a better view of the creature. "You think she's weakening, then?"

When I'd first met Sir Barnaby and his colleagues, they had looked at me in just such a way—as a curiosity, an oddity to be tested. Resentment flickered in me at the memory.

"If she is," I found myself saying, "maybe it's because the ropes are tied too tight."

"Too tight?" The King frowned. "Do you think that's so, Captain Ellis?"

The captain's jowly face reddened at the mere idea. "If we loosen them, she'll thrash herself right out of that barrel and into the sea, and then we'll all be at her mercy again. She's a killer."

"How exactly did she attack you?" I asked.

"She tried to wreck us," Captain Ellis. "She and her kin. And if Lord Walbrook hadn't been so quick-witted, they would've succeeded."

"Kin? You mean you saw more than one mermaid?" Penebrygg asked.

"Three by my count," volunteered Dr. Verney.

"By mine, too," Captain Ellis said.

"And this was near the mouth of the Thames, was it not?" the Lord High Admiral put in. "A treacherous place at the best of times, with sandbars and strange currents. A man must know what he is doing to get by them."

"Yes, my lord." Turning to me, Captain Ellis said, "I can show you the place later on the map, if you like."

"And when did it happen?" I asked.

"This morning, just after dawn." The captain's voice turned

grim. "I was steering the ship myself, with my best hands to help me. That's when we heard the singing."

"I heard it too," the ship's doctor said. "Such exquisite music—I have never heard the like." He glanced shyly at me. "Though I have never heard a Chantress sing."

"They're nothing alike," Nat assured him. "Chantress songs sound rather uncanny to our ears."

Norrie had always said they sounded eerie. I'd never known before what Nat thought.

"But the mermaids' song was beautiful beyond words," Nat went on. "Beautiful enough to drive men mad, in fact. Which is exactly what it started to do to us."

"To you, too?" Penebrygg asked.

"Luckily, I was below deck when it began, so I could barely hear it," Nat said. "It was only when someone in the cabin next to me shouted something about mermaids that I looked out through the porthole. When I saw them, I remembered the story of Ulysses and the sirens, the one in that dog-eared book you used to teach me Latin."

"Did you indeed?" Penebrygg seemed pleased.

Nat nodded. "And it's just as well I did. I didn't have any wax to hand, as Ulysses's men did, but the wool stuffing in my bolster served almost as well, once I tore it up. I shouted to the others below deck that they should plug their ears too, and then I ran up to the deck and plugged the ears of our captain here, and as many of the men as I could reach. Most of them recovered their senses quite quickly—and while they turned the ship,

I went after the mermaids, with the help of Dr. Verney and a few others."

"One of the creatures was by the shore, but the other two were just off the bow," Dr. Verney said. "We threw some fishing spears and hit one of them. The other we caught with a net."

"Once we got her on board, we gagged her," Captain Ellis said. "And then we had to figure out where to keep her."

"We wanted you to see her," Nat said to the King, "but I was afraid she would die if we kept her out of the water much longer. So we filled a barrel with seawater."

"A good thought," said Penebrygg.

"But she knocked it over the first time with her thrashing, so we had to tie her in—"

"And very slippery work it was too," Dr. Verney added. "Like an eel, she was . . ."

While they were talking, the mermaid came up for air. Her eyes were downcast, and the lids were red and puffy, as if she had been crying.

A trick or an illusion, perhaps. But the other thing I saw was most definitely not an illusion: the gray, wadded gag in her mouth, and the tiny spots of bright red blood where the water-soaked rope chafed against her cheeks.

So mermaids bled as we did.

"Three minutes and forty-eight seconds." Deeps clicked his timepiece closed.

"Fascinating," Sir Barnaby said. The ship's doctor made a note in his memorandum book.

No one else seemed to notice the bleeding.

Across from me, Nat said, "Some of the crew were all for killing her, but of course we didn't let them."

"Quite right," said Sir Barnaby. "Much better to study her while we can. Think of all we can learn. No one's ever had a chance to experiment with a live mermaid before."

My hands clenched. *She tried to drown the ship*, I reminded myself. *She tried to kill them all.* But killer or not, I felt ill. What kind of experiments did Sir Barnaby have in mind?

"That wasn't what I meant, Sir Barnaby," Nat said.

I was relieved to hear it, but my relief diminished as Nat continued speaking.

"I wanted to try to communicate with her." He looked at me over the top of the mermaid's head, his manner carefully impersonal. "Perhaps you can find out what her motives were, and if she and her kind have more attacks planned."

"An excellent idea," the King said.

I stared at the mermaid's bleeding face. "You mean you want me to interrogate her?"

"Yes," said Nat.

CHAPTER SEVEN

SISTERS UNDER THE SKIN

The mermaid raised her head and fastened her pale sea eyes on me. Could she understand what we were saying?

"I wouldn't know how to begin," I told Nat and the King. "Even without the gag—"

"The gag stays on." Captain Ellis crossed his bulky arms. "She's done enough damage already. Two of my crew still haven't recovered their senses. I'm not taking any chances with the rest."

"It seems the wool stuffing worked better for some than others," Dr. Verney explained. "Or perhaps they were just more vulnerable to begin with. Either way, we can't afford to let the mermaid sing again."

"Not on the ship, no," Nat said. "I propose we move her barrel to the Greenwich cellars. She shouldn't be able to do much damage there, even when the gag comes off."

The wind was picking up. I felt the *Dorset* rocking beneath me. The mermaid felt it too, I think. She turned her wan head in the direction of the breeze, and her tail fin swirled limply in the water.

"Are you sure she could tolerate the move?" I asked doubtfully. "She looks quite unwell to me."

"To me, too." Dr. Verney looked down at his memorandum book. "Judging from the evidence we've collected so far, she's weakening quickly. The strain of the move might kill her."

"Well, we can't have that," said Sir Samuel. "If she dies, we won't learn anything."

"True, true," the King said worriedly. "Chantress, can you suggest another course? Is there any other way we could learn her intentions?"

The mermaid was still watching me. Just looking into those sea-washed eyes was enough to make me feel that I knew her somehow, that we were sisters under the skin. . . .

But that was pure imagination.

"I can't read her mind without moonbriar," I said. "And we don't have any." The last vial had been destroyed in full sight of the King's Council last year.

Penebrygg said consolingly, "Never mind, my dear. There must be another way of approaching the problem."

"Yes, indeed." Sir Barnaby gave the mermaid a speculative glance. "If we could engineer it so that she could talk but not sing, we might be able to get something out of her. Perhaps if we experimented with her vocal cords . . ."

My own throat convulsed.

"No." The word flew out of me. Everyone turned to stare at me, and I realized my fists were clenched again.

"Chantress?" the King said.

"There must be another way." As I looked into the mermaid's eyes, I felt her fear almost as if it were my own. Her fear, and her longing for the sea.

"You're not going to take the gag off, are you?" Captain Ellis said, a little suspiciously.

"We've already settled that point, I believe," the King said. "Tell me, Chantress. What exactly do you have in mind?"

"I want to listen." Now, where had that idea come from? Never mind. It was worth pursuing. "To listen to the mermaid the way I listen to water."

Nat looked intrigued, and so did Penebrygg. Everyone else looked confused.

"But with that gag on, she can't make a sound," the Lord High Admiral protested.

"Not to your ears, no. But I can hear things in water that no one else does. I can sense what it wants and needs, and what tricks it might play—all without it speaking a word." I nodded at the mermaid. "The same might be true of her. She's a creature of the water, after all. And if Paracelsus is right, you could even call her the spirit of water."

Gabriel nodded at the mention of Paracelsus. "An interesting idea."

"Interesting, yes—but will it work?" Sir Barnaby questioned. "If you were going to hear something, Chantress, wouldn't you have heard it already?"

"It's hard to listen when there's so much chatter," I said. "We've hardly been silent a moment."

"Then from now on we'll be as quiet as monks," Nat said.

The others followed his lead, even the King. Captain Ellis sent an order down to the crew to keep still belowdecks. A few minutes later, all you could hear was the wind in the rigging and the quiet lap of the Thames against the sides of the frigate.

I looked at the mermaid, and she looked at me—and I gave myself over to listening.

At first I heard only the water in the barrel and its vexation at being contained. Round and round it went, an endless circling melody. But then I caught a glimmer of something else, a chilling music that told me that something in the barrel felt hunted; something felt afraid. And it wasn't the water.

Sir Barnaby leaned forward again, as if he wanted a closer look at the mermaid.

With a splash, she submerged, trailing a line of bubbles. The music came for me again, more powerful this time, panicked beyond reason.

"Back," I said. "Everyone needs to step as far back as you can."

Sir Barnaby looked annoyed, and so did the Lord High Admiral and Captain Ellis. But Nat and the King motioned for everyone to step well away from the barrel.

Safe, I tried to communicate to the mermaid. *It's safe*. But I'd lost all connection with her.

Frustrated, I wrapped my fingers around the edge of the barrel. She was right there in front of me, but I couldn't reach her, and I didn't dare touch her, not when she was so frightened already.

The water in the barrel bobbled. As it washed over my fingertips, a wave of feeling washed over me too, a bath of remorse so strong that it made me pull my hand from the water in shock.

The mermaid was sorry?

With a twist of her fins, she broke the surface again. Liquid streamed from her hair and down over her skin. It took me a few moments to see that it wasn't just seawater but tears.

I touched the water again, and again the tide of remorse washed over me—remorse and pain and fear.

She hadn't wanted to hurt anyone. I knew that now, without a doubt. And I knew something else as well. She was dying.

The gag wasn't just cutting into her skin, and it wasn't just stopping her from singing. It was suffocating her. The wadding had wound around her tongue, and now it was trailing down her throat, a little farther with every swallow . . .

Her panic felt like mine. I wanted to rip the gag off, then and there. But I knew there were reasons to be cautious. Besides, if I tried, I'd have to fight Captain Ellis, and likely most of the others, too—and though I could win that battle if I put enough of myself into it, there were better ways to save the mermaid's life. The gag was wet, after all. Could I find a way to compel the water in it to do my bidding?

Again I listened, this time not only to the mermaid but to the water all around her and especially in the wadding and the rope. The next time the mermaid submerged, I sang to the water, persuading it to float the wadding back up the mermaid's throat.

Then I used the weight of the water to stretch the rope fibers and slightly loosen the gag.

"Hold on there!" Captain Ellis started forward. "What's she singing?"

Nat and Gabriel pulled him back.

"She knows what she's doing," Nat said. "Give her the chance she's asked for."

His confidence surprised and warmed me. Distracted, I sang a moment too long, loosening the ropes more than I'd intended. Even as I drew breath to fix my mistake, the gag dropped.

"Stop her!" screamed the captain.

Nat lunged toward the barrel. And then he halted, dazed. They all did, every one of them.

The mermaid was singing.

The ship's doctor had spoken the truth: the song was exquisite, beyond anything I'd ever dreamed. Like the others, I was paralyzed by its beauty. Even as the mermaid wriggled out of the rest of the ropes that I'd so kindly—and so mistakenly—loosened for her, all I could think about was her music.

Unlike the others on the *Dorset*, however, I'd had long practice in dealing with bewitching tunes, and I had learned how to withstand some of their wiles. The best way was to go deep inside myself, to focus on my own heartbeat and not on external sounds. When I did this, the mermaid's song lost some of its power. I found I could move again, although it took tremendous effort.

Singing magic, however, was beyond me. For that, I would

have to open myself up and listen to the music around me again—and who knew where that would lead? I might end up singing the mermaid's song with her. Better to plug the ears of the men near me and get their help.

Even as I turned toward them, the mermaid thrashed and knocked the whole barrel over. It split as it fell, and water gushed out, carrying the mermaid halfway to the rail.

"No." I forced myself forward and grabbed hold of a slippery fin. "Stay. Talk to me."

Even as I touched her scales, I felt her anger. There was no remorse here, no regret, only a wild hatred.

You will pay, Chantress. Mind to mind, she spoke to me, even as her lips continued to shape the beautiful song. *The sea is coming. We are coming. And we will drown you all.*

In shock I clutched harder at the fin. *What?*

Let go. The mermaid's powerful tail slammed me against the deck. Stunned, I released her fin.

Still singing, the mermaid grasped the rail with her milky white arms and hoisted herself up and over it. With a great splash, she dived into the river and was gone.

CHAPTER EIGHT
STRANGERS

I raced to the rail. All was quiet and dark, and there was no sign of the mermaid, not even a slight glow under the waves.

But her song was gone with her, and that meant I could draw on my magic again. I listened to the Thames and found what I needed—a music to find the mermaid and trap her, a music to pull her toward us.

Behind me, the men were stirring.

"What was that?" someone said.

"She's escaped," the King cried. "The mermaid's escaped."

"It's the Chantress's doing," Captain Ellis snarled.

"It must have been an accident," Penebrygg said.

Nat strode to my side. "What happened?"

I couldn't stop to look at him, let alone answer; the mermaid was getting farther away with every moment. Shutting everything out except the music, I called on the river to help me.

My song traveled out into the night and then exploded into

cacophony. My head swam. It was as if my song had run headlong into a wall.

Something was protecting the mermaid, something unbelievably strong, something that in no way resembled the mermaid's own magic. Could it be the river itself? Or the sea currents within it? Could mermaids call on that kind of power?

"What's she doing?" Captain Ellis demanded.

"Keep quiet," someone said. Was it Gabriel?

The captain wouldn't be silenced. "Don't you give me orders. It's my ship, and I'll say what I like. How do we know she isn't helping the mermaid?"

Ignoring everything else, I sang again. Once more my music slammed into some sort of wall, throwing a surge of sound back at me. But this time, as the brief noise faded, I thought I heard something else deep in the water, the very faint traces of a powerful song, swirling with anger.

Strange and complex, it was utterly unlike the mermaid's song. Indeed, it was unlike any music I'd ever heard before. But there was something about the phrasing and the cadences that made me think of Chantress song-spells.

Could it be another Chantress?

In my shock, I must have made a sound, or moved in an odd way, because Nat said immediately, "What's wrong?"

A year and a half apart, and yet he could still read me plainly. Another time, that might have made me happy. Right now, however, it added to my sense of strain.

Should I tell him—tell everyone—what I thought I'd heard?

No. Not yet. I'd heard too little to be sure of anything. Instead I focused on what mattered most—finding out where the limits of my power lay. Would the river still do my bidding in other matters? Quickly I sang to it, a simple spell for creating spouts of spray.

It responded immediately, even enthusiastically, shooting off small fountains in all directions. I sang a spell to calm it, and they vanished. But when I tried again to call back the mermaid, I hit the same wall. I strained forward, listening for the strange new music. This time I heard nothing.

Behind me, Captain Ellis lost his temper. "I'll tell you what's wrong. Look at her!" I swung around to face him, but it was the men he was speaking to, not me. "The mermaid's gone off to shipwreck other vessels, and all the Chantress does is blow bubbles. And yet not one of you will speak a word against her."

"With reason, Captain," the King rebuked him. "She's earned our trust many times over."

"And we're not exactly blameless ourselves," Nat added. "Some of us should have worn earplugs, just to be on the safe side. I had mine in my pocket, but that wasn't good enough, not when she was singing just a few feet away."

I was grateful that Nat was helping to shoulder the blame. Yet when he turned to me, his eyes were full of questions—the same questions that were in everyone else's, even the King's.

What I had to tell them wasn't going to help matters.

"I'm afraid Captain Ellis is right." I steadied myself against the rail as the ship swayed beneath me. "The fault is mine. I meant only to keep the mermaid from choking, but it all went wrong." As dispassionately as I could, I explained how she had told me she was dying, how I'd tried to save her, and how I'd made a mistake with the ropes. "I chased after her, and just now I tried to use my magic to sing her back. But she outwitted me. I'm sorry."

My admission of guilt didn't take the edge off the captain's anger. Sir Barnaby also looked none too pleased, and Sir Samuel and the Admiral and Dr. Verney gave me reproachful looks. Nat had stepped back into shadow, so I couldn't even guess at what he thought. But at least the King, Penebrygg, and Gabriel were nodding sympathetically.

"I'm afraid there's more." I told them what the mermaid had told me: *The sea is coming. We are coming. And we will drown you all.*

"What does it mean?" the King wondered.

"Nothing good," Captain Ellis growled under his breath.

Sir Barnaby jabbed his cane at a bit of the broken barrel. "If you ask me, it's a pack of nonsense. She was lying to you, Chantress. Just as she lied about choking and dying."

Had she been lying about the gag? I still wasn't sure. And the vicious words of warning had felt like the unvarnished truth. "It didn't feel like a lie."

"You were fooled before," Sir Barnaby said.

To that, I had no good answer, except perhaps to mention the faint song I'd heard, so powerful and so full of ill will. But then I was unsure of that, too. I'd heard it for only a moment, and it was hard to remember now exactly how it had sounded, still less why it had put me in mind of a Chantress. Most likely it was more mermaid magic—and Sir Barnaby was right to point out that I'd been taken in by that before.

Before anyone could say anything more, the King intervened. "Well, whatever the truth of the matter, it seems that no one is drowning now, for which we should all be thankful. Captain Ellis, I am sure you and Dr. Verney will want to stay with your ship, but I suggest that the rest of you come with me now to Greenwich Palace. We will discuss this again in the morning."

The King spoke with a finality that kept even Captain Ellis from contradicting him. Orders went out that the ship's tender should be readied to bring us to the landing.

The Lord High Admiral shot a doubtful look at me as we boarded the tender. "Well, it's a shame the creature got away from you, that's all I can say. And there was one who escaped earlier too, wasn't there? So that's two of them on the loose. They could be anywhere by now."

I thought of Lady Gillian. That episode wasn't something I could keep to myself now, though I'd do my best not to bring Sybil into it. "I'm afraid there may be one in London," I told the others. "At twilight today, someone reported an odd creature swimming near the Whitehall landing. It may have been nothing, but now I wonder . . ."

"By Whitehall?" The King looked alarmed, and so did the others.

The Lord High Admiral looked thunder at me as I sat down across from him. "You didn't investigate?"

"No. At the time, it wasn't a priority." I wasn't going to explain why. "Of course, now I wish I had."

The Lord High Admiral narrowed his eyes. "I should think so. Quite an oversight, I must say."

Perhaps the others were merely busy finding their seats—Nat sat down in one well away from me—but no one came to my defense. And I couldn't defend myself without implicating Sybil.

Fortunately, Sir Samuel was only too happy to take advantage of my silence. Seated on the other side of the Lord High Admiral, he started conversing with him about the best way to defend London and the navy against this new threat.

As the oarsmen set out for Greenwich Palace, the others joined in the discussion. While they talked about the best way to procure earplugs and issue them to seamen, I kept quiet and looked out at the river. No matter how hard I listened, I could hear no sign of the mermaid. Nor could I hear anything of the strange force that had protected her.

† † †

When we reached the palace, the King asked to see any dispatches from London. We were all relieved to hear there were no reports of anything that could possibly be construed as mermaid magic. Heaving learned this, the King seemed disinclined to work into the small hours. At any rate, he didn't want to work with me. When I offered to stay, he said, "No, no. You've done a great deal already. I expect you could use a rest."

His expression was kind, and I had to assume his concern for me was genuine. Yet I noticed he stayed back to have a word with Nat and Sir Barnaby. Worried and confused and tired out from the magic I'd done, I said good night and left them.

The room assigned to me was a fine one. A maidservant had already laid the fire, and she returned to set down a tray of pastries and cold beef to tempt my appetite. But I could not seem to settle. Instead of eating, I stood by the oriel window that looked out over the Thames, just listening and listening.

Not one strain of the river's music seemed out of the ordinary. Yet still it worried me to see the *Dorset* floating at anchor, vulnerable in the dark. By letting the mermaid escape, I'd put the ship and her crew in danger. What if she returned and her singing drove the night watch mad? Or what if the power that guarded her chose to attack in the night?

We will drown you all.

Was it just an empty threat? Maybe. But if there was even a chance it was true, I ought to keep watch over the ship. Though not from here. The landing would be better; I could hear everything out there.

The maidservant made a token effort to dissuade me from going out, but she was in too much awe of my magic to do more. Cloaked against the damp river air, I slipped through the passageways, headed for the landing.

At this hour, few lights were left burning, but memory and touch guided me. A left turn through this doorway, and then down the steps.

Hands skimming the rail, I turned the curve of the staircase. A shadow loomed in front of me, but I was going too fast to stop, and I thumped straight into it.

The shadow turned out to be a person. At first I didn't know who—only that it was someone big enough to knock me off my feet and send me sliding down the stairs. Sprawled on the bottom step, head swimming, I heard an unmistakable voice.

"Lucy?"

"Nat?"

"Yes." He knelt beside me, still shadowy. "I'm sorry. I didn't see you. Are you hurt?"

I checked my ankle, which had borne the weight of my fall. "Nothing that won't mend." My head was still swimming, but for a different reason now. I could only just make out the lines of his body, but he was so close, I could feel the warmth of him there in the dark.

"You're still up?" I asked.

"The King wanted me to tell him everything I knew about mermaids. And you?"

"I'm going out to the landing." There was no reason to hide my plan; it wasn't a state secret. "I'm worried the mermaid will attack the *Dorset* again, so I'm going to keep guard over it."

"There's no need," Nat said. "We found some more serviceable earplugs here in the palace, and they've been delivered to Captain Ellis. The night watch is now wearing them, and the rest have them at the ready."

"Oh." That would go a long way toward keeping the *Dorset* safe. "But there are other ships . . ."

"Thousands," Nat agreed, "but no one can guard them all, not even you. Especially when you're exhausted. If a mermaid attacks, you can be sure we'll call on you. But for now, you should go back to your room and get some sleep." He reached for me. "Here. I'll help you up."

His steady hand wrapped around mine, pulling me to my feet. It was done in a moment, but it left me breathless. His rough chin brushed my forehead, and I felt him take a deep breath. He still had my hand, and we were so close that we could have kissed.

I lifted my head, and then we *were* kissing. So familiar this, and yet so new after all this time apart. When I leaned into him, his hands circled my waist and pulled me closer, as if to erase all distance between us. His lips were like music on mine, and I felt a rush of elation so intense, it was almost painful.

He still loves me. After all this time, he still loves me. The thought was as powerful and irresistible as magic itself. After so much sadness, so much loneliness, I wanted to drown in his kisses, drown and be lost.

He broke off the kiss and turned his head, his chin scraping my cheek. "Someone's coming." He pulled away, and then I heard it too, the tramp of boots coming close.

"You wait here," he murmured. His own boots made hardly any sound; I knew he was gone only when I heard a door click shut. A little later, I heard voices in brief conversation, though I couldn't make out the words. Soon he returned alone, a bright candle in his hand.

"Just one of the guards," he said quietly. "Nothing to worry about. I told him I was having a quick check of the place. I . . . er . . . didn't mention you were here."

"Oh." Was Nat simply trying to safeguard my reputation, or did he not want anyone to know that we'd been together?

I couldn't ask him. The interruption had made us awkward with each other. In darkness, it had been easier to believe that nothing had changed between us. The light gave that the lie. Suddenly we couldn't meet each other's eyes.

"This isn't going to work, is it?" Nat said.

Dread hit me in the pit of the stomach. He'd spoken my fears aloud.

Slowly I said, "I think we need to talk."

"Yes."

"You go first," I told him.

For a moment, I thought he wouldn't. But then, looking steadily down into the candle flame, he started to speak.

"The reason I was on that ship—the reason I was coming back to England—was to see you."

That was why he was here?

"Since we parted, I've thought of you every day, almost every hour," he went on. "I've hated being so distant from you, but I thought that in the end we'd be stronger for it. And I was hoping the time had finally come when we could be together again. But it's not that simple, is it? I saw that on the ship. The moment you saw that gag, you sided against me."

"I had questions, yes." I couldn't deny it. "But—"

"You gave the mermaid the benefit of the doubt, again and again. But not me."

I winced. I hadn't thought of it that way before. "That was a mistake. I'm sorry."

"It's not an apology I'm after, Lucy. I'm just saying that the trust between us is gone. I've been trying to tell myself it doesn't matter, that we can rebuild—but I'm not sure we can. The way you look at me, the way you speak to me, it's all changed. We might as well be strangers."

I was so upset, I couldn't speak.

More gently, he said, "You must feel it too."

And the worst of it was, I did. The Nat who had gone away wasn't the same as the one who was speaking to me now. And I supposed I wasn't the same Lucy, either. But that he thought of us as strangers—that was as bitter as galls to me.

I meant to stay calm, meant to choose my words carefully, but I suddenly found I couldn't. "If we're strangers, whose fault is that?" I said, my voice unsteady. "You're the one who left me. You're the one who asked me to stay away. You're the one who said I mustn't even write to you." I hadn't realized till this moment quite how angry I was about that. Or maybe I had, and I'd buried it. But there was no burying it now.

"I gave you everything you asked for," I said. "I let them all think there was nothing between us. Even when the Court gossips said that you'd left me because I was too cold, too inhuman to love, I said nothing—"

"They said *what*?"

I barely registered his words. "I didn't even tell my friends the truth. I couldn't; they might have given you away. I was more alone than I've ever been. And maybe you're right; maybe that's changed me. But in the name of all that's holy, Nat, how could you walk away from me for a year and a half and then come back and expect me to be the same?"

I turned my back on him and ran up the stairs.

CHAPTER NINE
LOVE SONG

I woke the next morning to a sore ankle and a sodden, weeping sky.

He didn't come after me, was my first thought.

And then: *What did you expect?*

His voice echoed again and again in my mind: *We might as well be strangers*.

By the cold light of morning, I had to admit the truth. He was right. I was a stranger to him, and he to me. There was no trust between us anymore—and no love.

I shut my eyes again. Whatever loneliness I had felt while on the road paled beside this.

The maidservant bustled in, bearing a cup of chocolate. "Good morning to you, my lady. Though *good*'s not the word for it, really. It's bucketing, it is. You should see the guards at the gates. They look half-drowned."

Drowned . . .

I sat up sharply. "The ship. The *Dorset*. Is she still out there?"

"No, my lady."

My heart thudded. I shouldn't have left her unguarded. "What happened?"

"She left for London on the dawn tide," the maidservant said. "The King and Lord Walbrook and the other councilors left too, on the royal barge. And a good thing, because the rain wasn't near as bad when they set out."

"They left without me?"

"Yes, my lady. I tried to wake you, but you were dead to the world. Must've been the tea I gave you last night, for the pain."

Vaguely I remembered the tea, a black concoction the maidservant had insisted on bringing to me last night after she'd seen me limping. I'd drunk the tea to placate her, and because I'd been desperate for sleep.

"But the King was going to hold a meeting." I waved away the chocolate that she was trying to press on me now. "I was expected to be there."

"He was told you were indisposed, my lady," the maidservant said. "The others urged him to let you rest."

The others? Did that mean Nat? Had he been hoping to spare himself the embarrassment of seeing me after last night's debacle? Did he think we could continue to avoid each other at Court?

If so, he had another think coming. I wasn't going to play that game any longer. Not when he thought of us as strangers.

"His Majesty sent his sympathies," the maidservant added, "and asked if you would follow him to Whitehall as soon as you're able."

I threw back my covers. "I'll go right now."

Now turned out not to be possible. My ankle was only mildly sprained, but it needed wrapping, which slowed me down, and the captain of the pinnace had to make his own preparations. When we finally did set sail, the weather was foul. Rain sluiced down without any letup, delaying our progress.

I hoped the sky would begin to clear by the time we reached Whitehall, but it was pouring there, too. After the pinnace deposited me on the covered landing, I looked back at the Thames. The rain was so heavy, it made London's houses and wharves and towers look gray and washed-out, like a city of watery shadows. Shivering, I covered my head with my cloak hood and hurried inside.

Rowan Knollys met me as I came in. "Chantress, we didn't look for you so soon. I heard you were unwell?"

"It's nothing to worry about, only a sore ankle." I pushed back my hood and shook off the raindrops. "Where is the King? Meeting with the Council?"

"The meeting is over, but I believe he's in the State Rooms."

"I'll go straight there then, and I'll meet you in the guardrooms afterward."

There was nothing straight about Whitehall, however, and that included the path to the State Rooms. Catching sight of myself in a gilded mirror along the way, I decided I would go to my rooms first after all. The trip upriver had left me bedraggled and windblown, and I wanted to be as composed as possible when I saw the King, especially if Nat happened to be with him.

Several twists and turns later, I heard the sound of singing.

I halted in my tracks, immediately on guard; the incident with the mermaid had made me vigilant. But then I heard a burst of laughter, and when it tapered off, a duet began—a tenor and soprano singing one of the new Italian love songs that were all the rage. I drew a sigh of relief. This was innocent enough.

The music was coming from a room around the corner—a large room near the Queen's chambers, where the younger set at Court could sometimes be found larking about. My route would take me past it, and I was curious and just a little wistful as I approached. Being a Chantress left little time for larks. Even when I was at Court, I rarely joined in, and every time I did the result was awkwardness. The ladies-in-waiting, the courtiers—everyone knew I didn't really belong there. And they were right. Forced to choose between Court capers and the demands of my magic, I'd have chosen the magic every time.

Still, I slowed as I came toward the open door. It was beautiful singing, by any standard, full of pleasing harmonies, plaintive and passionate by turns. Yet when I glanced through the door to see the singers, I had a shock. The tenor was Nat.

I didn't even know he could sing.

His partner was Lady Clemence. *She's been besotted with him for months*, Sybil had said. And there were other women there too. Now that the song was ending, at least half a dozen ladies-in-waiting were crowding around Nat, buzzing like bees around honeycomb. They all appeared to be on very friendly terms with him, and he with them.

The only stranger here was me.

Heart skittering, I backed away. But not quickly enough. Nat glanced up and saw me.

How must I appear, to have him look at me that way?

My cheeks throbbed. Averting my face, I darted back into the maze that was Whitehall. I thought I was well away, when I heard him call out to me.

"Lucy, wait."

I turned. He was alone—a small mercy, that. With easy grace, he loped up to me, till we were merely a few spaces apart on the checkerboard floor of the passageway.

Trying to hide my distress, I said as calmly as I could, "So you sing. You never mentioned that."

"It's not really something you say to a Chantress, is it?"

It was an honest response, and if things had been different between us, it might even have made me laugh. Instead I had to look away, remembering a time when I'd been Lucy to him, not "a Chantress."

"I owe you an apology," Nat said.

My heart seemed to stop beating.

"I thought I was doing what was best for us both," he went on. "I rode out into the world like a knight on a charger, willing to pay any price to prove I was worthy of you. But I didn't stop to think about what it would cost you. I had no idea how much you were suffering. I don't say that to excuse myself—I should have known, or guessed, or made it my business to find out. But I didn't. You're right. I was expecting we would come back together and have everything be the same, just better."

I could only shake my head. "It doesn't work that way."

"I know," he said quietly. "If I still thought it was that easy, I'd have come after you last night."

So that was why he hadn't followed me.

"What's done is done." Even in the dark passageway, I could see the sadness in his eyes. "We really are strangers now. Maybe something worse than strangers. It's not what either of us intended, but it's how it is."

He was only speaking the truth, but something gave way inside me. I hadn't realized that I'd still harbored a spark of hope, until it went out.

With a patter of light slippers, Lady Clemence appeared at the door. She gave me a half-fearful, half-apologetic look, but her face softened as she turned to Nat. "I'm so sorry to interrupt. It's just that the others are insisting we sing for them again."

"Not just now," Nat said, but there was a gentleness as he spoke to her, and a warmth in his smile that startled me. Perhaps the admiration was not entirely one way.

"Go," I said to Nat. "I don't mean to keep you."

The words were barely out of my mouth when the shouting started.

It was far louder than the cry I'd heard the night before when I'd been out on the landing—a shout that came not from one voice but dozens, perhaps even hundreds. Building to a terrible roar, it went on and on, fearful and agonized. I started running toward the commotion, and so did Nat.

Because of my ankle, Nat easily outdistanced me. When I

caught up with him, he was pushing his way through a crowd of guards by the entrance that led out onto the river landing. By now it was clear that the noise was coming from the river. I followed Nat out the door.

Outside, standing on the stormy embankment, I couldn't tell at first what was wrong. I could see only boats pulling hard for the shore and people running from the riverbank. But then, through the curtain of rain, I glimpsed a monstrous gray-green head rising out of the Thames, and a thick, coiled tail lashing behind it.

Bearing down on us was a creature straight out of myth and legend and nightmare—a sea monster.

CHAPTER TEN

HERE BE DRAGONS

Impossible to believe, and yet there it was, a sea serpent writhing in the river. Not a small snake, this, but a great eel grown to a monstrous size, its vast body longer than a man-of-war. For a moment I gaped at it. Then I started to sing, calling on the river to pull the beast down to its depths.

I thought it would work. And it almost did. But as the river swirled up against the monster, I felt the magic buckle and break. For a moment, I was swamped by cacophony. Something was stopping me, just as it had with the mermaid. Something with a magic stronger than mine.

The sea is coming. We are coming. And we will drown you all. Was this what the mermaid had meant?

"Can't you stop it?" Nat asked.

"The water won't listen," I told him. "I don't know why."

Maybe I just needed to find the right music. I tried another tune—a song meant to draw the water out of the monster itself and leave it parched and dry. The only thing my singing accomplished this time was to attract the attention of the monster. Through filmy eyes it searched for me, trying to find the source of the sound.

"Stop." Nat flung out an arm, as if to shield me. "If you keep singing, it will find you."

At another time, I might have been moved by his desire to protect me. But right now I didn't want to be shielded. While some boats had made it to safety, others were still midriver, full of terrified passengers. I needed to defend them. I needed to defeat the monster.

How could I do that? Looking out to the edge of the landing, where several skiffs were tethered, I had an inspiration. Ducking past Nat, I ran down and jumped into one of the boats. Even as my ankle bumped up against the bottom, making me wince, I was reaching for the oars.

As I cast off, Nat leapt into the skiff, nearly knocking the oars from my hands.

"What do you think you're doing?" I shouted through the rain. "Are you crazy?"

"No, but I think you are," he shot back. "You should fight the beast from land, where it can't get you."

"No good," I gasped out, pulling hard at the oars. "Must try and get closer, see what I can hear."

Maybe I'd convinced him—or maybe he simply saw there was no turning me back. At any rate he took up one of the oars, helping to take us through the choppy seas toward the monster.

I sang to the river to speed us, and when it obeyed, I felt hopeful. Yet before I could turn my magic on the monster, its fearsome jaws snapped at the nearest boat, a ferryman's sturdy craft. The gleaming teeth crunched through the timber, splintering off the prow. The passengers screamed as they went sliding into the cold, churning waters.

How could I not sing them to safety? Passing my oar to Nat, I knelt in the bottom of the boat. Soaked through by seawater and rainwater alike, I used my music to float the monster's victims to shore.

By the time I was done, the creature had me in its sights again, the long slavering tongue flicking like a battle flag in the heavy rain.

"Look out!" Nat cried. "It's turning!"

There was no time to think. The beast was racing toward us, open-jawed. As Nat pulled hard at the oars, I leaned out over the livid waters and let out a volley of song.

The monster writhed and dived under the water, as if anticipating the force of my blow. But when it came up, sleek and stinking, from the bottom of the river, I felt my music shatter on the back of whatever protected it. A sudden blare of noise made my ears ring. Then, from deep within the water, I heard the faint strains of music, a song with a cadence and resonance like Chantress magic but even richer, with odd tunings all its own. A song as slippery as water. A song full of rage.

Blasted by its intensity, I rocked back in the boat. For a moment, the smell of magic was so strong that I was choking on it. As I tried to catch my breath, the sea serpent thrashed its massive tail and set the waters whirling. Our skiff went spinning.

"The oars!" Nat clutched at one, but the other was lost.

Knocked against the bottom of the boat, I smelled a blast of putrid breath. Turning, I saw the monster closing in on us. It snapped its massive jaws, baring serrated teeth. I heard the glamour of the raging music glistening all around me. Was it one voice, or two, or three? The water distorted the song and magnified it. Or perhaps that was just the confusion in my own head.

How could I defeat this? We were done for.

"Stay down!" Pulling me back, Nat snatched a dagger from his belt. Against the coiling length of the great serpent, the dagger looked laughably small—a matchstick next to a dragon. But when Nat lobbed it at the scaly head, the beast shrieked.

Nat had aimed at the eyes, but at the last second the monster twisted away so that the dagger struck the scales on its back, well down from the head.

I winced in sharp disappointment. It couldn't possibly be a death blow.

Yet even as I braced myself for the crunch of its massive teeth, the monster started backing away. It was wailing, almost keening, in a language that I could not understand. More miraculously still, the great green coils were turning the color of water and dissolving, first around the spot where the dagger had lodged, and then out and out until the entire monster was gone.

Crouched in the boat, Nat turned to me, bewildered. "Did I do that?"

"It wasn't me," I said. "There was strong magic there, but I don't know what it was. I've never heard anything like it. If it weren't for you, we'd have gone down."

"But it was just a dagger." Nat looked out at the spot where the monster had vanished, as if he still couldn't quite believe it was gone. "Made of the best Toledo steel, but even so . . ."

"Maybe it was a lucky blow."

"But I only nicked its back. It wasn't exactly a mortal injury." And then, more slowly, Nat said, "Maybe that's it."

"What do you mean?"

"That creature wasn't something from the mortal world, was it? It was magic."

"Yes." The smell and the sound of magic had been all over it.

"And steel is mostly iron, and iron breaks magic, doesn't it?"

"Not mine." Iron had never stopped me.

"No, but lots of kinds, or so the old stories say. It's death to goblins, witches, faeries—why not sea monsters, too?"

"I don't know," I said doubtfully. "Could it really be that easy?"

Humor glimmered in his eyes. "I'm not sure 'easy' is the right word for what we've just been through."

I had to laugh, but even as I did, something wrenched inside me. For a moment, he no longer seemed like a stranger. That glimmer in his eyes, that quiet humor—they were part of what I had loved about him.

As he looked back at me, I felt the old spark leap between us. For one shining moment, I could believe that time had run backward and we were in a world where we had never parted. Anything seemed possible.

But then he looked away, and I became conscious once more of the cold rain and my river-drenched clothes and the lingering smell of putrid serpent breath in my hair. Romance on the river? Not here. It would take more than a spark to fix what had gone wrong between us.

"Ahoy there!"

I turned, startled. One of the royal pinnaces was bearing down on our small boat, and the captain was calling out to us through cupped hands. "Marvelous, the way you two finished off that beast! We've come to pick you up and tow your boat to shore."

Before either Nat or I could reply, an enormous cheer shook the waters. A crowd had gathered on the riverbank and was saluting the victory. "Hurrah!"

Moments later, the pinnace drew up beside us. In the commotion and fuss that followed, Nat and I were separated. We were back in the real world, the world of the Court—the world where we were strangers once again.

CHAPTER ELEVEN

MELUSINE

After we landed, Norrie, shaken and white, took charge of me as soon as she could. Exclaiming and making much of me, she bustled me off to our rooms and prepared a hot bath. "To warm you up," she said, "and to ward off colds."

Perhaps that was all it was meant to do, but I noticed that she sprinkled lavender and rosemary into the bath, and even slipped in a bay leaf—herbs of protection against harm. I could remember her making use of them on the enchanted island where I'd spent my childhood, but I hadn't realized she had them here in London, too.

At first the steaming water was white-hot on my chilled skin, but after a few minutes my muscles relaxed and the nightmare of the monster began to recede. As I washed the stink of the serpent out of my hair, Norrie came and sat beside me, speaking cheerily all the while. But when she stood to get the towels, she glanced out the window and shivered again over what might have been.

"Oh, lamb, I don't think I'll be able to look at that river for a month, it makes me that sick. When I think of that horrible creature—and you in that tiny boat, with nothing but your music to defend you . . ."

"I had Nat," I reminded her. "It was Nat who saved us."

"Did he?" Norrie shook her head. "I can't say I saw it all that clearly, not from so far back, and with the rain so heavy. But I did hear you singing. Surely your magic helped?"

I shook my head. "We'd have been lost without Nat's dagger." I was thankful beyond words that Nat had been there, and I wanted to give credit where it was due. But in the back of my mind, I felt chagrin, too—and worry. I was used to being the one who saved myself, and the one who saved others. Yet against that strange, impossibly strong magic, I'd been all but powerless.

I couldn't bring myself to say it in so many words, however. Not even to Norrie.

"The dear boy," said Norrie. Then, looking more closely at me, she added, "I hope I'm not speaking out of turn—"

"Let's not talk about it now." My face, already pink from the bath, grew pinker. I stirred a bit of rosemary with my hand. "Tell me about these herbs instead. Do you really think they work?"

Norrie hesitated. "Well, my own mother set great store by them, and people have been using them for time out of mind to keep themselves safe. Though I can't say they did much to protect you, back when you went singing us off our island. But who can tell? Maybe it would've gone worse for us if I'd done nothing."

"Lady Helaine said they weren't part of Chantress lore."

"Your godmother didn't have much time for them, it's true, but I don't see why Chantresses should scorn to use them. Especially now that we're coming up to Allhallows' Eve. Only a few days now till it's here."

Norrie had always been anxious about Allhallows' Eve, believing it to be a time when spirits walked and magical threats abounded. Her worries seemed to be based more on old traditions than anything else. According to Lady Helaine, however, Allhallows' Eve was indeed a dangerous time of year, at least for Chantresses, because that was when Wild Magic was at its strongest.

This warning hadn't affected me as Lady Helaine had intended. She'd taught me that everything in this world had its own Wild Magic, its own music—which could mislead or even kill a Chantress who opened herself up to it. Like most Chantresses, my godmother wore a stone that deafened her to Wild Magic—a stone that instead allowed her to work Proven Magic, a collection of safe song-spells that Chantresses learned by rote.

I had once had such a stone myself, but it was cracked and useless now. Wild Magic was the only way open to me. Fortunately, I gloried in it, finding it far more powerful and flexible than Proven Magic, and far less dangerous than my godmother had claimed. For a long time now, I hadn't given Allhallows' Eve a second thought, except to appreciate the greater intensity and clarity I heard in the music all around me at this time of year.

But perhaps I had been naïve. Perhaps Norrie's vague anxiety and Lady Helaine's solemn warnings contained more truth than I'd realized.

I thought of the furious singing I'd heard—so much like a Chantress, and yet so different. "Norrie, you don't happen to know of any connections between sea monsters and Chantresses, do you?"

Norrie looked at me over the towel. "What a question!"

I pressed her again. "Do you?"

"I'm the wrong one to ask," Norrie said. "You know that."

It was true. Norrie wasn't a Chantress herself, and she wasn't privy to Chantress secrets. Which suited her just fine, as magic had always made her uneasy. By preference, she had as little to do with it as possible.

"All I know is the Melusine story," Norrie said, "and you know that already."

So I did, though I hadn't thought to connect it with the monster I'd just battled. It was one of Lady Helaine's favorite stories—a lesson, as she saw it, in the importance of respecting one's elders and the awful consequences that came of not obeying their rules.

According to Lady Helaine, Melusine had been a first-generation Chantress, meaning that she'd been the daughter of a faerie mother and a human father. As a small child, Melusine went to live in the faerie realms with her mother, Pressina, but at fifteen she returned to the mortal world, where she tried to use her magic against her father. Pressina herself punished Melusine for this terrible act by cursing her. From then on, Melusine turned into a sea serpent from the waist down every Saturday, without fail.

For years, Melusine used her Chantress skills to hide the truth from everyone, even the man who became her husband. She was loved and respected, renowned not only as a mother and wife but as a builder of castles and walls and towers. But one Saturday her husband surprised her in her bath. When he saw her slick, green coils, he shouted out in horror, and Melusine turned on him in a rage, becoming a sea serpent from head to toe.

It was a tale that had given me nightmares when Lady Helaine first told it, for Melusine had ended her life as a monster, unable to claw her way back to human form. But of course there was no proof that Melusine had ever really existed. I'd heard other versions of her story elsewhere, and they were all different—and the very relish with which Lady Helaine had told her variation made me suspect she had embellished it mightily.

"I can't see what that story has to do with the monster you saw," Norrie said doubtfully.

I couldn't either. The story was probably no more than a legend. And there was nothing to connect it with what I'd seen on the river.

"It was just a shot in the dark," I said.

Norrie frowned. "But why are you asking about sea monsters and Chantress magic in the first place?"

I was saved from having to answer by a knock at the outer door. Norrie went to see who it was.

"The King's calling the Council together," she reported when she returned. "They won't meet for another hour, but the King sent a page to ask if you will see him in the meantime."

"Tell him I'm coming," I said, and reached for the towel.

† † †

A quarter of an hour later, nestled in a warm blue gown of soft wool, I was on my way to the King. My body was still warm from the bath, but I could feel the chill in the air as I hurried toward the State Rooms.

I'd gone only a short way when the King himself appeared around a corner, an anxious look in his eye. "Chantress! Well met."

"Your Majesty." I was surprised to see him so far from the State Rooms. Usually he was so busy that I was the one who had to find him. His reasons for seeing me must have been urgent indeed. "You wanted to speak before the meeting?"

"Yes. Now that you're dry, perhaps we could have a private word? I want to understand exactly what happened out there on the river."

"Of course," I said. "I can't vouch as to how it started, but by the time I came out onto the riverfront—"

"Why don't we go out to the river itself?" the King interrupted. "That way you can show me where you were standing."

Before I could answer, he was already hurrying forward and motioning for me to follow.

"As quickly as you can, Chantress," he said over his shoulder as I raced to keep up with him. "I know this isn't the ordinary route, but that's all to the good if we don't want everyone at Court tagging at our heels."

It was indeed an unusual route—Byzantine, even by Whitehall standards. Instead of emerging at the King's landing, we came out by the workaday wharf at the far end of the palace, where foodstuffs and coal and other supplies for the Court were unloaded. Not much work was going on now, however. Whether because of the continuing rain or because of the fright the sea monster had caused, there were very few people to be seen.

"There." The King seemed pleased. "Now we can talk in peace."

I nodded, still catching my breath.

He gestured for me to join him at the wharf's edge. "Tell me everything."

As I stepped toward the river, I heard a faint flicker of anger buried deep in its usual songs. I stopped midstride. "Your Majesty, be careful!"

"Why?"

"There's something wrong here." I listened again. "No, it's gone now." Gone—or buried still deeper, where I couldn't find it?

I sniffed the air. Was that a faint trace of magic?

With a worried face, the King turned again toward the water. "Could it be another sea monster? Come, tell me if you see anything!"

As I rushed over, I smelled magic again. Behind me, I heard a distant shout.

"Don't look," the King commanded me.

But I couldn't help it. I glanced back. Two people were coming out of the gate by the landing—Nat . . . and the King.

Two Kings? I froze. They couldn't both be real.

"Ignore them," the King beside me snarled.

Now I knew for certain who the false King was. Leaping back behind a pile of crates, I started to sing in self-defense. And that was when I had my second shock, because my song shattered on the false King just as it had shattered on the sea monster. After a moment of cacophony, I heard the raging music again, the same music I'd heard out on the river—and this time it sounded more like a Chantress than ever.

"You're coming with me." The false King seized a stick from the ground and came after me with it, nearly knocking me into the water.

I heard Nat shout, but he was too far away to help. A wall divided the wharf from the rest of the palace waterfront, and he and the true King were still trying to scramble over it.

The false King swung his stick again, this time whacking me on the shoulder. I stumbled, and my hands came down on something hard. A broken bit of chain.

Iron chain.

I scrabbled for it, fingers slick with mud and rain. As the stick came down again, I rolled away and flung the chain into the false King's face.

When it hit, he shrieked. For a second it looked as though his face were melting. Then his entire shape wavered and changed. He turned into something only half-human, and then into something not human at all.

A serpent writhed at my feet, its coils translucent where the iron had touched it. As I stood there in shock, it slipped over the wharf's edge and vanished into the Thames.

CHAPTER TWELVE

IRON

Still reeling, I tried to call the serpent back from the river, using every bit of magic I knew. None of it did any good. My music ran into a wall every time, just as it had with the mermaid and the sea monster.

"But at least you unmasked it," Nat said an hour later. "And now we know for certain that iron is a good defense against such creatures."

Our Council meeting was only just opening, but it was already clear to me that Nat was indeed the King's right-hand man. When he spoke, everyone listened, and most of them nodded in agreement. The only person who had trouble looking him in the eye was me. Too many emotions and thoughts were whirling inside me, and I was afraid he would see my turmoil.

"Before you say anything more, Walbrook, may I point out that we don't know if everyone here is who he appears to be." Eyebrows arched high over his sallow face, Sir Barnaby looked from the King to Nat to me to Penebrygg to Gabriel and on down the table to the Lord High Admiral, who had joined us for our deliberations. "For all I know, one of you is a snake in disguise."

"No," Nat said. "I've checked you all."

"What?" Sir Barnaby looked disconcerted. "How?"

"Most of you touched the iron door handle as you came in. I made a point of shaking hands with those who didn't, touching this iron ring to your skin." Nat pointed to a thick black ring on his finger. "No one here is a shape-changer."

Sir Barnaby's brow relaxed. "Well done, Walbrook."

"Hear, hear!" Sir Samuel raised a lace-cuffed hand in the air. "I say we should all wear something of the sort."

There was a rumble of general support.

"I could create an emblem for us," said Sir Christopher Linnet, well-known for his love of design. "We could have it stamped on rings for all the Council."

"That would take time," Penebrygg pointed out.

"Yes, we need a speedier solution." Nat opened a box that had been sitting in front of him. "With that in mind, I've brought an assortment of iron objects that I've borrowed from the palace with the King's permission. Each of you should take one."

The box was passed to me first. I selected a simple, flat bracelet and slipped it around my wrist. One by one, the others found something to suit them—a badge, a cross, a ring.

"Now we must arm the entire country," Nat said. "Here's what I have in mind."

He outlined his plans: all sea walls to be spiked with iron, all sailors and fishermen to be given iron spears and pikes, iron cannon to be set up along the Thames, iron bullets to be issued to new coast patrols . . .

Gabriel raised a well-groomed eyebrow. "A laudable plan, Walbrook. But where will we get all this iron, may I ask?"

"We'll have to boost production, of course," Nat said. "And in the meantime, we'll have to commandeer the iron that already exists, especially inland."

"People won't like that, you know," Gabriel said. "They won't give up their iron without a fight."

"I think they will, if the danger is great enough," Nat said. "We'll pull together, just as we did during the famine." He turned to the King. "At any rate, I'll do everything in my power to make it happen."

"And we all know that your powers of persuasion are considerable," someone called out from farther down the table.

Everyone laughed, even Nat. But then he added more soberly, "To fight this, we'll need all the powers at our disposal."

"Well, we shall give you all the backing we can muster," the King said. "I take it we're in favor of enacting Walbrook's plan? Very good. Walbrook, I put you in charge of our defense efforts. You may call on any man here to help you."

Most were eager to volunteer. But the King raised his voice; he wasn't done. "Keep in mind, however, that the nature of the task before us may yet change. We have no idea who our enemy is, or what he or she—or indeed, it—has planned for us." The King looked at me. "Unless perhaps you have some notion, Chantress?"

It was time for me to share all I knew, even though I was leery of the repercussions of doing so. "I can't identify our enemy, not at this point. But I can tell you this: There is some kind of singing involved."

"Singing?" Sir Barnaby's jaw dropped.

The Lord High Admiral half-rose from his seat. "*Chantress* singing?"

Even Gabriel looked alarmed. "Do you mean to say there's a Chantress attacking us?"

This was just the kind of reaction I'd feared.

I made every effort to appear calm and dispassionate. "Let's not leap to conclusions, please. I didn't say it was a Chantress—"

"But it might be?" It was Nat who asked.

I took a deep breath. "Yes. It might be. The music is different, but there are some similarities, especially in the phrasing and the resonance of the voice."

"When have you heard it?" Nat said, his face unreadable.

It was the question I least wanted to answer. "I heard it when I tried to go after the mermaid, and then again when the sea monster appeared. And once more, very clearly, when I encountered the false King."

"You heard it with the mermaid?" the Lord High Admiral barked at me. "And you didn't say so?"

"It was very indistinct," I said crisply. "For all I knew, it might have been mermaid music—and perhaps it was. Perhaps everything I've heard is. But the fact remains that I've heard it more clearly now, and it reminds me more of Chantress music than anything else."

"You should have said something at the time," the Admiral insisted.

He wasn't the only one who was annoyed. Sir Barnaby was frowning, and so were several other Council members. But the King motioned to the Lord High Admiral to sit down. "The Chantress has shared everything with us now, and that's what matters. The question is, what are we going to do about it?"

Everyone looked at me.

"I think we must start by finding out if any Chantresses besides me survived Scargrave," I said. "None have ever come forward, but that doesn't mean they don't exist."

"You mean a Chantress hunt," the Lord High Admiral said.

The words sent a chill through me. They called to mind all the terrors of Scargrave's reign, when Chantress hunting had been widespread and all of my kind—even my own mother—had been hounded and killed.

"*No.*" I turned to the King. "I promise you I personally will look into this, with the assistance of Captain Knollys and my men. But there must be no general hue and cry for Chantresses. It would only lead to panic and confusion in the kingdom—and I think we have enough of that to contend with as it is. Besides, if it really is a Chantress behind this, I'd rather she didn't know what our suspicions are. A general hunt would serve as a warning to her to be on her guard."

The King nodded. "We will leave this in your hands, then, and you can report your progress to me. We all stand ready to help, should you need us."

After he called an end to the meeting, everyone crowded around Nat, making suggestions and volunteering their services. Leaving them to it, I started on my way down to the guardrooms, pondering what I should say to Captain Knollys. I'd insisted to the Council that this was not a Chantress hunt. And yet the fact remained that I was about to order my men to track down Chantresses, and to consider them our enemies.

I could quibble over words all I wanted to, but there was no getting around it. I was a Chantress about to turn Chantress hunter.

CHAPTER THIRTEEN

QUESTIONS

My men had been chosen for their discretion as well as their strength. Accustomed to delicate and secret undertakings, they took this one in stride. The only problem was in knowing how best to deploy them. After ordering them all to carry iron, I dispatched some to places where Chantress families had once flourished, with instructions to search for descendants whom Scargrave might have overlooked. The rest I kept with me at Whitehall—including young Barrington, who was still recovering from the injuries he'd sustained at Charlton Castle.

"But you can count on me," he told me eagerly. "My left shoulder still catches me, but my sword arm is fine." He slashed in the air to prove it.

"Put that down, Barrington." The last thing I wanted was for him to start hacking at potential Chantresses. "It's not your sword I need right now but your brain." I turned to Captain Knollys and the rest of the men. "And that holds true for all of you. Our best scouts will go out into the taverns and meeting places of this city, where they will listen for any talk that may be useful to us. The rest of you will wait here for further instructions."

"And where will you be?" Knollys asked.

"I will be having a word with someone who might be able to help us," I said.

Knollys, who had plenty of discretion of his own, didn't ask any more questions. Which was just as well, because I didn't want to say that the person I had in mind was the Queen. I made my way alone to her chambers.

Under the circumstances, it might not have been best to remind people that Sybil was the granddaughter of a Chantress, but that was why I wanted to see her. Although she couldn't work magic herself, she knew all kinds of odd facts about Chantresses. Well, perhaps "facts" was putting it strongly, since much of her knowledge came from hearsay or family tradition or stories that were close cousins to fairy tales. Still, she'd helped me in times of trouble before, and she might be able to help me now.

As I reached the Queen's chambers, I found myself tensing. Behind the gilded door, someone was singing beautifully—Lady Clemence, with another love song. When I entered the Queen's chambers, she broke off and bowed her head, not meeting my eyes.

Everyone else stared at me, even Sybil. Sitting in an opulent chair, she looked more like a portrait than a human being, a painting of elegance personified. But when she rose and held out her hand, I saw she was wearing an ugly iron ring among her jewels, as were her ladies. Evidently, word of iron's powers had reached them.

After I touched Sybil's ring, she gave me a strained smile. "How delightful. Shall we take a stroll in the garden, under the loggia?"

She spoke the words as if she were playing a role—as of course she was, I realized—the role of Queen. Her wish, it seemed, was our command. Taking it for granted that I would say yes, her closest attendants ran to fetch the Queen's cloak and a pair of elaborately carved pattens to protect her brocade shoes from mud and rain.

"No, we wish to be on our own," Sybil said in answer to their murmurs as they dressed her. Stepping daintily forward, she nodded at me. "Shall we go?"

She maintained her queenly bearing until we were just outside the garden and no one else was around. Pattens clattering on the wet pavestones, she threw her arms around me. "Lucy! I'm so glad to see you. Everyone keeps talking about your battle with that dreadful serpent, and how you and Nat fought it off together, and I feel so stupid because the guards sealed us away the moment it began and wouldn't let me go to you. Then they told me you were in a meeting, and—"

"Never mind." I hugged her. "I'm glad to see you, too."

"Oh!" She jumped back, blond tendrils bobbing under her hood. "Something stung me."

"What?" I said in alarm.

"I think it was that." She pointed at me.

I looked down and saw the cloudy red jewel that was my

birthright as a Chantress, the stone that had once deafened me to Wild Magic. Swinging on its silver chain, it had slipped free of my bodice and was visible in the gap of my cloak.

"You're sure it was this?" I was skeptical. An intact stone could give a horrible shock to anyone who touched it—though not to its Chantress, or to any person she willingly gave it to. But my stone was riddled with cracks; I wore it only as a keepsake. The most it could muster up was a slight pinprick, and even that was rare.

"I'm sure." Sybil eyed my stone warily. "I thought you told me it didn't have any magic left."

"It doesn't."

"If it can sting me, it must," Sybil said with assurance. "Let me try again." She put out a cautious and perfectly manicured fingertip. When it touched the stone, she jerked back. "Yes, there's something there. It's not deafening you, is it?"

"Not a bit," I said cheerfully. "Ever since it cracked, everything sounds just the same whether I have it on or off. But I'm sorry it hurt you." I tucked it safely away. "Look, let's go into the garden, and then we can talk more freely."

"Yes." Sybil slipped her arm through mine. "On an afternoon like this, hardly anyone will be there."

She was right. In the soaking rain, the garden was empty save for one man who was resolutely trudging at the far end with a wheelbarrow. Giving him a wide berth, we walked along the loggia, the rain beading up on our cloaks as it blew in through the pillars.

"Was it love at first sight?" Sybil murmured.

I looked at her blankly, my mind on the questions I needed to ask her. Love? What was she . . . Oh. My meeting with Nat on the *Dorset*.

"No," I told her. "It was an utter disaster."

Her radiant face lost some of its glow. "Oh no. Did you argue?"

"Yes," I said. "But it wasn't just that. We've been apart so long that we hardly know each other anymore. I've changed, and so has he."

Sybil brightened. "Well, really, that's only to be expected, isn't it? You'll soon get used to each other again. And in the meantime"—she dimpled—"there can be something rather exciting about a stranger, can't there? I've known Henry since I was a child, and yet when he puts on his crown and his robes of state and holds court, it's as if I'm seeing a whole new man. It's quite a delicious experience."

I shook my head as we continued down the loggia. "Maybe for you. But not for me."

Even as I said it, I wondered if that was true. Did I really want to turn back time? Much as I hated the distance between us, I admired the man that Nat had become. More than admired, if the truth were told.

"You still love him." Sybil squeezed my arm. "I can see it in your face."

I hadn't meant to reveal so much. Halting by a pillar, I looked out at the perfect squares of the garden, the hedges trim and glistening with rain. "Maybe I do. But love alone isn't enough."

"Why not?"

I glanced at her in surprise. "You of all people should know, Sybil. I mean, look at you. You married the King, and that defines your life, just as marriage to a Chantress would define Nat's life. You aren't free to live by your own rules anymore. You have to be Queen, whether you like it or not. And you don't like it, do you? It's making you very unhappy."

Sybil bit her lip. "Is it that obvious?"

"To a friend, yes. And who could blame you? You're a free spirit, but now you have to follow protocol every minute of the day. You're under the scrutiny of the Court and the broadsides all the time."

"Oh, the broadsides," Sybil said miserably. "Don't remind me." We started pacing down the loggia again. "One unguarded remark, and they pillory me. And the ladies-in-waiting can be just as bad. Half of them are political appointments, you know, and they're always looking for evidence that I really am the 'Mad Queen,' just as the broadsides say." She paused, and added softly, "But I love Henry. And that makes it all worthwhile."

Did it? I thought of her frustration the other night, when she'd said Henry and I treated her like an idiot, and I wondered how she would feel in the long run.

"It's worth it," she said again, as if I'd argued the point.

"But Nat and I aren't like you and Henry," I reminded her. "We never have been. Even at the best of times, we've argued more. And that would make it even harder to be on public display, with everyone watching our every gesture. We'd have to be very sure of each other to cope with that. And we're not."

"So you're going to give up?" Sybil looked upset. "Just like that?"

I stopped short at the end of the loggia. "Sybil, please." It hurt too much to keep talking about Nat. "This isn't why I came looking for you."

She glanced at me in surprise. "It isn't?"

"No." The gardener was coaxing his wheelbarrow toward a square of lawn that was altogether too close to us. I tugged on Sybil's arm to guide her back down the length of the loggia. "You've heard about the serpent—the second one?"

"The one that looked like Henry?" Sybil shuddered. "Yes. The story's all over the Court. The very idea makes me sick."

"I think Chantress magic might be behind it."

"Chantress magic?" Sybil's smooth forehead wrinkled in doubt. "But how—"

"I've heard music." We were well away from the gardener now, and I couldn't see a sign of anyone else. Still, I spoke as quietly as possible.

Sybil too kept her voice down. "What kind of music?"

"I've heard it three times now, with the mermaid, and the sea monster, and the serpent that looked like the King—"

"They sang to you?"

"Not exactly. Well, the mermaid did sing—but the music I'm talking about was quite different. It came from the water around her, and it completely blocked my own magic. I heard it with the other creatures too—the serpents." Even the memory of the song chilled me. "It's an angry music, Sybil. Full of fury. And there's something about it that makes me think of Chantress singing. Not the melody, or the tuning. But there's something about the voice itself, and some of the cadences—"

"And yet iron broke the magic?"

"We didn't try it on the mermaid," I said. "But it struck down the other creatures, yes."

"That doesn't sound like Chantress magic to me."

"But the singing does, at least a little. Have you ever heard anything to suggest that another Chantress might be out there? Even the merest ghost of a rumor?"

"Never." Sybil had a beautiful voice, but it went rough as she spoke. "Scargrave was very thorough, Lucy. My cousins, our old friends—everyone who was a Chantress was killed so quickly. The only reason you survived was because your mother hid you and hedged you all about with enchantments."

Was it my imagination, or was the rain growing heavier? In the distance, I saw the gardener heft his spade and fork into the barrow and wheel them away.

I quickened my pace. "But perhaps there was someone else like me, someone else who was hidden—"

"Who's never been heard of from that time to this? It seems unlikely."

Sybil stumbled, pattens clicking, and I realized I was walking too fast. I slowed down. "But what about the singing I heard?"

"Are you ready to swear it was a Chantress?" Sybil asked.

"Well, no. But I was sure . . . At least, I thought at the time . . ." I trailed off. The truth was that the memory was fading now, and

I wasn't sure of much of anything, especially in the face of Sybil's skepticism.

"I don't doubt you heard something," Sybil said gently. "But I question whether it was a Chantress."

"What else could it have been? Do you have any ideas?"

Sybil laughed a little wryly. "My upbringing being what it was, I have a hundred and one ideas. Mama used to say that all kinds of creatures could sing—goblins, demons, faeries, sprites—the list was endless."

We reached the end of the loggia again and turned toward the garden.

"I don't know," I said doubtfully. "It's true there was something unearthly about the music I heard, but there was something human about it too."

"I see." Sybil looked thoughtful. "Well, Mama also used to say that Chantresses weren't the only humans who could work magic with music."

"Really?" This was news to me. Lady Helaine had never mentioned there were others.

"Oh, yes. She adored telling stories about them—the high priestesses of ancient Egypt, the druids, various Greeks, the occasional prophetess. She even ran across a sect of wise women here in England who swore they could work magic by singing."

"They weren't Chantresses?"

"Apparently not. Just an odd little group that worshipped water and called on its powers through incantation." She smiled, though her eyes were sad. "Of course, what you would have thought of them, I can't say. You know how my mother was . . ."

She didn't have to finish the thought. We both knew better than to accept Sybil's mother as a reliable source. Sybil's grandmother had been a Chantress, but the power hadn't passed to her mother. She had spent much of her life seeking out the advice of charlatans, willing to listen to anyone, however disreputable, who had promised to give her magic.

Still, I wanted to know more about the water worshippers. "Where did she find these wise women?"

"Mostly in London, I think. She used to slip down to the Thames to meet them. There were all kinds of strange rituals involved, though Mama wouldn't tell me much about them."

"She thought their singing truly had power?"

"Oh, yes. Though whether it really did is anyone's guess. Mama was always ready to see magic in anything." Sybil looked out at the great sundial in the center of the garden, its concave bowl awash with rainwater. "That said, Mama once brought their leader to the house to pray over me when I was ill, and I must say she was quite uncanny. Tall, with the kind of voice that goes right through you, and the oddest sea-green eyes. And I did get well again."

"Do you know if she survived Scargrave?" I asked. "If any of them did?"

"It's possible," Sybil said slowly. "He did go after all kinds of magic-workers, but what he wanted most were Chantresses. He didn't pursue the others with quite the same vengeance. So I suppose the wise women might have escaped him, if they were lucky. Though more likely they were killed along with all the rest."

A distant clock chimed the three-quarters hour.

"Oh dear." Sybil put her hand on my arm. "I'm sorry, Lucy, but I have to get back. Otherwise my ladies are bound to come looking for me."

"I understand." I hurried away from the loggia with her. "I ought to be going too."

"I'm sorry I wasn't more help."

"You *were* a help." It was disconcerting to think my senses might have misled me about the nature of my enemy, but I was pleased to think that the culprit might not be a Chantress after all.

Sybil gave me a quick hug and pattered away. I stood for a moment in the rain, watching her go, her shoulders stiffening under her cloak as she took up the burden of being Queen again.

It pained me to see the change in her. But then I had my burdens too—and they wouldn't be lessened by my standing there in the rain. I strode off, determined to see what else I could discover about Sybil's wise women.

CHAPTER FOURTEEN

WISE WOMEN

"Wise women?" Gabriel's well-arched eyebrows shot up, and his skeptical voice echoed loudly in the anteroom of the Great Library. "You want me to research *wise women*?"

"Yes," I said crisply.

After one too many clashes with Nat and Sir Barnaby over the best way to proceed with the riverside defense efforts, Gabriel had offered his services to me. I'd gladly accepted, but I was beginning to think that I'd made a mistake. Captain Knollys and my men hadn't given me this kind of reaction when I'd raised the matter of wise women with them.

"You mean cunning women?" Gabriel said, eyebrows still raised. "The ones who sell charms and fake love-potions?"

"How do you know they're fake?" I countered.

"They must be. Most of those women can't even read. It's all superstition."

"I wouldn't be so quick to judge," I said. "Just because they're poor and unlettered doesn't mean they have no power. And anyway, I'm not looking for love-potions. I'm looking for wise women who claim to have a special influence over water."

Gabriel's face told me what he thought of that.

I looked up at the coffered ceiling of the anteroom and told myself to be patient. "You're the one who wanted to help," I reminded Gabriel. "And right now this is what I need—someone to search the Great Library for any references that might be useful. Someone with a knowledge of old languages and arcane texts. I think you could do it. Will you?"

With a small sigh, Gabriel bowed. "Very well. Anything for you, Chantress."

† † †

Was I right to put so much weight on what Sybil had told me? I wasn't sure. Perhaps I was headed down the wrong path—and perhaps listening to the water would put me on the right one. That night, while Gabriel researched wise women, and Knollys and my men went looking for them, I stationed myself down by the river, paying especially close attention to the places where the strange sea creatures had appeared.

I had to concentrate quite hard to hear anything, however, for Nat's plan to arm England with iron was proceeding at a dizzying pace. All along the riverfront, men were hammering in spikes by lantern light and calling out to each other as they mended iron rails and chains. Here and there, blacksmiths had set up temporary forges where their anvils rang out like bells in the night. Meanwhile Sir Christopher, Penebrygg, and their friend Robert Rooke labored over a new design of water pump in the shadow of Whitehall itself. The hoses made a ghastly sound as they sucked.

I kept as far from the sound and fury as I could, the better to listen to the river. Mischievous as ever, it was full of songs, but they told me nothing I didn't already know. If the Thames was privy to any magic secrets, it didn't share them with me. At last, a few hours after midnight, I gave up and went to bed.

† † †

The next morning came much too quickly, and it brought more rain. A gloomy prospect, but at least my ankle was feeling better. I dressed as quickly as possible and gulped down some porridge with Norrie while I went over the night's reports. No sea monsters or mermaids had been sighted overnight, which was cheering.

From Captain Knollys, there was nothing but a brief note asking me to come see him. Done with breakfast, I rushed off to the guardrooms to find out what was happening.

Halfway there, my hastily pinned-up hair slipped loose. Clapping a hand to the unraveling coil, I went in search of a mirror and found one in a tiny jewel box of a room nearby. While I stood before the mirror, twisting my hair up again, voices filtered through to me from the next room.

"You think Lord Walbrook will marry the Chantress? My dear Clemence!"

I couldn't see the speaker, but I knew her by her tone alone. It was Lady Clemence Grey's older sister, Ardella, who was married to the Lord High Admiral.

"It's not so ridiculous," another woman said. It sounded like Lady Gillian. "Didn't you see the way he looked when they came off the river?"

"I heard someone say he's never stopped loving her," Clemence said wistfully.

"Nonsense," Ardella said. "She has some kind of hold over him, perhaps. But you needn't worry. He won't marry her. Who would? No man wants to wed a woman who has the power of magic, trust me. Walbrook, least of all."

Under my frozen hands, my coil of hair sprang free and tumbled down my back. I wrenched it tight and started putting it in order again—but an angry curiosity kept me listening to what was said about me.

"I suppose you're right," Lady Gillian conceded. "She's a strange creature. Really, when you come down to it, she's not even human, not fully."

"Yes," Ardella said. "And anyone who marries her has to think of the children."

"Children?" Clemence sounded confused. "What do you mean?"

"Haven't you ever heard the story of Melusine?" Ardella's voice sank low, as if she were relating a juicy bit of gossip. "She was a

Chantress too, or so they say—daughter of the faerie Pressina. She tried to hide her true nature from her husband, but her blood betrayed her. Her children were monstrous. One son had a lion's foot growing out of his face. Another had a tusk for a tooth. And when her husband finally confronted her, she turned into her true form, a sea serpent."

That wasn't the way Lady Helaine had told the tale. According to her, Melusine's sons had been perfectly normal on all counts, and she'd had a Chantress daughter as well.

What was the true story? I didn't know. But I did know I'd heard enough of Ardella's sly scandal-mongering. The woman was poison. I jabbed the last pins in, eager to get away.

"Ugh," said Lady Gillian. "Who would want to marry a creature like that?"

"No one," Ardella said emphatically, still in that malicious voice. "Not even dear little Lucy's father, from what I hear."

A pin slipped in my fingers, piercing my scalp. My father? I knew he'd been a musician, and little more. What did Ardella have to say about him?

"I know someone who used to be friends with her mother, Viviane," Ardella went on. "She loved the man desperately, even ran away from her guardian to marry him. But when she told him she was expecting their child, he got cold feet. Maybe he thought she'd bear another tusked wonder. At any rate, he left her."

I felt dizzy; the mirror seemed to wobble. I'd been told that my father had died before I was born, but the details had been vague. Was it just a story? Was Ardella telling the truth?

"How awful," Clemence said.

My whole head burned. I had to get away.

Desperate for a refuge, I stabbed the last pin in and retreated toward my room. Then I remembered: I needed to see Captain Knollys. Still dazed, I turned myself around—and almost bumped into Gabriel.

"Chantress! Just the woman I wanted to see." He flashed a smile at me, then looked more closely. "Are you all right?"

I wasn't all right, but I worked to hide it. I touched my bracelet to his outstretched hand—a gesture of greeting that was starting to become almost routine. "I'm fine. I was just on my way to the guardrooms, and then I was planning to look for you. Did you find anything in the library?"

"Nothing much," Gabriel said. "Though I was there till almost dawn."

Till dawn? He didn't look it. Freshly shaved and fashionably tailored, he wore boots so polished that I could almost see my reflection in the black leather. People said that Gabriel's valet was the best in all England. I believed them.

"Let's sit down, and I'll give you my report." Gabriel steered me into the next room and gestured toward a velvet couch—high-sided, soft, and intimate.

Thinking it looked a little too cozy, I sat myself down in the nearest chair instead. "This will do."

"Very well." He pulled another chair close. "I did find a reference in a fourteenth-century chronicle to wise women who talked to the creatures of the sea. A century later, another writer speaks of a group called the Well Women who practiced certain rites on the banks of the Thames."

"Rites?"

"Chiefly wading into its waters and making offerings. There's one mention of a wicker Flower Maiden that was set alight and given to the river. But there's not a word about singing."

"Nothing at all?" That was disconcerting. Of course, early chronicles were notorious for missing out important details. "Did they mention any kind of music?"

"No." Gabriel stretched out his legs, jaw tightening as he suppressed a yawn. "One of them talked about the music of the spheres, but that was in a different section entirely."

"The music of the spheres?" I'd heard the phrase before, but I had no idea what it meant. "What's that?"

Gabriel, who enjoyed playing the expert, was happy to explain. "Well, some scholars argue that all heavenly bodies—the sun, the moon, the planets, even the stars—have their own unique music. Pythagoras wrote about it, and so did Plato, and plenty of others. Some think they meant it just as a metaphor, a way of talking about theories of mathematics and astronomy. But the rest say no, it's actual music." His hand, idly running down the chair, came close to mine.

I pulled my own hand back. "No one suggests that it's connected with water, do they?"

"Not that I've read," he admitted. "But the moon is the force behind the tides, so that's a connection to the ocean. Come to think of it, it might be worth seeing if there's anything about music in Paracelsus—"

"He's the man who wrote about elementals?"

"Yes. Although he's better known for his books on alchemy and medicine."

The mention of alchemy made me sit up straighter. That too was something I hadn't considered—but perhaps I should have. "Did Paracelsus think alchemy could give people power over elementals?"

Gabriel's fingers restlessly explored the chair arm. "He thought a true master might be able to make the invisible visible. And yes, perhaps even give him control over some elementals."

"Does he say how?"

"No."

A dead end, then. But a suggestive one. Could alchemy be part of the puzzle I was trying to solve? Who better to ask than the man beside me? Gabriel was one of the best alchemists in the kingdom, even if he'd sworn off active pursuit of it after his talents had gotten him into serious trouble last year.

"Gabriel, do you know of anything in alchemy that might explain what's happening now?"

His brown eyes flashed. "If I did, don't you think I would have said so before?" There was hurt as well as anger in his face. "I've expressed my loyalty in a thousand ways, not only to King and country but to you personally. What more do I have to do to prove myself?"

Seeing how distressed he was, I forgot my caution and laid my hand on his. "I didn't mean to question your loyalty. I was just hoping that you might remember some small detail that could help us now. Or that you might have heard some rumor from your alchemist friends—"

"I have no such friends." He clasped my hand, his dark eyes fervent. "Not anymore. I swear to you that I've turned my back on the art forever. You must believe me."

"I do, Gabriel. I do." I released his hand, but he didn't let me go.

"I don't think you understand how I feel." His eyes turned soulful. "Chantress—"

Behind us a library door flew open. As I pulled away from Gabriel and spun around, young Barrington galloped into the room like a stallion on the loose.

"Come quickly, Chantress! We've been looking for you everywhere." Bright-eyed and panting, he gave me a brilliant smile. "We've found something."

CHAPTER FIFTEEN
BEHIND THE VEIL

The "something" my men had found turned out to be a woman.

"We haven't taken her in yet." Captain Knollys's voice rang out robustly in the confines of the guardroom, but he stopped short when he caught sight of Gabriel, who had followed me down.

At a nod from me, he accepted Gabriel's presence and went on. "The scouts say she's what you're looking for—a wise woman with a reputation for working water magic. Keeps herself pretty much out of sight, but we've tracked down where she lives, in rooms right by the river."

"People call her a miracle-worker," Barrington added. "They pay fees for her help."

"And there's talk of some odd rituals, too," Knollys said. "Riverside offerings and suchlike. Melisande's the name she goes by."

That took me by surprise. "Melisande" was said to be another name for Melusine. Maybe there was a Chantress connection here after all.

"Do you want us to bring her in?" Knollys asked. "Or do you want to go there yourself?"

"I'll go." I'd learn more that way. And if it was magic she was using—whatever it might be—then I didn't want my men facing her without me.

Leaning languidly against a stone wall, Gabriel had listened to Knollys in silence. Now he turned to me and spoke. "I'll go with you."

I hesitated, not sure this was wise. Perhaps he saw my doubts, for he continued, "In fact, you could send me in first. I could pretend to be someone seeking her services. That would put her off her guard."

"That's not a bad idea." Knollys looked at Gabriel with new appreciation. "Might be a better chance of taking her by surprise that way."

I had to agree. "It's worth considering."

Barrington glanced at Gabriel, clearly annoyed at him for stealing the limelight. "I could do it, Chantress. Send me."

I shook my head. An actor Barrington was not. His open face revealed every emotion he felt. But Gabriel had the gift of theater; I knew he could pull off a role with aplomb.

"I want you in the crew that surrounds the house," I said to Barrington. "I need you ready to fight." Raising my voice, I spoke to the men ranged behind him as well. "But you all must keep back and well out of sight until Lord Gabriel and I have gone inside."

"I thought I was going in alone," Gabriel said.

"I have a better idea," I told him.

And so we made our plans.

† † †

My men had reported that Melisande lived in the darkest part of the filthiest alley in the disreputable riverside neighborhood of St. Katharine's—and they hadn't been lying. When Gabriel and I finally reached the place, he rapped on the door and winced as he stepped on something repulsive with his once immaculate boots. Behind him, I was grateful for the gauzy scarves and oversize hood that covered most of my face. They had been meant solely as a disguise, but they helped screen out a little of the smell. The whole alley was full of stinking trash and scraps, and the rainwater that pooled everywhere was turning them into a foul-smelling stew.

A flap in the door opened up at eye level. Through my scarves, I caught the scent of magic—teasingly brief and faint.

If I'd had my godmother's keen nose, I might well have been able to identify the type and source of magic from that single whiff. I wasn't Lady Helaine, however, and for me the smell was impossible to categorize. All I could tell was that magic of some sort was here.

Still, that was enough. It meant we were on the right track.

Through the flap, beady amber eyes squinted at what little they could see of us. "What d'ye want?"

A gruff tone, but I was pretty certain she was female. Was it Melisande?

"Well?" Beady-eyes was growing impatient.

"My sister's had a bad accident," Gabriel said in a low voice, starting on the story we'd concocted. "She's not healing, and I fear she may be disfigured for life. She needs help." Lowering his voice still further, he added, "From Melisande."

The beady eyes swept over me, then fixed on Gabriel again.

"I can pay." He held up a gold sovereign.

He'd hit on the right password. The slot shut. The door opened.

"In with you," came the gruff order. "Be quick."

The room inside was even darker than the alley, but there was enough light to see that I was right. It had been a woman at the door, though she was younger and slighter than I'd expected. Behind my veil, I sniffed the air again. This time I smelled no magic.

The woman put out a scrawny hand and said to Gabriel, "Your sword."

We'd expected this, but he gave a show of reluctance before pulling it out of its scabbard and turning it over.

The woman clenched her hand around the hilt. "And the gold?"

Gabriel handed it to her.

She tested it with her teeth, then eyed us both. "So what's behind the veil?"

I shrank back, feigning maidenly shyness.

"Cat got your tongue?" She chuckled—not a pleasant sound. "Melisande's used to grand visitors like you, you know. Even gets highborn Court ladies coming to ask for help."

Court ladies? I wondered who.

"It's usually love-potions they want, of course," the woman went on. "Perhaps that's what you really want too."

I shook my head violently.

"No?" The woman cackled. "Well, your money's good, so we'll let Melisande ferret the truth out of you. I'll see if she's ready to receive visitors."

Turning away from us, she opened the door to the back room. I couldn't hear anything that sounded like magic, but I caught the scent of it again, and that was warning enough. I tensed, ready to sing at any second.

Rustles and whispers came from the back room. Then the beady-eyed woman returned. "She'll see you now. But you've interrupted her work, and she's not best pleased, so mind your manners."

She ushered us into an even darker room, lit only by scattered candles floating in bowls, which threw weird shadows on the cluttered walls. As my eyes adjusted, I saw a steamy white plume of smoke rising from a squat cauldron in the center of the room. My head clouded as a strong smell overpowered me. *Not magic*, I thought dizzily. Was it incense?

Veiled by the smoke, a shape stepped forward from the darkest corner. The beady-eyed woman curtsied so low, she was almost bent double. "Melisande," she breathed.

Trying to see the figure through the smoke, I stepped forward. For just a moment I caught sight of her. She was a woman, and very tall, but what I noticed most were her intense sea-green eyes.

At the same time, she saw me—even through the veil. She turned on her servant. "You fool! It's the Chantress."

Through the smoke, Melisande lunged for me.

CHAPTER SIXTEEN
WATER AND WALL

Even before Melisande came barreling toward me, I started to sing. The boiling water in the cauldron leaped up, forming a wall around her like searing, bubbled glass. Trapped, she looked at me in fury.

As I finished singing, I heard Gabriel say, "Oh, no, you don't! That sword is *mine*." When I turned, it was safely in his hand. The servant, however, was gone.

Gabriel pointed downward. "She went out through there."

Squinting hard, I could just make out a hole in the floor. Leaving Melisande behind her boiling wall, I knelt by it and heard the river. "It goes out to the Thames."

"I can't fit through the hole, or I'd follow her," Gabriel said.

I probably would fit, but if I went down there, it would mean leaving Melisande behind. It was too big a risk to take.

Moments later, my men piled in, crowding the room. "We heard you sing," Barrington explained.

"Well done." That was what we'd agreed beforehand: If I sang, they were to come immediately to our aid. "Simpson, Uddersby, you're the smallest. See if you can get through this hole. Lord Gabriel, if you could tell them what to look for?"

Leaving them to it, I turned my attention to Melisande, still trapped behind the wall of water. My men had brought torches, and in their light I could see her clearly—a woman who had several inches on me but whose bearing made her look even taller. Her hair was a rich brown flecked with silver, and her age was hard to place, especially now that the fury had ebbed from her face, leaving it cool and curiously blank.

"Is Melisande your real name?" I asked.

She looked right through me.

I sang softly, and the wall of water sizzled and steamed. When it cleared, there was an angry light in Melisande's green eyes—and also a touch of fear.

"I can make it even hotter," I warned her. "Answer me. Is Melisande the name you were born with?"

She spat the answer at me. "Yes."

"Some would say that's a Chantress name. Are you a Chantress?"

"See for yourself." She let her drooping sleeves fall back, revealing arms that were smooth and white. She had no Chantress mark, as I did—that small, bone-white spiral at the base of the forearm that set a Chantress apart.

Well, that was one issue settled. "What kind of magic do you practice?"

She gave me a wicked grimace. "Wouldn't you like to know?"

"How many of you are there? How long have you been meeting?"

"How long?" A snort of contemptuous laughter. "Since the dawn of time, Chantress. We've been here before you, and we'll outlast you."

"Do you sing?"

Silence.

"Are you the one who called up the sea creatures?"

She still didn't speak, but I saw a gleam of sly satisfaction in her eyes.

"Talk, or I'll sing," I said. "I can make that wall a lot hotter, you know."

A look of pure hatred. "You and your walls! That's the Chantress answer to everything. You did it to the Mothers, and now you're doing it to me."

"What are you talking about?"

"Don't pretend you don't know." Her mouth twisted with venom. "The old wall let us slip through, but you put a stop to that, didn't you? You Chantresses built a wall between us and the Mothers. We honored them; we respected them; we worshipped them in the way our own mothers taught us. But not you, oh no! You Chantresses were too high and mighty for that."

I stared at her in confusion. What wall was this? And who were the Mothers?

"But all things come right in time," Melisande said, eyes alight behind the bubbling wall. "We have been faithful; we knew this hour would come. Your wall is breaking down, Chantress. There's a crack in it, and the Mothers are coming for you. And this time, you cannot stop them!"

After that, Melisande would say no more. Even when I made the water wall boil again, she only laughed more and more wildly.

"She's mad," Gabriel said behind me.

Maybe so. But even if Melisande were mad, it didn't mean she was powerless. I'd smelled magic here. And her wild words about the Mothers sounded uncannily like the vicious warning the mermaid had given me: *We are coming.*

"Who are the Mothers?" I asked Melisande again.

Her only answer was crazed laughter.

I turned to Barrington. "Your pike, please."

He gave it to me without hesitation, and I drove it through the water wall. Melisande shrieked, but I was careful not to let the point touch her, just the iron side of the shaft.

Iron didn't damage her, still less make her disappear. She looked exactly the same as before, only angrier.

What now? It wasn't easy for me to keep the wall up, and she had the kind of light in her eyes that said she was prepared to die rather than give in to me. We'd have to find something else to do with her.

I motioned my men forward. "We'll take her to the Tower."

† † †

Rising up from the east end of the city, the Tower of London was England's stronghold. Officially it was a royal residence, and some even considered it beautiful, with its domes and battlements and its white-walled central tower. But as we passed through the gatehouse, I shivered. I could never forget how the Shadowgrims had made it a place of horror and death. For me, the Tower would always be more prison than palace. There was no question it was the most secure jail in the city, however, and I wasn't willing to settle for less when it came to Melisande.

Not that she was any more forthcoming here. As we put her into her cell and bound her with an iron chain, I noticed that she wore a strange ornament around her neck. Made of silver, it was shaped like two snakes, each swallowing the other's tail. I no sooner started to question her about it than she began rocking and humming, making the stone cell echo with a strange sort of sound that reminded me a little of the sea monster's keening.

Was she attempting to work magic? I sniffed the dank air but smelled nothing.

"Watch out!" Barrington cried as Melisande writhed backward.

She collapsed on the straw-covered floor.

"She may be pretending," Knollys grunted.

"I'm not so sure." Gabriel had his hand on her wrist. "Her pulse is very weak."

For almost a full hour, we tried to revive her. We shook her. We splashed water on her face. We waved smelling salts under her nose till the room reeked with them. Nothing worked.

Gabriel, still monitoring her pulse, said that it was even weaker than before. "It's steady, though. Almost as if she were in some sort of trance."

Barrington crossed his arms. "We could put her to the rack."

"No." Looking down at Melisande's slack, dead-white face, I saw for an instant the ghost of my godmother, who had died in this place. *It isn't the same,* I told myself. *This woman is dangerous.* Yet it took me a moment to speak with the authority my men expected of me. "Leave her here. The rest of you, come with me."

Out of earshot of the cell, I gathered them in a tight circle. "We still haven't found any trace of her servant, have we, Captain Knollys?"

"No sign at all. The trail leads to the water and then stops."

"Then all we have is Melisande, so we'd better treat her well. Give her plenty of blankets, and have some food and drink sent down. We'll question her again later."

Knollys and Barrington looked less than satisfied, but they didn't try to argue with me. Nor did the others. I knew, however, that they would be happier if I were harsher with Melisande—and perhaps I should be. At any rate, I couldn't be as lax as I'd been with the mermaid. Yet the dark history of the Tower was itself proof that torture wasn't the high road to truth. People would say anything to end the pain. What if Melisande told us lies? What if we pushed her too hard and she died? We wouldn't have learned anything, then.

Even if the others saw it as weakness, I was going to choose another way.

"There is plenty to do while we wait," I said. "The men who are searching her rooms may have more to tell us, and we can continue the search for her servant. I myself must go to Whitehall;

I promised the King I would keep him informed of our progress."

"I could send a messenger," Knollys said.

"He'll want to speak with me himself." Which was probably true, but the real reason I wanted to go to Whitehall was to tell Sybil about Melisande and see what she made of what the woman had told me so far. Perhaps Sybil would know who the Mothers were. Perhaps she would even be willing to come here and see if Melisande was the same woman she'd met long ago. Though how we would manage that, I wasn't sure, when Sybil was so carefully encircled by her ladies, and her every movement was a cause for gossip. Still, it was worth a try.

"I'll return as soon as I can," I said. "I don't know what tricks she might have up her sleeve, so don't interrogate her without me. And keep her chained and guarded." I wasn't going to have her escape as the mermaid had.

I left, with solemn assurances from Knollys, Gabriel, and the others that they would keep close watch over Melisande until I came back.

CHAPTER SEVENTEEN
WESTMINSTER

I traveled by well-armed boat from the Tower to Whitehall, making good time. My plan to visit Sybil, however, was forestalled by the guards who greeted me at Whitehall. The King wanted to see me right away.

I hurried to the State Rooms, only to discover that the King was nowhere to be found.

"He did ask us to summon you a little while ago," one of his secretaries said worriedly. "He wanted to speak with you. But then he and Lord Walbrook hurried off, and we haven't seen them since."

"Where did they go?" I asked. "Do you know?"

"To see one of the river walls in Westminster, I think. But to tell the truth, I'm not sure exactly where." Grimacing, the secretary ran a hand through his thinning hair. "We've been at sixes and sevens ever since the removal orders went out."

"What removal orders?"

The secretary looked surprised. "The King has requisitioned all rooms overlooking the Thames, my lady, so that they can be used for defense. Hadn't you heard? We announced it an hour ago."

"I've been rather busy," I said.

"Of course, of course." He gave me a wan smile. "Well, the river-facing rooms here at the palace are being evacuated as we speak, and the cannons are being moved in. But it's a job working out where to put everyone, with so many rooms out of bounds. And the King's papers have to be shifted too, and all his correspondence. And then there are all the people coming in from other parts of the city. Everyone along the riverside has been ordered to move out, and some of them are coming here. So I'm afraid everything's rather chaotic right now—"

"Never mind." Westminster lay just southwest of Whitehall, an easy walk from here. "I'll find the King myself."

† † †

A little while later, I located the King by the river's edge in Westminster, huddled in the drenching rain with Nat and Sir Samuel. The King's shoulders were hunched, and Sir Samuel cut a mournful figure, his lace cuffs sopping wet at the ends of his overcoat sleeves. Nat's back was to me, but when he turned, I saw iron-dark circles under his eyes.

"Chantress!" The King greeted me warmly, but it was only when we touched iron to skin that his shoulders went down a notch. "I was beginning to think we'd never see you."

I explained that I'd been at the Tower, and why.

When I finished, he said, "So you think Melisande is the one causing all this trouble?"

"She certainly knows something about it," I said. "Whether she's behind it is another matter. We'll get the truth out of her, I promise you. But that's all there is to tell for now."

He looked disappointed, and so did Nat and Sir Samuel, but there was nothing I could do about that. "What's been happening here?" I asked. "Have there been more attacks?"

"Yes." The lines in the King's face deepened as he spoke. "Late this morning a sea serpent attacked boats downriver from here, near Tilbury. And there's been a terrible attack at the Royal Navy at Portsmouth."

"The dispatch came in this morning," Sir Samuel said morosely. "Yesterday evening a sea serpent destroyed four ships of the line. Some three hundred men drowned."

Three hundred men? Sorrow and anger engulfed me. I started to wish I'd pushed Melisande harder.

"That's the worst of it for now," the King said, "but there are reports coming in from all over the country of mermaids singing, and monsters being sighted from shore, and fishermen's boats vanishing."

"Which makes it all the worse that we've gone and ruined the wall that protects Westminster itself." Nat pointed upriver. Through the driving rain, I saw a point a few dozen yards ahead where Westminster's embankment all but disappeared.

Dispassionately Nat explained what had happened. "Most of

the river walls are sturdy enough, but when we tried to reinforce this one with iron, the mortar crumbled, and we were left with this enormous gap. Now there's nothing to stop the river from flooding the whole district at the next high tide."

I saw what he meant. Long ago, all of Westminster had been an island—and a low-lying, marshy island at that. Since then, it had been developed and protected from the river by a series of embankments. Nothing, however, could make it high ground. Once the river rose above the gap, there was nothing to stop it from inundating all of Westminster—including Parliament and the law courts and the hallowed precincts of Westminster Abbey.

"We need to mend the gap before the next high tide," Nat said. "But that's only hours from now. And that isn't really enough time to get the job done, even if the weather were perfect. And in rain like this, I don't see how it can be mended properly at all."

"That's why I called you here," the King said to me. "The wall. Can you help?"

If I did, it would delay my return to the Tower. But there was no telling exactly when Melisande would revive—and a great many lives were at stake here. I looked down at the long gap and listened to the rain and the river. "I think I could hold back the Thames for you," I said at last. "Just by a few yards, but that should be enough. I can divert the rain, too. And once the new wall is up, I can make the mortar set fast."

The King immediately looked happier, and so did Sir Samuel.

Nat, however, gave me a troubled glance. "Didn't you say yesterday that the river wouldn't obey you?"

"Only when I try to use it against the creatures that are attacking us. It wants to protect them somehow. Other than that, my magic is as strong as ever."

"Strong enough for my men to trust their lives to it?" Nat asked soberly.

It was hard to be questioned like this, but I knew he was asking in all good faith, for the sake of the men in his command. I would do as much for my own men.

Since our battle with the sea monster, I'd avoided meeting his eyes, but now I looked straight at him, commander to commander. "I believe the water will listen to me. If I have any doubts, I'll warn you. I don't want to put any lives at risk."

As his eyes searched mine, my pulse kicked up. But I couldn't look away. He had to understand that I was telling him the truth.

"All right," Nat said. "We'll try it."

† † †

While the King and Sir Samuel went back to Whitehall, I stayed by the wall in Westminster with Nat and a small army of bricklayers and ironworkers. After talking a bit with the chief bricklayer, Nat came over to me. "How do you want to start?"

"I'll sing the water away first," I said. "It's the kind of songspell that will need constant replenishing, but I'll keep it up as long as I can. I expect I could do it for several hours, if need be."

Nat still looked worried. "If anything goes wrong, we'll need to get the men out of there fast. Can we work out a warning signal, just in case?"

He wasn't doubting me, I told myself. He was just being sensible. We settled on the waving of hands overhead, and then I gave myself over to the task at hand.

I listened hard, but to my relief I couldn't hear even the faintest echo of the furious song I'd heard yesterday, only the usual strains of Wild Magic. When I sang to the river and the rain, coaxing them away from the wall, they were as docile as lambs. Within minutes, the entire face of the wall was dry, down to the pilings.

"All right, men," Nat said. "Let's get to work."

The men looked at the river, openmouthed, and then at me. No one moved.

It was a lot to ask of them, to trust me with their lives.

I moved to the far end of the wall, where a rope ladder dangled over the edge. Still singing, I stepped onto it.

Alarmed, Nat came after me. "Lucy, no. There's no need for this."

I couldn't spare the breath to answer him, not even when I saw him following me. Everything in me was bent on keeping the water back—and on placing each foot carefully on the rungs, until at last I stood at the foot of the wall.

I looked up at the men, and they looked down at me.

"Can't leave a lady on her own like that, can we?" one of them called out. Within moments, there were ladders being lowered all along the line, and the men followed me down.

† † †

For the next three hours they laid bricks as fast as they were able, using pulleys and scaffolding and teamwork to speed the job. It must have been an amazing sight, but I hardly took in any of it. All my attention was trained on the watery wave that I was holding back with my music. Even at the start, it had towered over our heads. As the tide came in, it grew still higher—and not only higher but stronger.

It took all my skill to keep the wave back. Chantress singing didn't tire the voice as normal singing would, but it required enormous strength and patience to keep it going for so long. As I listened carefully to the liquid nuances of the river's songs, I became all but deaf to every other sound. The slap of bricks, the squeal of pulleys, the banging of hods—none of it made a dent in my concentration. And so I didn't notice that the work was done, until Nat came up and gestured to me to turn around.

The men were back on land now, leaving behind the new wall, perfectly mended and riveted with iron spikes. Which meant I needed to rise to a new challenge, that of singing the wall dry while still holding back the river. Turning so I could see both the wave and the wall, I slowly began to weave the two songs together.

The drying couldn't be done too fast; otherwise the wall would crack. That was the trick of it, listening to get the pacing just right. I didn't rush. Standing in the riverbed, I took my time and let the mortar grow white, grow dry. And then, just as I was all but done, I heard what I'd most dreaded—the faint echo of fury coming from the water.

I waved frantically at Nat. The water was turning on me, and my wave was about to crash down on top of us.

CHAPTER EIGHTEEN

THE DROWNED LAND

Nat understood my warning signal right away, but despite the alarm in his eyes, he didn't rush to the ladder.

What was he waiting for? For me to get out first? Of all the misplaced notions of gallantry! It was my song; I should be last out. He wouldn't budge, however, and I couldn't argue while I was singing. So I ran to a ladder—there were several still up—and started to climb.

To my relief, he did as well, and he quickly reached the top. I made slower progress, hampered by skirts and the demands of singing and an ankle that was still giving me twinges. As I grabbed the last rung of the ladder, the water broke loose.

Above the roar of the wave, I heard Nat call out to me. "Lucy!"

His hands reached down, seized me, and hauled me bodily up to solid land. Drenched by the spray, I held fast to him, gasping for breath. Then I looked up into his eyes, and the world dropped away. The wall, the wave, my narrow escape—I forgot them all as we stood there, aware of nothing but each other.

A terrible shouting came from the men. "Watch out!"

As Nat and I sprang apart, I glanced over my shoulder. Three slimy gray snakes were rising from the waters. They lashed at the air, eyeless and as thick around as trees. There were four of them now. No, five . . . six . . .

Half-hypnotized, I stared at the sinuous, bubbled flesh. Snakes? No. They were tentacles. Which meant . . .

With a horrible slurp, the fleshy head surfaced, all gaping mouth and teeth.

"Giant squid!" someone screamed.

"Kraken!"

The tentacles reached for the wall.

As Nat seized the iron-tipped spear he'd brought with him, I saw other men reaching for their weapons. The creature must have seen this too, or perhaps it simply sensed the iron embedded in the wall. It reeled in its tentacles and plunged underwater.

"Hold on," Nat called out to his men. "Wait till the creature comes up."

A few of them let loose their spears anyway. The wooden shafts twisted as they hit the water. I heard the sound of the water steering the spears away from the monster—and beneath it, scattered notes from the furious song.

"The water's protecting it," I said to Nat. "Just as it protected the others."

"It'll have to surface again if it wants to attack us." Nat scanned the waters, spear at the ready. "And when it does, we'll get it."

But he was wrong. At the foot of the wall, the currents of the river were shifting. Small waves appeared, then larger ones. I leaned out over the new bricks, listening. What was happening down there?

And then I had it: "The kraken's pulling on the pilings!"

Nat paled. We hadn't put iron down there, only on the brick part of the wall. "How do we stop it?" he asked.

"I'm not sure we can. Tell the men to warn the neighborhood. Get everyone out."

Nat shouted out the command, and within a minute, the rainy waterfront was all but empty. Only a couple of the younger masons remained, determined to show their courage.

"Let's see if we can save the wall," Nat told them. Together they probed the water with their spears, but the river twisted the staves and wrenched them away.

"Nails," Nat called out. "And the leftover spikes!" We hurled them in, but the water must have carried them off, because the kraken kept pulling at the pilings.

While Nat and his men cast around for other things to try, I sang to the water, pleading with it to turn against the kraken. But I wasn't surprised when the water ignored me. I put my hands against the wall and felt it tremble.

"It's about to go down!" I shouted to the others.

As they turned back to look at me, the wall cracked.

"Run," I screamed.

The masons were already sprinting inland, but Nat waited

for me, pacing himself to my stride. Through the deserted, rain-soaked streets of Westminster we ran, past the abbey and its great Tudor chapel, and the ancient Gothic arches of the old palace. But we still hadn't quite reached the embanked wall around the precincts of Whitehall when we heard a terrible groan and crash behind us.

Had the kraken succeeded?

I couldn't help it. I glanced back through the sheets of rain, only to see the river streaming down the street behind us. And was that a gray tentacle?

Nat yanked me forward. "*Run.*"

Breath burning in my lungs, I raced up the street with him, my ankle jolting in pain. The dank smell of the sea was everywhere.

By the time we reached the embankment, the gates were shut tight. Shouting for help, Nat and I scrabbled at the rough wall, trying to find footholds before the waters closed in.

Spying us, the King's guards threw down some ropes. When we grabbed them, the guards hauled us up and over to safety, just as the tidal river raced in behind us.

Standing with the guards and the masons who had reached Whitehall before us, we watched the Thames take Westminster. The first waves rippled out, swirling around corners, filling every path and inlet, until the abbey and the palace and all the ancient buildings were nothing more than islands in the midst of churning waters.

Here and there, in the stormy gloom, lights burned in windows. Did they mark people left behind? Or were they untended candles and lamps that might catch fire, compounding disaster on disaster?

I saw no sign of the kraken.

I didn't realize I'd spoken out loud until Nat answered, "It'll be out in the deeper reaches of the river, I expect, looking for more walls to pull down. We'll need to warn the riverbank patrols to watch out for it. Maybe they'll land a blow where we failed." He turned to have a word with one of the King's guards, who went running back into the palace.

We failed. It was not a thought I wanted to dwell on. But the evidence was pooled out in front of me.

As I stared at the churning expanse of water, I heard the furious song again, faint and horrifying. Only this time, as I listened, the song swelled, stronger than ever, and I heard an eerie counterpoint beneath the angry music:

Come, Chantress. Come into the water . . .

Who was singing? Wise women? The Mothers that Melisande had claimed were coming? Whatever the source, it was menacing. I backed away.

Nat must have seen the distress in my face, though he didn't understand its cause. "Remember, the tide will go out soon," he said. "In just a few hours, we'll be able to start rescuing people and putting up new defenses."

I tried to nod, but the song was still there, calling to me, no matter how hard I tried to block it out.

"Never mind that now. You're shivering." Nat drew me toward a door. "Let's get you indoors."

Once I was inside the thick walls of Whitehall, the music

dimmed until it thinned out altogether. I came back to myself, and the first thing I noticed was that Nat was still there, only inches from me. I raised my head, and when I met his warm hazel eyes, it was as if we were standing by the wall in Westminster again, lost to the world. . . .

"Lucy." There was a tender edge to his voice that made my heart turn over. "I—"

"Chantress!" The cry came from the far end of the passageway.

I whirled around. A palace guard trotted toward me, iron pike in hand. "You're needed at the Tower," he called out. "Your prisoner has escaped."

The world rushed back with a vengeance.

There was no time now to talk with Nat, no time to find out what he had been about to say to me. I said a distressed good-bye to him and rushed off to the Tower.

CHAPTER NINETEEN
PERFECT CIRCLE

At the Tower, Knollys met me with a look of chagrin on his broad, ruddy face. "I'm sorry, Chantress," he said as we touched iron—my bracelet to his hand, his ring to my palm. "We've been searching for Melisande for almost two hours now, and there's no sign of her." He added, with gruff hope, "Unless you can detect something?"

"No." Ever since I'd heard the news, I'd been sniffing the air for magic and listening for singing. Even here at the Tower, however, there was nothing. If magic had been involved in Melisande's escape, I had missed it. Though I knew I ought to check her cell as well.

When I suggested as much, Knollys offered to take me there, and we crossed the innermost ward in the rain.

"How exactly did she escape?" I asked.

Knollys told me that they'd kept a close watch on Melisande until a sea monster had been sighted from the Tower walls. "We rushed out to defend the Tower, of course. Melisande was still unconscious, so I thought there was no danger in leaving her, especially as I left young Barrington on guard." Knollys shook his head in frustration. "But when we came back, she was gone."

"And Barrington?" I said as we entered the tower where Melisande had been kept.

"Left his post, the young fool," Knollys said with a flinty gaze that did not bode well for Barrington. "Says he heard singing outside and he went to see what it was."

"Singing?"

Knollys shrugged. "That's what he says. But he can't describe it, except to say it didn't sound like any singing he'd ever heard before, including yours. When I questioned him, he admitted that it might have been the echo of all the shouting and screaming out on the river while we fought the monster."

I made a mental note to question Barrington myself.

"I take it you drove the monster off?" I said.

"Uddersby drove a spear right through it," Knollys said with grim satisfaction. "It turned as clear as ice and sank like a stone. And here we are." He unlocked the cell door and pushed it open.

I looked around the stone-walled room, bare of all but a rumpled straw pallet and some blankets. "This isn't where I left her."

"No, we moved her on Lord Gabriel's advice. He thought she'd recover more quickly in a warmer room."

As indeed she had. "You're sure you locked her in?"

"Yes. Indeed, the door was still locked when Barrington returned."

"Then how did she get out?"

Knollys's voice was tight with frustration. "I don't know, Chantress. It's possible she had help from someone else. Some tradesmen made deliveries to the Tower kitchens just before the monster was sighted, and we're trying to find out if they had anything to do with it, or if they saw anything amiss." He walked over to the cell's tiny barred window. "And some of the men have another theory."

"They do?"

Knollys pointed to a damp corner of the room. "See the rain-water coming through there? It comes down from the roof, then drains out of the room through tiny cracks in the stone."

I looked. The cracks were minute.

"They think she found a way to magic herself into the water and leave the room with it," Knollys said. "And who's to say she didn't?"

† † †

Had Melisande used magic to escape? Or had someone come to her aid? Either way, I was determined to hunt her down. Over the next few hours, I questioned everyone involved, and I led another full search of the Tower. I sat for a long while by the dripping corner of the room, listening to the water's songs, in case they held a clue of some kind. But none of it was any use. Melisande had well and truly vanished.

"What now?" Knollys asked me.

"We return to Whitehall." Much as I hated to concede defeat, it was time to go back. In another hour or so, it would be nightfall, and the Thames was still high and swollen. I hated to think what Westminster looked like now.

Before we left, Knollys and I discussed how best to deploy the men. Some had been stationed in and around Melisande's rooms since the morning, searching for information about her and her followers; they needed to be relieved. I dispatched other men to various points around the city. The rest of us went to Whitehall.

It was a long trip. An edict had come through from the King, forbidding boats from taking to the river, so the warders at the Tower had arranged for us to travel by carriage instead. Even at the best of times, I was not fond of carriages, and this journey seemed endless, for we stopped frequently as the wheels became mired in muck. By the time we finally jounced through the palace gates, my head was pounding.

Gritting my teeth, I made a last few arrangements with Knollys, then jumped out of the carriage, my mind full of all I must do. Deciding to check in with the King first, I made my way toward the State Rooms. Torches had been lighted against the encroaching twilight, but they were smoking and fizzling in the rain, and the courtyard stones were dark and slick. When a guard loomed out of the next passageway, pike in hand, I nearly slipped in front of him.

"Begging your pardon, Chantress," he said, blocking my way, "but I have orders not to let anyone through."

I looked at him in surprise. "Why ever not?"

"Evacuation orders, my lady."

Blast. I'd forgotten about the evacuation. "Where would I find the King?"

"Couldn't say for certain, my lady. The whole place is topsy-turvy today. But the Royal Steward's set up a station by the Banqueting House with lists of all the changes, and if you go there, I'm sure they'll help you."

Pulling my hood tight against a particularly ferocious burst of rain, I started off for the Banqueting House, only to find myself in the midst of widespread chaos. At the Banqueting House itself, scores of people pleaded for directions. When I finally attracted the attention of a guard and asked him for the State Rooms, he was kind enough, offering me a lantern to light my way. But he must have misunderstood what I wanted, for when I reached the door he'd sent me to, I found nothing but my own belongings behind it, mixed up with Norrie's.

In the flickering light of the lantern, I stared around the room in dismay. Norrie's and my possessions were heaped in piles on and around the bedsteads. Evidently guards had been detailed to move us, but they hadn't set anything in order. Probably there had been no time.

I was about to pull the door shut on the mess and start again on the wearying hunt to find the King. But what did I have to tell him, except bad news? Now that Melisande had escaped, I truly had no idea how to get to the root of these attacks and put a stop to them.

I knew Sybil would help me if she could, and so would Gabriel, but talking with them hadn't done any good so far. None of us had any real idea what magic was at work here. All I knew for certain was that it was somehow connected with water and the sea, and it was stronger than me.

If only the water itself could tell me what was happening! But it wouldn't or couldn't speak to me of that. It was as if the element I best understood had become my enemy. It was even worse than last year's silence, when I'd been hardly able to hear anything at all, and the only way water had spoken to me was through scrying.

Scrying.

Now, that was something I hadn't tried. In fact, I hadn't done any scrying at all since I'd gotten my powers back. At best, it was a poor substitute for singing and listening, yielding mysterious images that were more riddles than answers.

But even a riddle was better than no clue at all.

I rose and started to paw through the piles behind me. A bowl, that was what I needed. I could fill it at one of the outdoor troughs down in the courtyard. And perhaps I should light a fire, too.

It took me an age to get everything ready.

At long last, however, I was sitting before the flames, my blue-and-white delftware bowl brimming. The room was perfectly quiet, except for the crackle and sigh of the fire. The perfect conditions for scrying, except that my mind was restless.

Clear your mind. That was the first rule of scrying.

Instead my mind flitted to the wall I'd called up around Melisande . . . her strange keening in the Tower . . . the spiraling tentacles of the kraken . . . Nat's strong hands pulling me to safety. . . .

Concentrate.

I stared hard at the water. Too hard. Now my eyes were picking out every detail of the bowl's decoration—the dark blue blossoms, the curving latticework, the swirling vines along the lip.

The magic isn't in the bowl, I reminded myself. *It's in the water.* I could hear it there, a swirl of playful melodies, but that only made my task harder. Last time I'd scried, I hadn't been able to hear magic. Now I had to tell myself sternly that I wasn't here to listen but to look.

I blinked, softening my gaze, and pushed the bowl an inch closer to the fire. This time it caught the flames in just the right way, drawing my gaze under the shimmering surface. All at once the water was like a river running through my hands, carrying me down to the sea. And as it swept me along, I heard a music I'd heard once before, a music that horrified me: *Come, Chantress. Come into the water . . .*

My first instinct was to fight free of it, but I was in too deep for that. The water and the music wouldn't let me go. They spiraled around me, pulling me down and down, until everything blurred—sea-green to deep blue to black. And yet still I went down, plunging headfirst, until far below me I saw something at the murky bottom of the sea—a stone wall even broader and stronger than the one I'd destroyed on Lord Charlton's lands, a wall that stretched out into shadows. Along one section of it, two massive green serpents spun round and round, chasing each other until they formed a perfect circle, tongue to tail.

As I plummeted toward them, the circle began to glow with

an unearthly green light. Except now I saw that it wasn't a circle but a hole—a hole in the vast wall. And it was from that hole that the music was coming. I flung out my arms, trying to stop myself from falling into it. But with a flick of their tails, the serpents caught me around the ankles and started to pull me through.

Come to me . . .

I couldn't breathe, I was drowning, and still the serpents wouldn't let go.

Kick.

I jerked my legs as hard as I could. Something cracked, and the song and the serpents vanished.

Blinking, I saw my feet splayed out in front of me, soaking wet, and the bowl in pieces on the clay-tiled hearth. An expensive accident—delft bowls were not cheap—but what I felt as I stared down at the shards was relief. I was no longer at the edge of that terrible hole.

It wasn't a real hole, I reassured myself, head spinning. And the serpents weren't real either. They were only symbols and signs. That was how scrying worked.

But what did it all mean? As I sat there by the dwindling flames, trying to work it out, I felt more and more confused. Melisande had worn a necklace with tongue-to-tail serpents, and the hole in the wall might have been the crack that she had talked about. With scrying, however, things were rarely what they seemed. My vision might mean something else entirely.

Perhaps Sybil could help me make sense of things. Although she didn't have the power to scry, she was the one who'd introduced me to the technique, so there was a chance she'd know how to read the pictures I'd seen, or at least have a guess about how to interpret them. Cheered by the thought, I pushed the shards of the delft bowl to one side with the coal scuttle, then rummaged in the nearest pile for dry stockings.

Five minutes later, lantern in hand, I was on my way out the door.

CHAPTER TWENTY
IRON CROSS

Where exactly I was to find Sybil, I didn't know. The Banqueting House seemed a good place to start asking for directions, but I wasn't even halfway there when Sybil's maid Joan spotted me.

"My lady!" Wizened though she was, her voice was strong, and evidently the rest of her was too. She pushed through a throng of bemused courtiers and came up to my side, holding out an iron amulet.

"So it really is you," she said with satisfaction as my fingers brushed against it. "The Queen's been wondering where you were at. There's horrible stories about the kraken—"

"I'm fine, truly. What about the Queen, and you, and Norrie?"

"The Queen?" She gave me a pockmarked grin. "She's running the entire outfit, she is, with Norrie's help. We're all taking orders from them, over at the Great Hall." She drew her scarf tighter. "I'm off to the kitchens right now, but you should go in and see them. They've been that worried about you."

She disappeared into the crowd, leaving me mystified. What on earth were Sybil and Norrie up to?

Only when I reached the Great Hall did all become clear. The huge space was rigged out like an infirmary, with pallets laid out everywhere, and men, women, and children crowding onto them. Many of them wore plain iron crosses, or clutched amulets like Joan's in their hands.

"See if you can find me another dozen blankets," Norrie was saying to a young woman as I walked up. "More if you can get them."

"I'll do my best." The young woman turned, and as she scooted past, I saw to my surprise it was Lady Clemence. Both she and Norrie were wearing iron crosses.

"Lucy!" Norrie's face lit up. "I'm so glad to see you, child."

"And I to see you." I offered up my bracelet so that she would know for certain that it was me. "But what's happening here?"

"Oh, we've been busy for hours, ever since the evacuation started. Some poor souls have nowhere to go, or couldn't be moved far, so the King opened up the Great Hall to them. And the Queen thought we ought to see what could be done for them. Who'd have guessed she'd be such a dab hand at setting up a hospital? But she is. Has the whole place running like clockwork."

"Is she here now?"

"She's somewhere about, I expect." Norrie looked about the crowded hall. "Mind you, I'm not sure just where at the moment. Come to think of it, she may be off talking the King and the Royal Steward into giving us some more supplies. I expect she'll get them too. She's the one who dug up these crosses for us, you know. Packed away at the back of the chapel, they were."

Before she could say anything more, a hollow-cheeked man stumbled up and asked for help for his wife.

"In pain, is she?" Norrie asked. "Well, let's do what we can to set her at ease." She motioned for me to come with her, murmuring, "Chances are, the poor dear's suffering as much from shock as anything else. Sometimes a reassuring word does a world of good. All the more so if it comes from the Chantress, I should think."

I followed without protest. Although I needed to find Sybil, surely this wouldn't take long, and the man's wife did indeed appear to be in great distress. Lying still on a pallet, staring with glazed eyes at the ceiling, she was as gaunt as he was, and at first she took no notice of me.

When Norrie made a point of introducing me, however, the woman glanced fearfully in my direction and shrank away. "You're the one who's calling up the monsters."

"Calling them? No, I'm fighting them—"

"Magic calling to magic. I heard it. Yesterday on the Thames, I did." She scrabbled at her kerchief and pulled out an iron cross. "Leave me alone!"

She held the cross in front of her, but when I moved to touch it, she jerked back and shrieked louder. "Begone!" She raised the cross, as if seeking to exorcise me.

Didn't she understand what the point of wearing iron was? "There's no need to fear me." I showed her my bracelet. "See, I'm wearing iron too."

She yelped again and cowered back "Get away!"

Her cries were attracting attention now, as her neighbors looked to see what was wrong.

"Maybe you should go, Lucy dear," Norrie whispered into my ear. "She's obviously quite disturbed, and it'll only upset her more if you stay."

"But she—"

"Never mind." Norrie gave my hand a squeeze. "You go on. I expect you have more important things to do. I'll let the Queen know you were looking for her, shall I?"

As I turned away, it felt as if everyone were watching me. Although some of the people smiled or bowed, I saw others step back. Did they, too, harbor suspicions about my role in all this?

Don't be ridiculous, I told myself. *They have worries of their own, that's all. You've had the people's goodwill ever since you freed them from the Shadowgrims. That woman's just a troubled soul who deserves your sympathy.*

But as I made my way through the crowded hall, I saw at least a dozen people quietly reach for their own crosses and hold tight to them as I went by.

† † †

Outside the Great Hall, it was growing darker, and for once I was glad of the gloom. I pulled my hood up high; I didn't want to be recognized. Ignorance, that was all it was, I told myself.

Ignorance and superstition. But I still felt hollow inside when I thought of those crosses.

Scrying, I reminded myself. *That's what you should be thinking about. And Sybil.* I still needed to find her. Norrie had mentioned she might be with the King and the Royal Steward, but I had no idea where they were meeting. The relocated State Rooms, perhaps? Should I go back to the chapel and ask for directions again?

While I stood deliberating by a puddle, I caught sight of a familiar silver-bearded figure shuffling past one of the smoldering torches—Penebrygg. Perhaps he would know where the State Rooms were. Pleased to have spotted him, I rushed over to greet him—but as I came closer, my pleasure vanished. The velvet cap he always wore was gone, and his black robes were stiff with mud, while he himself looked as if he'd added a decade to his already considerable age since I'd last seen him.

He started when I addressed him. "Oh, my dear. I didn't see you."

With a faltering hand, he touched my iron bracelet. Only then did I notice that his spectacles—so carefully fashioned and almost part of the man, with lenses he had ground himself—were missing.

I reached out to steady him. "Dear Penebrygg, what's happened to you?"

He blinked as if trying to clear his vision. "The wall by old Bridewell Palace gave way. My house is not far from it, you know." His voice sounded as battered as the rest of him. "I stayed perhaps a little too long, trying to find a book I wanted. But I'm afraid most of my library is beyond recovery now. And Nat's books as well, and all his papers besides. He will be so distressed—"

"He will be very relieved that you are safe," I said firmly. "As am I. Tell me, do you have a place to sleep?"

Again he blinked, owl-like. "I'm not quite certain, my dear. A guard directed me to the Great Hall, but I didn't like to take a pallet when there were so many in need. Nat has rooms here now, you know, and I thought I might stay with him. I've done so before, from time to time, and I have a key—but I'm so blind without my glasses that I can't find his staircase."

I remembered how Penebrygg had offered me refuge during my first days in London, when very little had stood between me and a terrible death. Surely I could spare the time to help him find shelter now.

"Come with me," I said.

Finding Sybil could wait.

CHAPTER TWENTY-ONE

TRESPASSER

I hadn't realized that Nat had rooms of his own in Whitehall, but Penebrygg remembered enough about where they were located that I could find them easily. Deep inside the palace, they did not have a view of the river—which meant they were still accessible.

As we walked over there, I saw several people shy away from us. Was it me they were avoiding? Were they holding iron crosses?

Ignorance and superstition, I told myself again. *Don't take it to heart.* But still they unnerved me.

Once we reached Nat's rooms, Penebrygg had trouble with the key, so I handed him the lantern and unlocked the door myself. Penebrygg went straight in, but at first I held back, standing self-consciously on the threshold. Given where I stood with Nat, I wasn't sure he would want me in such a private place. But when Penebrygg looked back at me, his weary face heavily shadowed in the light of the lantern, I cast aside any reservations.

"I'll get a fire going," I said.

A half hour later, the coals were burning merrily, and I had Penebrygg tucked up in a chair close by them. I'd made free with Nat's possessions, grabbing a counterpane from his bed, pears from a basket, and cider and cheese from a well-oiled cupboard. Penebrygg was looking more like himself now.

And I? I was caught between warring emotions. It felt like trespass to be here when Nat hadn't invited me in—and yet it felt perfectly right too, especially since I was ministering to a man who meant so much to both of us.

Nat's role as the King's special envoy meant that he was often on the road, so it made sense that his rooms were neat but plain; they had an air of a place that wasn't much used. Yet here and there I saw the stamp of his presence: books on astronomy, microscopes, and philosophy; a treatise on the potato; a letter addressed in his incisive hand. And when I'd gathered up the counterpane, I'd caught the scent of him in it, as immediate and fresh as an embrace.

Penebrygg finished his pears and cheese and set the plate on the small table next to him.

"Can I get you anything else?" I asked.

"No, no, my dear." He rubbed the place on the bridge of his nose where his spectacles usually sat. "I've had as much as I care to, thank you. And in any case, you must have plenty of other things to do than look after one rather doddery old man. Where were you off to when we met?"

Worried about all he'd been through already, I started to deflect the question, then realized I was doing him a disservice.

Without his spectacles, he looked fragile and unfocused, but his mind was still as sharp as ever, and his spirit as curious. So I told him not only that I'd been looking for Sybil but why.

"Scrying? How fascinating, my dear." A bit of color came into his cheeks. Magic had always excited him. "I remember you mentioning that you had done something of the sort before, but I'm afraid I know very little about how it works. What kind of pictures did you see, exactly—if you don't mind my asking?"

I didn't mind at all. In fact, it was possible that Penebrygg would be able to cast some light on them. Although he didn't have Sybil's deep knowledge of Chantress magic, he was a keen researcher and reader, and his interest in magic meant that over his long lifetime he'd consulted all kinds of rare books—some of which no longer existed, having been burned in Scargrave's time. I sat down on a bench by the fire and carefully described what I'd seen, hoping he might have a clue as to what it all meant. For good measure, I told him about Melisande, too—about her necklace, and what she'd said about a wall and the Mothers.

"And now here you are seeing a wall with a hole in it, and a green light on the other side." Penebrygg stroked his beard, something he did only when troubled. "I wonder . . . could it be the wall between the worlds?"

"The what?"

"Didn't I once tell you about it? Years ago it would be, back when we first met, when you asked me what I knew about Chantresses. It's how your kind came about, you see. So the old stories say. I've heard a few different versions, but it boils down to this: There is—or was—a wall between the faerie world and ours, and both we and they used to cross it now and again, and to mingle. And those men who took faerie wives had Chantress daughters."

If he had said something about this, I'd forgotten it in my rush to understand more about the threat posed by Scargrave and his Shadowgrims.

I said slowly, "The old stories? You mean it's only a legend?"

"A legend, yes. But that doesn't mean there's no truth in it, my dear."

My godmother had warned me that Penebrygg's stories about Chantresses weren't necessarily to be believed, and she herself had never mentioned any kind of wall. Still, I was curious. "You say people used to cross it? They don't anymore?"

"So the stories go. Something sealed us off from each other; I've never heard anything about how or when or why. From what you say, I gather Melisande believes it was Chantress magic of some sort, though why Chantresses would want to cut themselves off from the faerie world, I don't know. I seem to remember reading once that Chantresses used to cross the wall to renew their powers. Apparently visiting that world strengthened them, though, it was said that they had to be careful never to take their stones off while they were there, or terrible things could befall them."

I couldn't help shaking my head. I'd never heard of such a thing before—not from Lady Helaine, not from anyone else.

"Well, all that's by the by," Penebrygg said. "My point is this:

I wonder if what we are dealing with now is a hole in the wall—and some kind of terrible magic from the other side. You said the light coming from the hole was green?"

"Yes."

"In the old stories, green is the color of the faeries. Who, it is also said, can be held off with iron."

"But it's not faeries we're seeing," I objected. "It's sea serpents and kraken."

"For all we know, that's what they look like." Penebrygg stretched his hands toward the blue-orange flames of the fire. "The trouble is, you're thinking of faeries as tiny winged creatures who dance around the woods. But that isn't what they are at all. You should think of them instead as masters of illusion. The old stories say the creatures of faerie can be anything they want to be."

I thought of the moment when I'd seen two kings. Maybe there was something in what Penebrygg was saying.

"And here's something else for you to consider." He fished in his sleeve and pulled out a bedraggled scrap of paper. "I've been doing a bit of research about ondines, and I found something I thought you would want to see. It's based on an old Norman manuscript from the time of the Conquest, but I've translated the passage for you." He pulled the paper close, then stopped and blinked, looking bereft as he missed his spectacles again. "Well, I can't read it properly now. But perhaps you can, my dear?"

I took the paper he held out to me and spoke the words aloud: "*It is well known that the ethereal spirits of air were never very strong, and the spirits of earth and fire have long since been weakened by humans, who have done so much to tame their elements. But water spirits by nature are nimble and strong and ambitious, and their domain includes the oceans, which cover most of the globe. They take many forms, and they are by far the most dangerous kind of elemental, greatly feared even by Chantresses."*

"For 'elementals,'" Penebrygg said, "I think you could perhaps substitute the world 'faeries.' Or perhaps even Melisande's 'Mothers.'"

I stared down at the tattered paper. Was that the explanation? Were we at war with a whole host of watery beings? If so, was Melisande their agent—or their leader?

"What about the two snakes?" I asked. "The ones I saw, and the ones on Melisande's necklace. How do they fit into this?"

"Ah, yes, the snakes." Penebrygg stroked his beard again. "They would appear to be a version of the ouroboros. A very ancient symbol, most often used to signify immortality and eternal rebirth. It was known to the Greeks and even the ancient Egyptians. You see it in alchemy, too."

I looked at him in surprise. "In alchemy? Why?"

"Because immortality is one of the great goals of alchemy, my dear. Some also say the ouroboros embodies the mingled acts of destruction and creation that are part of the alchemist's work."

I sat up straight, the scrap of paper forgotten. "Then maybe it's not magic we should be worrying about. Maybe it's alchemy." I told him about my conversation with Gabriel.

"How interesting," Penebrygg said, clearly intrigued. "I suppose the green light you saw could represent the first stage of transmutation."

I tried to remember what I'd learned about alchemy last year. "The first stage—that's what you call the Green Lion, isn't it?"

"Yes. And in alchemy, the Lion devours the sun, you know."

"Does it?" As always, the arcane terminology of alchemy made little sense to me, but Penebrygg sounded very sure of himself. "Well, it's true we haven't seen the sun for days. But what about iron?"

"There, I must admit I'm less certain." He was stroking his beard again. "But iron is important to alchemy. When you combine it with sulfur, you get sulfuric acid, the destroying fire. So it's possible it has a destructive force that interferes with power over water."

He closed his eyes for a moment, and I saw how weary he was. This discussion was taxing him.

"Thank you," I said. "You've given me a lot to think about. I should leave you now, but can I first help you to bed?"

"No, no." He waved me away but couldn't help yawning as he did so. "Must leave the bed for the boy."

"He's so busy, he probably won't come back tonight. And even if he does, I'm sure he'd want you to have it." I tugged at the counterpane. "Come, let's make you comfortable."

He really was exhausted, which made it easier for me to persuade him to do as I directed. I'd barely gotten him tucked into the bed before he was fast asleep.

Making as little noise as possible, I closed the door to the bedchamber before banking down the fire in the main room. My hand was on the latch of the outer door when I remembered my lantern. Looking back, I saw Penebrygg had set it down on a desk strewn with papers.

I was reaching for it when I heard quick footfalls outside. My pulse picked up as I recognized the tread.

The door swung open, and Nat walked in.

CHAPTER TWENTY-TWO

BROADSIDE

Nat stopped short when he saw me. In the dim light, it seemed as if his face were covered with bruises, but as he came closer, I was relieved to see it was only mud.

"Lucy?"

"It really is me," I assured him, holding up my bracelet. As he briefly touched his iron-ringed hand to it, I swallowed hard. What must he think, finding me here in his rooms?

"I brought Penebrygg here," I told him quickly. "His house is flooded, and he had nowhere to sleep except your rooms. I hope I did right—"

"Of course you did." His face was full of concern. "Is he still here?"

"Yes, fast asleep in your bed. But he's heartsick about the flood, Nat. He couldn't save your books and papers—"

"No matter. As long as he's safe."

It was exactly what I'd thought he would say, but it warmed

me all the same. It seemed he hadn't changed that much after all, at least not in the most important ways. "And what about you?"

"I've just come back for a change of clothes before I have a quick word with the King." He set some sodden papers down on the desk and shucked off his dripping coat. Draping it over a chair by the banked fire, he added, "There's more bad news, I'm afraid. You know Westminster's flooded, and I expect you'll have heard about Bridewell from Penebrygg. And now St. Katharine's is underwater too, and most of Southwark and Lambeth."

That *was* very bad news. "And the kraken?" I asked.

"An archer up at the Tower shot it down two hours ago; there are plenty of witnesses. But on my way here, I saw Sir Christopher Linnet, who says he spotted it—or another just like it—not half an hour ago, surfacing near London Bridge." Nat rubbed the mud off one cheek with the back of his hand. "But what worries me most is that we're only two hours off low tide, and yet the waters haven't gone down."

"Not at all?"

"Not so much as an inch. Sir Barnaby's been keeping track of that for us, and I don't doubt his measurements. I've told the King that if it continues this way, I think we may need to evacuate the whole city." He looked at me with hope in his eyes. "Unless you've found a way to stop all this?"

"Not yet." I hated to disappoint him, but that was the hard truth. "I may have found a clue, though. I'm just not sure what it means, but I'm hoping Sybil can help me. I was looking for her when I ran across Penebrygg."

"It was good he found you."

Our eyes met, and there was a light in his that made me blush. But before either of us could speak, something shot through the gap between door and sill: a cheap printed broadside on a page of foolscap.

I was closest to the door, so I picked it up for him. I read the title in disbelief.

THE WICKED CHANTRESS
or, The Melusine-Monster

Nat tried to grab it from me. "Don't read it, Lucy. You don't need to see this."

"I think I do." I yanked it out of his reach, into the full light of the lantern. Beneath the huge black letters of the title, a crude woodcut showed a dark-haired woman dancing in the sea while a serpent snaked around her. In the background, three ships were wrecked on rocks, and a sea monster was attacking London.

Heart knocking in my chest, I scanned the lines. According to the ballad, I was a magic-maker who was now betraying my country. Like Melusine before me, I had revealed my true nature and made alliance with my own monstrous kind to destroy England.

I shut my eyes for a moment, trying to remain calm. I failed. I read the lines again. These things spread like fire on thatch. Already half of London had probably read it or heard it sung. I thought of the people in the Great Hall holding up their crosses.

"Lucy, don't look like that."

I didn't look up. "You knew what this was, didn't you?"

"Yes, but—"

"Is it everywhere?"

"I don't know. I've gathered up all the ones I've found." He gestured toward the soggy papers he'd laid facedown on his desk. It was a thick pile.

"You should have told me," I said.

"I had other things I wanted to say to you first."

I shook my head, hardly hearing him. I was still staring at the broadside.

Nat covered the ugly title with his hand. "Lucy, listen to me. Please."

He touched the curve of my cheek, as if I were a bird he feared would fly away. "I said we were strangers, but I was wrong. I could never feel about a stranger the way I feel about you. I'm not going to let you face this alone. From now on, I'll be right by your side—if you'll let me."

Everything blurred before me. I ached to say yes to him, but how could I? The world was so much against me—and it would turn against him, too, if he stood with me. Loving him as I did, how could I possibly let him in for that? Especially when I was half-afraid he was making the offer out of pity.

Biting my lip, I pulled away. "Nat, you can't afford to be paired off with someone the whole world thinks is a monster."

"It's just one broadside," he said gently. "It's awful, I know, but it's not the whole world."

"It's not just the broadside, Nat." The foolscap crinkled in my hands. "People are screaming when they see me. They're holding up crosses. They hate me."

"It's because of this flood," he said. "It's made everyone lose their heads."

"It's *not* just because of the flood. People mutter things and gossip behind my back even when everything's fine. At best, they say I'm different, but most don't stop there. I'm not human, they say. I'm a witch, a harpy, a she-monster. And if they see us together, you can be sure they'll smear you right along with me."

"I can live with that," he said steadily.

"That's easy to say, when they haven't done it to you yet." He started to protest, but I stopped him. "You've worked so hard to get where you are. I won't let you throw that away." I thought of Sybil and how unhappy she was. I couldn't bear to do that to Nat.

There was a stubborn set to his jaw now. "I'll do what I please."

But I was stubborn too—stubborn and exhausted and worried half out of my mind about how to save us all. I had to work hard not to sound sharp. "And what about me? Do you think I want to live with a man who's sacrificed everything for me? Because reputation is the least of it, Nat. Think of all you stand to lose. As long as we're together, your life will never be comfortable, never be normal. I'll always be traveling for the King, for one—"

"He makes you travel too much," Nat said.

This was exactly the kind of argument that would make life together a misery. "I need to travel, Nat, and anyone who marries me is going to have to accept that."

"I can accept a lot," Nat said. "But that doesn't change the fact that the King is becoming too dependent on you, and that's not good for anyone. It would be better for us all if your magic were used more sparingly."

I'd secretly wondered as much myself, but somehow hearing Nat say it didn't help. My grip tightened on the broadside. "Look, if you want a normal life—"

"It's not a normal life I'm after." The amber light of the lamp caught him full in the face, and his gravity took me aback. "I thought I'd made myself plain, Lucy. What I want is you."

There was a directness in what he said, and an honesty, that made my throat ache. But it didn't change how things were.

"Maybe you think that's what you want now," I said quietly. "But sooner or later, you're going to wish you'd chosen someone else—someone who's easier to live with, someone you haven't given up so much for. You'll want your independence back. You'll want to leave." *The way my father left my mother.*

"I won't."

I looked straight at him. "You left me before."

That silenced him.

"I can't live through that again." I was still raw from the first time. "I tell you it won't work."

His face grew fierce. "So you're saying we're done? That I should go find someone else?"

My head pounded. I felt as if I were teetering on the top of a precipice, and everything hung on what I said next. But I couldn't take the words back, any more than I could change who we were, or how the world worked.

No man wants a wife who works magic.

"Yes," I said. "I think you should find someone else."

He turned away from me and went to stand by the dying fire. "If that's really how you feel, maybe I will."

There was nothing more to say. Feeling sick, I picked up the lantern and walked out. Down in the courtyard, the dark sky was still weeping with rain. I trudged on shaky legs across the flooded cobblestones.

I'd saved the person I loved from a life he would hate. I'd saved us both from a painful mistake. That had to be right.

Why, then, did it feel as if I'd just laid waste to everything that mattered?

CHAPTER TWENTY-THREE

FINDING THE QUEEN

I didn't dare let myself stop; if I stopped, I would cry. Instead I marched myself off to the Great Hall to talk to Sybil about the scrying. If people chose to hold up crosses when they saw me coming, I would just have to deal with it. I had work to do.

But the trouble started before I even had a chance to enter the Great Hall. Just outside the doors, half a dozen ladies-in-waiting were standing in a tight gossipy knot. When they saw me approach, they broke apart. Had the gossip been about me? Had they seen the broadside?

By the look of them, they had. Before this, they'd never been friendly, but now they were overtly hostile. I saw some of them fingering crosses. For the first time, it occurred to me to wonder who had pushed the broadside under Nat's door.

I wasn't going to ask; I had my pride. But I wasn't going to retreat, either—even though they had arranged themselves so that my way forward was blocked.

I brandished my iron bracelet to prove my good faith. "I need to speak with the Queen. Do you know where she is?"

Silence. But then, from behind me, someone spoke up, shyly but with courtesy. It was Clemence. "The Queen? Why she's in the little room around the back, where we're keeping the supplies."

"Thank you." I could reach that room without going through the Great Hall—or past the line of ladies-in-waiting.

As I walked away, I heard the others chide Clemence for speaking to me. There was clearly more to her than I'd realized, a certain kindness and independence of mind that the others lacked. Was that why Nat was drawn to her? Would he turn to her now?

I knew I should feel grateful to her for helping me, but what consumed me was pain.

† † †

Sybil was counting out blankets when I came in. For a moment I almost didn't recognize her. No longer the perfect portrait of queenly elegance, she wore heavy boots and a gown that had been ruined by the rain. Her curls were disheveled, and her neck and arms and ears were bare, save for her iron ring.

Her eyes, however, were as warm as ever—and livelier than they had been in ages.

"Lucy!" She didn't leave her work but beckoned me over. "Joan told me you were all right, but it's good to see you with my own eyes."

She hugged me, then frowned anxiously. "Oh dear. What is it?"

"Nothing. I'm fine."

"No, you're not," she insisted. "Do you think I can't tell?"

It was no use trying to hide the truth from Sybil. "I had an argument with Nat, that's all."

"Oh, Lucy! What about?"

"It—it doesn't matter." Quickly I broached the real purpose of my visit, telling her about Melisande and the scrying and what Penebrygg had said about them both.

"The wall between the worlds," she said slowly when I was done. "That rings a bell somewhere—and the two snakes, too."

"You recognize them?"

"Nothing so precise as that, I'm afraid. But I have this idea that Chantresses were involved in sealing some kind of wall, or widening it, or something like that. I don't know what they did exactly, or even when, but Mama once said that the Chantresses did it to keep the Others at bay."

"The Others? Is that what she called them?" I asked. "Not the Mothers?"

"I think she said the Others, but I'm not certain. She was talking to someone else, you see, and I just happened to overhear her. So I didn't catch everything."

"Did you hear her say anything else about this wall?"

"Not that I can recall," Sybil said slowly. "Though I think . . . maybe . . . she said the sealing of the wall had something to do with Melusine."

"With Melusine?" I was surprised. "Are you sure?"

"Well, that bit I'm really not certain about," Sybil admitted. "And of course Mama never let the truth get in the way of a good story."

I felt as if we were going around in circles. But then I thought to ask, "Who was your mother talking to?"

Sybil looked down, thinking hard. "Do you know, I think it was when that odd woman came to the house to heal me, the one with the sea-green eyes."

I felt a leap of excitement. Could it have been Melisande? "Can you remember anything else?"

Sybil closed her eyes. "I think . . . I think it was the woman who was asking the questions. And she reminded my mother that if Chantress magic made something, then only Chantress magic could destroy it." She sighed and opened her eyes. "And I'm afraid that really *is* all I remember. I wish it were more."

"It's a great deal," I assured her, though I was sorry it wasn't more too. If only Melisande hadn't escaped! I could try describing her to Sybil, but there was no way she could identify the woman for certain without seeing her. And even then, could such a distant memory be trusted?

I looked at Sybil, who had gone back to her blankets. "The woman you saw, was she wearing a necklace like the one Melisande had today? With the two snakes?"

"If she was, I didn't see it. She was all wrapped up." She scribbled a note on a list, then paused. "But as I said, there's something about those snakes that sounds familiar." She shook her head. "How frustrating. I can't quite place it."

"Maybe it will come to you later. Will you find me if it does?"

"Of course—as soon as I can get away, that is. Or I'll send Norrie. She's planning to stay in the Great Hall with me tonight." Sybil stretched and set down her list. "What a rock that woman is, Lucy! Honestly, she's had the strength of ten today."

I remembered how confident Norrie had looked when I'd seen her, calm and in charge. Of late I'd been reluctant to lean on her, fearing she was too old and frail, but it seemed I'd underestimated her.

I'd clearly underestimated Sybil as well. Standing here in her plain clothes, busy about her work, she had a serenity and sureness I'd never seen in her before. And there was something more I saw.

"You look happy," I said wonderingly.

Sybil looked abashed. "It sounds dreadful to say it, when people are suffering so much, but I am. I can't tell you what a gift it is to be able to do something practical for once, something real. No one in the Great Hall cares about Court etiquette. They just want a bed and some food and a friendly word—and I can make that happen." Her eyes crinkled in amusement. "In a way, it's rather like my old life with Mama. I cajole supplies out of the steward; I sort out arguments; I calm the kitchen staff . . ."

It was good to see her so happy, but it was also disconcerting. "And the King? Does he know how much you've been doing?"

"Oh, Lucy, he's so *proud* of me." She gave me a glowing smile. "He's sharing reports with me now. And we've talked—really talked—about what's happening in the city and what we should do about it."

"That's good." My voice sounded all wrong, but it was hard to know what to say.

"Oh, I know it won't sound like much to you," Sybil said. "You're used to having Henry seek your advice. But for me, it's new—and wonderful—to have him trust me like that." She shook her head. "I've been trying so hard to be a proper queen; I didn't want to humiliate him. But I'm starting to think I should have just been myself all along."

A knock came at the door. Sybil gave me a quick hug. "I need to get that. But you're welcome to stay, Lucy."

"You're kind to offer, but I should go." If I stayed, she might want to talk about Nat again, and I couldn't bear that.

The person at the door turned out to be Clemence, who blushed when she saw me. Sybil didn't seem to notice. Warmly she drew Clemence in, and they started to discuss the ins and outs of supplies, and even to joke with each other about some of the trials of the day.

"Good night," I said, and slipped out.

In the darkness, I let the cool rain fall onto my burning face.

What have I done?

I had been so certain I was doing the right thing in pushing Nat away. I'd taken Sybil's unhappiness as a warning. And now Sybil's situation was changing . . .

Was it too late to go back to Nat? To tell him that maybe I was wrong? To say that I loved him and wanted to find a way forward?

My feet made the decision for me. I found myself turning back to his rooms, first walking, then running, then racing. There was a light in his window. I bounded up the stairs and knocked on the heavy door.

No one opened it.

I knocked again, harder. "It's Lucy," I called through the keyhole.

Nat didn't answer.

Maybe he isn't there, I told myself. *Maybe he's asleep.*

But there was another, more awful possibility that I couldn't ignore. *Maybe he knows I'm here but he's done with me.*

I knocked twice more, so loudly that I was half-afraid I'd wake Penebrygg in the inner room, but no one came.

I forced myself to turn away. No matter how desperate I felt, I couldn't stand there all night, not when I was needed elsewhere.

The rain lashed at me as I crossed the dark courtyard again. I wasn't giving up, I told myself. I might have to wait until later, but I was still determined to talk to Nat, to ask for one more chance to set things right between us. Deep inside, however, I couldn't help fearing that I'd already been given that chance—and I'd thrown it away.

† † †

Weary and aching with sadness, I set off toward the guardrooms to see Captain Knollys, hoping he might have some new clue about Melisande's whereabouts. Much to his frustration and mine, however, Knollys had nothing to report.

"There's no sign of Melisande anywhere," he said. "Or of that servant of hers. And no one's approached those rooms since we went there this morning. Whoever—or whatever—those women are, they've gone to ground."

It wasn't good news, but I knew I needed to bring it to the King anyway. It had been many hours since I'd last seen him, and he would be wondering what progress I'd made.

It took me another half hour to find where the new State Rooms were located, in temporary quarters by the tiltyard. When I arrived there, everything was in confusion. The most valuable trappings had been carried across from the old State Rooms, but the Brussels tapestries were still rolled tight, the King's gilded throne sat forgotten in a corner, and paintings by Holbein, Raphael, and Gentileschi were stacked against the walls. Crates of documents were piled up everywhere, and mobs of clerks and secretaries were scrabbling to put them in order.

The King, haggard but alert, touched iron with me, then drew me into a small alcove filled with yet more crates, six Turkey carpets, and an ivory-inlay writing desk. "Your captive—has she been found?"

"I'm afraid not," I said. "But my men are still doing their best to trace her. And I may have found another clue that will help us."

"A clue?" He looked hopeful.

"Yes. Here, let me draw it for you." With the pen and paper he offered me, I sketched out the joined snakes. "Have you ever seen anything like this before?"

"No. Not at all." His blue eyes clouded. "Should I have?"

"Not necessarily." I folded up the sketch and tucked it into my sleeve, trying to sound more confident than I felt. "Don't let it worry you. I'll work it out. But perhaps you could tell me what's going on elsewhere? I hear there's been another sighting of a kraken."

"Three at least, by now," said the King. "The only bright spot is that it seems that the attacks are slacking off elsewhere. As far as we can tell, we're bearing the brunt of things here in London."

Was that because our enemy was bent on destroying the country's seat of power? Or was there another reason? I thought of how the sea serpent had honed in on my singing, how the kraken had come to just that part of the river where I had been working magic, how the river kept calling to me.

Could it be that *I* was the target?

The King was skeptical. "If you're the target, then why aren't all the monsters lining up outside Whitehall? And what about those mermaids that came before, and the attacks at Portsmouth?"

The Lord High Admiral huffed up to us, holding up his iron ring. "Your Majesty, if I might have a word?"

"Of course." The King gestured for him to speak.

The Admiral coughed, glanced at me, then shook his head. "In private, Your Majesty."

"Very well." The King motioned for us both to follow him.

The Admiral stayed where he was. "In *private*, Your Majesty."

"Yes, yes, we'll find somewhere," the King said, not catching his meaning.

The Admiral skirted around me and barked into the King's ear. "I want to speak to you without *her*."

The King stopped still. So did I. So did half the clerks and secretaries in the room. The Admiral may have meant to be discreet, but his voice carried.

"You wish to speak to me without the Chantress?" the King clarified.

The Admiral gave a curt nod. He wouldn't meet my eyes.

The King frowned. "Whatever you wish to say to me can be said to her as well. There are no secrets between us."

"I'm not so sure of that, Your Majesty," the Admiral growled. "She let the mermaid escape, didn't she? And now another captive of hers has slipped the net. And there's some strange talk at Court and in the city—"

"Enough." The King silenced him. "I trust the Chantress absolutely. You will speak before us both."

It was a stirring defense, and I deeply appreciated it, but the Admiral remained stubbornly silent. Glancing around, I saw that he wasn't alone in doubting me. Some of the clerks and secretaries were watching me with suspicion. They might not be holding up crosses, but they'd been swayed by the gossip about me.

Insisting that the Admiral speak in front of me would not help my cause. I curtsied to the King. "You are very kind, Your Majesty," I said, "but I must ask your leave to go. I have much to attend to."

I wasn't sure the King would accept this, but after a moment he nodded. "Very well. We are grateful for all you are doing to defend us, Chantress." As I left, he called after me, "Please take care. We would all be lost without you."

I nodded because he expected me to. But I knew it would take more than being careful to defeat our enemy—and to prove to all the doubters that I really was on their side.

CHAPTER TWENTY-FOUR
FLOOD TIDE

I meant to do another round of scrying that night, and then hunt up Gabriel, talk to Captain Knollys, and look for Nat again. But as soon as I opened the door again on my dark and cluttered rooms, exhaustion and grief washed over me. It had been a hard day by any reckoning—and the hardest part had been what had happened with Nat.

Was there any way to fix things between us? I wanted to believe there was, but I wasn't sure. Some things couldn't be unsaid. Some things couldn't be mended. And maybe this was one of them.

I pushed the door shut behind me, desolate to my bones.

A rest, that was what I needed. I let myself lie down on one of the mattresses. *Only for a minute, and then I'll build a fire and find a bowl for scrying.*

The next thing I knew, Norrie was shaking me awake, touching her hand to my iron bracelet. "Lucy, you need to get up." Her voice was full of alarm. "The waters are rising."

I blinked. The room was still dark, but the sky outside was deep gray, not black. Pushing myself up from the mattress, I tried to slough off sleep. "The river's rising?"

"Since sometime after midnight," Norrie said. "Slowly at first, but faster and faster now. It's come up at least two feet in all, and it shows no sign of stopping. And here it is Allhallows' Eve. Not a good omen, that."

"What time is it now?"

"Just before six. The order's just gone out—we have to leave Whitehall."

I was fully awake now. "They can't hold the palace?"

"No. And they may not be able to hold the rest of the riverfront, either," Norrie said somberly. "Already Whitehall is practically an island, and it's only going to get worse from here. We all have to go to higher ground."

And here I'd been sleeping all this time. Hurriedly I smoothed back my hair and shook out my gown.

"Nat's the one who's organizing us all," Norrie said. "It's like moving a mountain, but he's doing it."

I winced. Merely hearing Nat's name was enough to bring the pain rushing back.

Fortunately, Norrie didn't see. Turning away, she grabbed a basket from the top of a pile and started stuffing it with clothes, candles, and other necessaries. "I came here to get a few things before we left," she told me. "They want to move the refugees up to Marylebone, and they've asked the Queen and me to go with them. We have to leave right away. I didn't know you'd be here;

I thought you'd already gone. Someone said you'd left earlier, with the King and Sir Barnaby."

"No. I saw the King late last night, but I had things I needed to do here." And I'd left them all undone—the scrying, seeing Gabriel and Captain Knollys and Nat.

I looked up to find Norrie looking back at me. "Child, are you all right? Do you need me to stay with you?"

"No. No, I'm fine. Just worried by the floods. And about you. Will you be all right, going up to Marylebone?"

"Of course. Which isn't to say I wouldn't be happier if you were coming too, but that's for your sake, not mine." She set her full basket down by the hearth, then leaned down to pick up a piece of paper. "What's this?"

For an awful moment, I thought it was another copy of the broadside. But of course it was much too small for that. As I came up to her, I saw it was the sketch I'd made for the King, showing the two snakes. It must have fallen out of my sleeve when I'd been asleep.

"Just a drawing," I told Norrie. And then, because I thought I might as well ask: "Do you recognize it?"

"I should think so." Norrie had already turned back to her basket. "It's those snakes from Audelin House."

"You mean Lady Helaine's place?" I was torn between excitement and consternation. Audelin House had been deeded to me along with the rest of my godmother's property, and for a long time now Norrie had been trying to get me to visit it. She'd had it in mind that I might someday want to set up my own household there. But by her own reports the house was in sad shape, so it had seemed an unlikely plan to me, and I was so busy on the few occasions I was in London that I'd never actually gone to see it. "You saw them there—just like this, in a circle?"

"I have indeed." Norrie rose to get another basket. "And you would've seen them too, if you'd gone there with me. All over, they are, tucked away in the strangest places. I first saw them years ago, back when your godmother still lived there." She smiled, remembering. "The footmen said there were secret doors behind some of them, but I think they were just pulling my leg. It's just decoration, I expect—some kind of family crest, or maybe an old Chantress symbol. Not a very nice picture, is it? But it does stick in the mind."

Secret doors? I snatched up my cape. "I have to go there, Norrie—right now."

Norrie swung around, basket in hand. "To Audelin House? Lucy, you can't. It's too close to the river. Likely it's flooded already—or if not, it soon will be."

"Even if it's half underwater, I still need to go." I was frantically filling a sack of my own now: candles, tinderbox, a ball of twine . . . anything that might be useful for exploring an abandoned, half-flooded house. "Those snakes could be the key to everything."

"I don't see how," Norrie said.

"I don't see exactly how either. But I saw them, Norrie. I scried and saw them, so I know they're important. If I could just figure out why, I might be able to stop this flooding and save us all."

Norrie still looked worried, but she stopped protesting. She knew that scrying had saved my life before; inscrutable though it was, it wasn't something to be ignored. "You'll need the keys, then." She reached for her chatelaine and slipped them off—two iron keys, dark and heavy and fearsomely notched. But instead of handing them over, she held them tight in her hand. "Please don't go alone, Lucy. It's dangerous out there. Talk to Nat. If he can't go himself, I'm sure he'll find someone to go with you."

I couldn't possibly go to Nat, not after what I'd said last night. When I saw him next, it needed to be when we were alone and I could take back my hasty words. I couldn't go to him when he was in the thick of things, surrounded by others, and ask him for a favor. But I had to accept that Norrie had reason on her side. Going in company would be safer. "I promise I'll find someone."

She gave me the keys. "And do be sensible, child."

"Of course." I hugged her, then flew to the door, only to turn back on the threshold. If Norrie could help me unlock one mystery, perhaps she could help with some others. "Norrie, did Lady Helaine or my mother ever talk to you about a wall—a wall between the worlds?"

"No." Norrie shook her head slowly. "No, I can't say as they ever did. But do remember, child, they'd not have shared any Chantress secrets with me."

True enough. I blew her a kiss and went on my way.

† † †

The moment I stepped outside, I realized everything had changed. It wasn't raining anymore, but the sky glowered, ominously gray, and even in this inner courtyard I could smell magic everywhere, mixed in with the dank and tidal scent of the Thames itself. The river's everyday melodies of mischief and exuberance were now a mere froth above deeper and stronger and more malevolent tunes. Some of this music I recognized as being the river's own, or songs I'd heard from the sea—from currents that pulled unwary swimmers down, from depths that kept tight hold of whatever they found. But there were new songs here as well—strange and opaque melodies that I could not even begin to understand.

Part of the difficulty, of course, was that I couldn't hear them properly. The whole palace was in an uproar, and there were too many competing sounds. Trumpets called men to order. Guards bellowed. Everywhere people were calling out in panic and commiseration, lugging sacks and baskets with them.

Skirting past them, I went down to the guardrooms to find someone to go with me to Audelin House. I was dismayed to find the place empty. All I could do was leave a brief note to let Knollys and my men know where I was going, but I couldn't be certain they would get it. Had they too been told that I was already with the King? Had they gone there to meet me? Or were they out helping with the evacuation? I didn't know, and I couldn't spare the time to find out. If I wanted to make good on my promise to Norrie, I'd be better off going straight to Gabriel—provided he hadn't left yet.

Like Nat, Gabriel had rooms away from the river, so he'd

stayed put during yesterday's upheavals. When I reached his rooms, his door stood open. Inside, Gabriel was handing two books to his agitated valet.

"My lord, the time is growing short," the valet pleaded.

"I don't care, Quittle. We can't leave these books behind. You'll have to—" Seeing me, Gabriel broke off. "Chantress, I thought you'd gone already."

"No." Like Quittle, I was worried about the time, so I didn't stop to explain myself but merely touched my iron bracelet to his hand. "I need to go to Audelin House. Will you come with me?"

"Now?"

"Yes."

He didn't hesitate. "Of course." He turned to Quittle, who was wedging the desired books into a bulging bag. "So you can get them in? Excellent. Take all the bags to Cornhill, and I shall meet you there later."

"Cornhill?" I repeated.

"Yes, we're all going there, the whole Council," Gabriel said. "Didn't you hear? The King is assembling us in one of the Crown properties there."

"I'm afraid the message missed me."

"You and plenty of others, I expect. Whitehall's a nest of confusion this morning."

I nodded. Cornhill made sense as a destination, though. It was the highest point within the London city walls, a district favored by goldsmiths and bankers.

"Never mind. I'll take you up there after we've been to Audelin

House." Gabriel donned his overcoat and ushered me out the door. "Let's go—and on the way, perhaps you could explain why you have such a pressing need to see the place?"

I did explain, as briefly and quietly as I could. Not that there was much danger of anyone overhearing. This part of the palace had emptied out already, and the few people we saw on the staircases and in the galleries were in too much of a hurry to eavesdrop.

"Well, I can see why you have to go," Gabriel said when I'd finished. "But if that fails, I think you ought to look again at alchemy. Anyway, I'm glad you came to find me."

Gabriel knew a shortcut to the stable yards, where a temporary causeway linked Whitehall to the higher ground near Charing Cross. The small crowd there was too anxious to pay any attention to us, but once we were safely across, Gabriel drew me aside. "From now on, you'd better keep your hood up and your face down."

I looked at him, puzzled. "Why?"

"Haven't you heard? There are broadsides all over London blaming you for this. People don't know whether to pray to you or burn you."

"*Burn* me?"

"There's been some ugly talk like that, yes. Not from most people, of course, but I'd just as soon we didn't attract attention." He surveyed me. "You've got some kind of a wrap on under that cloak, haven't you? Maybe you could try pulling it up over your mouth."

Silently I did as he suggested.

"Much better," he pronounced. "We shouldn't get any mobs screaming for your blood now."

Maybe not, but still I felt tense as we joined the crowds heading for Charing Cross and points north. I breathed more easily once we left the pack and headed east into the maze of streets that led to Audelin House.

These streets were very close to the river, and for the most part they were deserted. But when we rounded one corner, I heard wood splintering and glass breaking and men shouting and singing.

"Looters." Gabriel pulled me back. "Let's go a different way."

Twice more we had to change our route, but soon we were approaching Audelin House.

Although I had never been inside the house before, Norrie had pointed it out to me a number of times, so I recognized it as soon as I saw it: an imposing residence of stout timber and fancy pargeting, so large that it took up the entire end of one street. At first glance, the house looked very grand, with carved beams and a double bay of oriel windows that jutted out from the front. It was only when you came closer that you saw the cracks and the fallen-away plaster and the boarded-up windows.

The house stood at the very edge of the flood. Even now, the river was lapping at the muddy street in front of it. Quite possibly its cellars were already awash. But the situation was better than I'd feared it might be.

I went forward and pushed my keys into its immense old

locks. They took some convincing, and Gabriel and I had to push hard at the heavy door, but finally it opened. As we stepped inside the dark entryway, a damp, moldering smell enveloped us.

Behind us, I thought I heard shouting, coming from somewhere not too far away. And I heard something else, too. Something much closer. Something I was desperately trying not to listen to.

Come to me, the river called.

I swung the door closed, and Audelin House swallowed us up.

CHAPTER TWENTY-FIVE
AUDELIN HOUSE

The house seemed impossibly dark at first, but pinholes of light picked out the edges of a door ahead of us. After I found the latch, we walked into what once must have been the grandest room in the house.

"Once," of course, was the critical word. It had been only a decade since my godmother had lived here, but it felt like a hundred years. Would she have recognized it? Would she have wanted to? Chunks of ceiling plaster now covered the floor, and the paneled walls that weren't scorched were pockmarked and splintered.

The place had stood empty ever since Scargrave had arrested my godmother and seized the house as attainted property. He'd ransacked every corner for contraband magic and Chantress secrets. And when he'd finished, he'd had its contents burned.

People don't know whether to pray to you or burn you.

There had been a great deal of burning in those years. Books.

Buildings. Even sometimes Chantresses themselves, and those who were thought to have truck with them. Judging from what I could see of the walls and floor, one of those bonfires had been right here in this room.

Yet if you had the eyes to see, you could imagine what it had been like once, back when it had belonged to my godmother. There were two oriel windows and light poured in where the shutters were broken. Not an inch of wall or ceiling had gone undecorated. You could even make out the original designs: carved circles that overlapped and interlocked.

When I looked more closely, I saw that over half those circles were made of snakes.

Norrie was right. They were everywhere.

Gabriel looked to me for direction. "So what do we do now?"

"I'm not sure," I admitted. "Investigate the snakes, I suppose. Norrie said there were hidden doors behind some of them."

We wandered from panel to panel, pushing, pressing, fiddling with heads and tails. Nothing sprung out or slid back. When we knocked, nothing sounded hollow.

I lifted my head to the high ceiling. "There are dozens more up there."

Gabriel peered into the next room. "And even more in here."

He wasn't exaggerating. The walls positively writhed with snakes.

I felt overwhelmed. "It could be any of them."

"Your magic isn't telling you anything?"

I shook my head. Now that the walls of Audelin House stood

between me and the river, I'd been letting myself listen for magic, but I hadn't heard anything yet. Perhaps Scargrave had destroyed every trace of it.

"What if we take a quick walk around the whole house?" Gabriel suggested. "Maybe something will stand out."

That sounded sensible enough. But by the time we'd finished surveying the floor we were on, we had a rough count of three hundred snake circles.

"And I'll wager there are even more behind this," Gabriel said, working at the lock of a heavy door in the back of the house. "Are you certain there's no magic keeping it shut?"

There was so much magic in the air this morning that it was a little hard to tell, but I couldn't smell anything. "I don't think so. It's probably just mechanics—or rust. Let's not waste any more time on it. We still have the whole upstairs to see."

Gabriel poked at the lock again with one of the keys he'd grabbed from other doors. When it didn't yield, he followed me up the staircase.

Upstairs the rooms were much darker. As we walked into yet another dim, snake-ridden room—this one with only a few damaged window slats to let in light—I started to regret the impulse that had brought me to Audelin House. "There's no end to them," I said to Gabriel. "And look at those scorch marks on the walls. For all we know, Scargrave burned away the circle we need."

"Keep going," Gabriel urged. "The right one might be just around the corner." He cracked open a door in the darkest part of the room. "Or then again, maybe not."

His voice sounded odd. I hurried over. "What's wrong? What did you see?"

"Not a thing. The room's too confounded dark." He pulled back the door, revealing an opening as black as pitch. "The room doesn't have any windows, I gather. Or if it does, they've been shuttered over."

The darkness in that room seemed to be more than a matter of shutters. There was a stillness there that I hadn't felt elsewhere, a watchfulness. It felt as if the darkness were waiting for us.

Part of me wanted to slam the door shut. But what if the right snake was somewhere in there?

If only I could still conjure up a light to see by, as my godmother had taught me. But like all other Proven Magic, that song was now out of my reach—and I'd yet to find a reliable way of controlling fire with Wild Magic. Here in Audelin House, with its history of burning, I thought I'd better resort to more prosaic means of making light, even if it took more time.

"I've got a tinderbox," I said, digging into my sack. "And candles."

"Hand them over," Gabriel said. "No one can strike a flame faster than I can. Not even you, Chantress."

I'd long since discovered that kindling flame from a tinderbox was not half so interesting as kindling one from song, so I was happy enough to let him have the honors. But evidently my tinderbox was not what he was used to, because he took a long time over the job. While he fussed with the flint, I investigated some of the snake circles on the blackened walls.

"When did you last use this tinderbox?" he finally asked me.

"Last spring, I think. Maybe longer." Traveling as I did with my own men, I was rarely called upon to light a fire.

"Well, you need a new charcloth. It's smothering the sparks, not catching them. We'll need some other kindling." He stood up, tinderbox in hand. "There was some straw by that door downstairs, the one that wouldn't open. That would do. And I might have another quick look at that lock while I'm at it."

"Shall I come with you?"

"No need—unless you want to."

"Then I'll stay here and keep checking this wall of snakes."

"All right, then. I'll be back soon."

After he left, I peered into the dark room again. Beyond the dim shadows at the door, the darkness was so complete that I felt for a moment as if I were looking out on nothing at all. A desolate chill went right through me. There was something more than mere darkness here.

I reached to pull the door shut, but as I did, I heard music coming from somewhere deep inside the room—a sweet, golden song that sounded familiar. A song sung by someone I never expected to hear again.

My mother.

It wasn't a living voice, of course. The Shadowgrims had turned my mother to ash. But a Chantress could sometimes leave a song behind her—a song-spell only another Chantress could hear. My mother had done that in a letter she'd written to me on the eve of her death. It contained not only her wisest advice but also the very sound of her voice, forever echoing in a song-spell of protection around it. For a long time I'd listened to that letter every day. And here was that same voice, singing to me now.

Without a second thought, I crossed the threshold and plunged into the darkness. Blind now, I had a moment of panic. But then I heard the song again, a little louder this time. Groping with both hands outstretched, I followed it deep into the shivering blackness of that room, stumbling over warped boards, and even once falling to my knees.

Eventually my fingertips touched stone. Beneath a heavy lip, there was a hollow and the bitter scent of smoke. A fireplace, cold as death—and the singing came from inside it.

I ducked down and followed the song to the very back of the hearth. Ashes crumbled against my fingertips, and the smell of soot choked me. But as I ran my hands up over the iron fireback, I felt a familiar curve, the circle of snakes. When I brushed my fingers against their heads, the golden music swelled and the upper part of the fireback swung loose.

There was a hole here, smelling of magic. Inside it, my fingers touched stiff vellum—the cover of a book.

I snatched it up and retreated to the outer room—a place that had seemed barely lit before but that now appeared as bright as day after the darkness. Stopping to peek through a broken slat in the shutter, I was reassured to see that the waters hadn't risen noticeably higher. I had a little time, then—and now I could see my prize plainly: a dove-gray book streaked with soot, about as wide as my hand and somewhat taller. The song wafted up from its pages, sweet and fresh, as if my mother had just sung the tune.

The book might be smeared with ashes, but I couldn't help hugging it. I had so little of my mother left to me. Bad enough that she should have died when I was eight—but even worse, she'd sung a song that had taken away most of my memories of her. She'd done it to protect me, to keep me safe from Scargrave, but even now, all these years later, I still felt a colossal sense of loss.

Had I known this book was hidden here, I would have come to Audelin House long ago. And perhaps I should have suspected something of hers might be here. Lady Helaine had been my mother's guardian, after all. But like everyone else, I'd heard that there was nothing left in Audelin House, that Scargrave had taken it all.

And all this time, this book had been waiting for me to pull it out of the fire.

Still rejoicing in my mother's music, I rubbed my grubby fingers clean on my petticoat and turned to the first page. In the letter, my mother's writing had been so faded as to be illegible, but this book was blank—or nearly so. Only if I turned it in exactly the right way could I see something shimmering there.

This was a stronger spell than the one she'd used for my letter. Still, I expected it worked more or less the same way.

I closed my eyes and let myself sink into the music. I knew I had to be careful, because this meant opening myself up a bit more to all music, including the river's strange songs. Could I keep them apart in my mind?

It seemed I could. There were no holes in the windows here; the river's music was muffled. Cautiously, I picked out the notes of my mother's song. As I sang it back to the book, faint writing appeared, then darkened, page after page of it, until at last I knew what I held in my hands.

My mother's diary.

CHAPTER TWENTY-SIX

IN HER OWN WORDS

Some diaries are merely ledgers of daily activities. Some record only the weather. But not this one. Judging from the scattered dates, my mother had kept it when she'd been about my own age—and she had poured her heart into the writing. As I flipped quickly through the pages, the emotions leaped out at me.

She'd been frustrated with Lady Helaine's rigid teachings:

I shall go mad if that woman makes me practice another scale.

She treats me like an imbecile. Again, she says. Again. Again.

She'd been overjoyed to discover Wild Magic:

Everyone is wrong about the stones. I was so weary of following rules all day that I took mine off last night, just to see what it felt like. Instantly I heard the most glorious music—melodies everywhere, as thick and bright as stars in the night. Oh, the beauty of them! I sang one, and the dew leaped into my hand. And Lady H. still has me singing scales. What would she say if she knew? . . .

Did more experiments with Wild Magic tonight. It's hard to control. I have to listen very carefully, and even then it can sometimes go horribly wrong. But there's far more power in it than the Proven Magic that Lady H. has taught me.

I don't think fire likes me. But water—oh, water is my friend. And every day I understand it better.

And when Lady Helaine tried to stop her, my mother was furious:

She found me out today. As always, I waited till I was sure she was fast asleep before I took my stone off, but this time she woke up and smelled my Wild Magic and came down on me like the old dragon she is. I've never seen her so furious! She shouted at me and grabbed my stone and half-choked me when she shoved it back over my head. I must never take off my stone again, she says. If I do, then Wild Magic will be the death of me. According to her, everything in the world has a song, and some of those songs are not safe for Chantresses to sing. But I don't believe her. It's all just a ploy to make me do what she wants. And I won't give Wild Magic up. I won't.

I shut my eyes for a moment, overwhelmed. When I'd opened this diary, I'd expected to find the gentle mother I dimly remembered: wise, patient, ever watchful. But the girl who'd kept this diary was someone else entirely. Someone much more fiery and stubborn and impulsive. Someone much more vulnerable. Someone who seemed to be speaking just to me.

I too had chafed at Lady Helaine's strictures. I too had found the lure of Wild Magic irresistible. And I too had found water a friend.

My mother had been gone for ten years, and yet I was still finding new ways to miss her.

I opened my eyes, wishing that I could see her just one more time. But at least I had the next-best thing—her book, open on my lap, and her words echoing in this quiet room.

I knew that time was going by and we should probably leave for the safety of high ground. But it was hard to close the diary when my mother's words were calling to me.

I couldn't help reading just a few pages more.

. . . she knows I'm defying her, but she hasn't caught me at it yet. When she questions me, I deny everything.

She says my stone will crack if I keep doing Wild Magic, that I won't ever be able to do Proven Magic again. As if I cared about that! Thank goodness Auntie Rose has written and asked that I visit her. I have to get away from here.

Auntie Rose. I hadn't heard the name for a couple of years, but I knew who she was. Her real name was Agnes Roser, and she wasn't a true aunt but my mother's much older cousin. I'd met her once, when I was small—a doughy woman with puffy hands and a kindly smile, who'd patted my face and offered me gingerbread. A cozy woman, easily underestimated. Only much later had I learned that she had been the guardian of some extraordinary Chantress secrets.

Had she said anything to my mother that might be useful to me now? I started to read more carefully.

Lady H. told her about the Wild Magic, and even Auntie Rose wants me to stop. But instead of screaming at me the way Lady H. does, she sat me down and said that she was going to tell me something that most Chantresses had forgotten, something that even Lady H. doesn't know. And then Auntie Rose said that the real reason Chantresses wear stones is to protect us from the music of the Others.

I'd never heard of the Others before, but Auntie Rose says that they're our ancestresses, our ancient Mothers. What some call faeries or fae or elementals. And the ones who come from our line—from water stock—are the most dangerous ones.

So Penebrygg was right. The Others, the Mothers, the faeries, the elementals—they were all one. And the greatest danger came from the water spirits.

Was that the enemy we were facing now? Still searching for answers, I dipped back into the diary.

I asked why the Others would want to hurt us. After all, we're their descendants—their own kin. Auntie Rose doesn't really know. All she could tell me was that centuries ago the Others decided it was a mistake that any of their kind had ever bred with humans. They made it their mission to destroy us. And they were powerful enough to twist the songs of Wild Magic and use them to lure Chantresses to their deaths.

But the Chantresses fought back.

First, they stopped practicing Wild Magic. Then they created the stones to deafen us to it. Auntie Rose says it was Melusine herself, the great Chantress who was raised in the world of the Others, who worked out how to make the stones. She invented Proven Magic, too. (Which means she's the one to blame for all those safe songs I hate so much.)

But even the stones and Proven Magic weren't enough to hold back the Others. They kept finding new ways to attack us. So the Chantresses had to strengthen the wall between us.

The wall. My heart beat faster.

Auntie Rose says there always was a wall between the worlds, but it waxed and waned with the seasons. If you were clever and you timed it right, you could get through. But the Chantresses made the wall so strong that the Others couldn't cross it anymore. Even Chantresses couldn't pass through it. Ever since then, we've been sealed off from each other.

When Auntie Rose told me this, I was delighted. I thought it meant that Wild Magic was safe now.

But Auntie Rose looked very stern when I told her this. "No, no," she said. "Quite the contrary. Chantress lore is very clear on that point. The wall can't be broken by the Others, or by ordinary humans, or even by Proven Magic. But it can be broken by Wild Magic. I don't know exactly what kind of Wild Magic it would have to be, but I do know that the Chantresses back then feared it could happen by accident. And they decided we must all avoid Wild Magic forever. So you must stop, Viviane. Not just for your sake but for us all. If you break that wall down, then there will be nothing to stop the Others from rising up against us . . ."

I stopped reading. Heart pounding, I went back again to read the last few sentences.

Was Auntie Rose right? Was it possible for a Chantress to break the wall between the worlds by accident?

If so, then maybe we really were at war with the Others. And maybe the person who had broken the wall—the person who had let them through—was me.

CHAPTER TWENTY-SEVEN

KEYS

I turned back to the diary, desperate for answers. Could I really have taken the wall down—and not even known it?

My mother's account of the conversation with Auntie Rose ended there. Maybe something had interrupted her as she'd written? I scanned the next pages quickly. It seemed my mother hadn't been sure whether to believe what Auntie Rose had said about the wall, but for a while she'd stopped working Wild Magic—

Was that a shout from below? I broke off from reading. Yes, and now quick footsteps . . .

Apprehensive, I shut the diary. As I stood up, Gabriel dashed in, breathing hard, his dark eyes alarmed. Barely stopping to touch my hand with his ring, he beckoned me forward. "I think we'd better go, Chantress. There's trouble outside. A mob. They must have heard you singing."

How loud had my song been? Truth to tell, I had been too entranced to notice. Such a stupid mistake. "Where are they?"

"Banging on the windows at the back, trying to break in. They're too afraid to go around to the front, because that's where the river is. So we'd better go out that way ourselves. It's our best chance."

Even from here I could smell the river's magic. Was it really wise to go rushing out toward it? "Couldn't we just stay here?"

Gabriel shook his head. "If we do, we'll be trapped. The water's rising fast. We really need to get out of here now."

"Just give me a moment." I reached around to put the diary into my sack.

"What's that?" he asked.

"My mother's diary."

His eyes flared with interest, and I wished I hadn't been so frank. I wasn't ready to share the diary yet. But all he said was, "Come on. We need to get out of here before the mob gets in." He raced to the door.

He was right. Sack bumping against my back, I sprinted down the stairs after him, worried about what we might find waiting for us. But all was quiet as we went through the grand room with the burn marks and the fallen plaster.

"I don't hear them," I said. "Maybe they've gone away."

"You can't hear them because this house has walls three feet thick, and they're way off on the other side. You'd hear them well enough if you walked over there." With grim humor, Gabriel added, "Though, I suggest you don't."

"No," I agreed.

When we reached the dark entranceway, he stepped back so that I could go first. "I don't know how this lock works."

"The usual way, I imagine." As a rule, Gabriel was eager to claim technical mastery, so I was a little surprised by his diffidence. Perhaps he was feeling discouraged because he hadn't managed to pick that stubborn lock we'd encountered earlier.

I felt my way toward the door and scrabbled at the ancient mechanism. It resisted at first, then gave way. I heaved the door open.

Gabriel shot past me onto the steps, but I stopped dead at the threshold. The bottom steps were flooded now. So was the entire street. Everywhere I looked, there was water—and the furious music half-deafened me.

"We shouldn't go this way," I said.

"Of course we should," he insisted. "It's just a little water, and it's the safest way out. Look!" He sloshed into the muddy current with his shining boots and held out his hand. "Come on!"

I followed, but slowly. There was something wrong here, and not just with the water. Even before I figured out what it was, my hands were working of their own accord.

He wants me to come into the water. And he wouldn't touch the lock. And that ring on his hand doesn't look like iron out here in the light.

I flung the keys of Audelin House at him. When the hard iron hit him, he shimmered, blond hair darkening, jaw shrinking, face blurring. Watching in shock, I glimpsed sea-green eyes and a woman's red mouth.

"Melisande!"

As I spoke the name, a snake tongue flickered out of the red mouth. Hands like claws reached for me.

I leaped back, but she followed, tongue darting. Before my horrified eyes, her shape changed again, and a glistening sea serpent reared up in the water before me.

Bounding for the door, I slipped on the step. As my feet went out from under me, the monster's mouth opened wide. In the blast of its hot, stinking magic, I defended myself in the only way I could. I flung my heavy sack at its coils.

Even as the sack sailed through the air, the creature shifted again, becoming almost translucent. When the sack hit its mark, I heard a crunch like breaking glass.

Was it dead? Careful to stay out of the water's reach, I leaned over to see.

Before I could tell for sure, a wave swirled over the serpent with an angry hiss, and the water in the street started to churn. Was it coming after me? I leaped back up to the door, which was still gaping wide, and ran inside, slamming it shut behind me.

When I looked out the window, I saw the waters had settled. If anything, they looked a little lower than they had been. But the glassy serpent was gone.

Something else had vanished too, I realized with a lurch—the sack I'd thrown in self-defense, with my mother's diary inside it.

CHAPTER TWENTY-EIGHT

LOW TIDE

As awful as the encounter with the snake was, the loss of the diary shook me even more. I retreated from the window, reproaching myself. How could I have been so careless with something that meant so much to me?

At best, I'd only skimmed a third of what my mother had written. If she'd had more secrets to share—and no doubt she had—I would never learn them now. Her voice was silenced forever.

Still shaken, I heard glass shatter somewhere close. At the back of the house? Men shouted, and a great thud shook the floorboards under my feet.

I whirled around. A mob! So that part of the story had been true.

I couldn't escape out the front, not with that water there. I'd have to stay put and use magic to defend myself. Heart hammering, I wondered where I should make my stand. Right here, where they'd find me in minutes? Or upstairs, where I'd have more time to prepare but a greater chance of being trapped?

Before I could decide, the men shouted again. This time, however, I could hear them more clearly, and the loudest voices sounded familiar. I ran to the windows at the back of the house. The tiny glass panes made the world outside look peculiar—all gray-green and curved—but if there had been a mob, it was gone now. Instead I saw Captain Knollys and my own loyal men ramming at the back door with their iron pikes.

"I'm all right," I shouted through a crack in the window. "I'm coming to meet you."

I raced through the house to get to them, but halfway there I jerked to a stop. My tinderbox was lying upended on the floor in front of me. Behind it, the door that had been so stubbornly locked now hung open, revealing a tiny room that smelled dankly of the river. A staircase led downward to the cellar, and at the top of its steps, Gabriel lay in a heap, his bright hair matted and bloody.

From the look of it, he'd been dragged there and left for dead, but I approached him with caution, fearing more deceit. It was only when I spied his iron ring, and touched my own bracelet to the back of his hand, that I stopped worrying.

By the time Knollys and the others came rushing in, I was holding my kerchief to Gabriel's head. "He's hurt, and badly," I told them. "If we can't stop the bleeding, he'll die."

After touching iron with me, they stanched Gabriel's wound and bandaged it. Helping them as best I could, I told Knollys about the false Lord Gabriel, and what it had turned into before it had disappeared under the waves.

Had it really been Melisande I'd seen? Or had it been a trick of the Others? I wished again that I hadn't lost my mother's diary. Perhaps I'd have found answers in there.

"It's a pity it's gone," Knollys agreed as the men carried Gabriel out on a makeshift litter. "But the King will be thankful you're safe, my lady. We were concerned when we learned that you had gone to Audelin House. There were several reports of disturbances in this neighborhood."

"I'm glad you came." Even with magic, it would have been a job to get both myself and Gabriel out safely.

"The King asked that you come to Cornhill," Knollys said as we reached a cross street, "and then—"

He broke off as Barrington came running up to us, shouting excitedly. "Chantress, Captain! Come see!" Motioning us forward, he pointed down the cross street. It resembled a shore at low tide, dotted with seaweed and soaked driftwood, its mud and cobbles slick and wet.

"Incredible." Knollys seemed just as amazed as Barrington. "The river was halfway up this street when we came through earlier, but now it's pulled back."

"Check the other cross streets," I told Barrington.

The men who were carrying Gabriel had already gone ahead, but the rest of our company fanned out to investigate what was happening. Soon the report came back: The river was definitely in retreat.

Knollys turned to me, eyes bright above his grizzled cheeks. "I think you've done it, Chantress. You've won the battle. You've defeated the enemy."

I thought of the horrible smack I'd heard when my sack had hit the glass snake. "I'm not sure I killed the creature," I said uncertainly. "It disappeared, just like the others."

"Even so, you must have won." Knollys gestured at the cross street. "There's your proof. The river's going down."

† † †

It might be proof enough for Captain Knollys, but I needed something more. I walked down the street with Knollys until we found the edge of the flood. We were still a good way out from where the river normally flowed, but even as we stood there, I could see the waters ebbing away.

"At this rate, it'll be back within its banks by nightfall," Knollys judged. "I've never seen a flood go down so fast. But then it was a magic flood, and magic works by its own rules."

I was surprised by the speed of the withdrawal too, but perhaps Knollys was right. Magic had its own rules. Although I listened long and hard, I couldn't hear even a trace of the fury that had ruled earlier. Indeed, the river sounded normal in every way, except that it was slightly subdued—almost as if it were ashamed of the trouble it had caused.

Perhaps we really had won the battle.

"We should tell the King," Knollys said.

"Yes," I said.

As quick as we were, the good news traveled even faster. By the time we reached the summit of Cornhill, people were turning out to cheer for me. Apparently patrols all across London were reporting that the river was going down. Thanks to our scouts, who had been instructed to run ahead and tell the King and Council all that had happened, the story about my encounter with the serpent was spreading like wildfire.

When we entered the King's temporary headquarters—part of an entire block of buildings that the Crown had requisitioned—a crowd of happy faces hemmed me in. The King, his freckled face glowing, seized my hand and raised it into the air. "My lords and ladies, three cheers for the Chantress!"

Everyone joined him in enthusiastic ovation. Even the Lord High Admiral was saluting me. If there were any holdouts, I couldn't spot them. As the huzzahs finally died out, someone started singing, and the crowd took up the refrain—one of the old broadside tunes celebrating my fierceness in defense of the kingdom. Here and there, people began dancing.

The King led me away from the crowds into a small chamber that had evidently been set up as his study. I asked how Gabriel was doing.

"He was starting to revive by the time he arrived here," the King said. "He's been put to bed upstairs, and the Royal Physician says that with care he should recover fully within a week or two."

That was a relief. "Good."

At the King's request, I gave a full account of what had happened at Audelin House and what I'd seen of the river and the city. "We should be careful about how we lift the evacuation order," I finished. "Even if the river keeps going down at this pace, it's done terrible damage. Some streets won't be fit to live in, or even safe to visit."

"There will be time to sort all that out later," the King said. "I've called a Council meeting for three o'clock, and we'll go over everything then. In the meantime, I must find Sybil. I've not seen her all day—and I'm sure she'll have some ideas about what should be done with the refugees."

"I'll come with you," I said.

He grinned at me, looking not so much like a king but like any young husband in love with his wife. "To tell the truth, Chantress, I'd rather see her on my own. You stay here and celebrate."

If I'd wanted to celebrate, this certainly would have been the time. When I returned to the crowd, I discovered that the party had spilled over into half the house. Casks of beer were being meted out, and the music and dancing were more jubilant than ever.

Amid the joyous clamor, I found myself feeling strangely hollow. Victory wasn't half so sweet when I couldn't share it with Nat. Oddly enough, he didn't even seem to be here. No, wait. . . . Was that Nat over in the corner there, in that crowd of ladies-in-waiting?

I forced myself to turn away. I couldn't go to him, not in front of all those Court ladies. Later, if I could find him on his own, I could talk to him.

In the meantime, I tried to hide my true feelings. I'd had plenty of practice at that, so it ought to have been easy. Yet as people swarmed around me, offering their thanks, I found myself thinking about Nat again. What if he didn't want to listen to me? What if I'd already burned my bridges?

As soon as I could, I pushed my way to the edge of the crowd and left the party.

† † †

Much as I wanted to escape this temporary Court, I couldn't leave the house without checking on Gabriel first. Not only was he a friend, but he'd also been injured while trying to help me. I had to make sure he was really recovering. If he was, that would be good news in itself. And if he could talk, perhaps he could tell me more about his attacker.

A few minutes later, with the help of a royal page, I found Gabriel's room—a makeshift infirmary at the very back of the house, where Quittle was attending him. The valet looked as anxious as ever, but I was delighted to see that Gabriel was sitting up now—white-faced and wrapped in bandages, but otherwise an only slightly shaky version of his usual debonair self.

"It seems we were the object of a cruel deception, Chantress."

"Especially cruel to you," I said.

He raised a hand to the back of his head but stopped short of touching the enormous goose bump there. "It was hair-raising, I must admit. And rather nasty to see a copy of myself coming at me, a rock in his hand."

"So that's all you saw—someone who looked just like you?"

"Yes." Gabriel's pale face grew a shade whiter at the memory.

"And I hardly even saw that. I was kneeling on the floor, scrabbling around for straw for the tinderbox, when I heard that locked door click open. The creature stepped up behind me, and I had only a second's warning before it slugged me. Not what you'd call a fair fight."

"No. I'm so sorry. When I asked you to come with me, I never meant for this to happen."

"I'm just thankful you weren't hurt," Gabriel said, reaching for my hand. "Quittle, will you leave us? There's something I must say to you, Chantress, and to you alone."

There was a light in Gabriel's eye that worried me. I tried to extract my hand. "There's no need for you to go, Quittle. I'm sure you want to keep an eye on your patient."

But to Quittle, his master's word was law. He was already slipping out the door.

Gabriel gripped my hand more tightly. "They tell me I almost died, Chantress. And when I went down, do you know what I was thinking of? You."

I couldn't look at him. "Gabriel, please."

He ignored me. "The last time I proposed, you said what you most needed was a good friend, and I've done my best to be that. I've been patient; I've been loyal; I've been what you needed me to be. But my mind hasn't changed. Please tell me I have a chance with you."

I stopped trying to pull away. There was no getting around this; I would have to face it head-on. It was an honest question, and it deserved an honest answer.

"Gabriel," I said gently. "I'm sorry, but no."

He went very still. The other times when I'd refused him, he'd shown great equanimity, even a certain cheerful buoyancy. Was it because of the accident that he looked so confused, so pained?

"I was sure I had a chance this time," Gabriel murmured.

"I'm sorry," I said again, and pulled my hand away. He didn't resist; he still looked dazed. *Maybe I ought to find Quittle.* I started for the door.

"You do know that Walbrook has gone and chosen someone else, don't you?" Gabriel said. "I thought that would make a difference."

My hand faltered on the door. "What?"

"He's kept it very quiet, I must say," Gabriel went on. "But I heard it this morning from Lady Clemence's father, the Earl of Tunbridge himself. They're working out the marriage contracts now."

So Nat had made his choice. And he hadn't wasted any time.

I yanked at the door, desperate to get away.

Gabriel's voice followed me. "Don't go, Chantress! Walbrook may not have any sense, but I do. You know I adore you—and your magic, too. And I have more to offer than he does—a time-honored name, a great estate . . ."

"I can't," I whispered.

Shaking, I shut the door.

CHAPTER TWENTY-NINE

A QUIET FURY

Fleeing Gabriel, I ran up the stairs, wanting to get as far from everyone and everything as I could. Coming across a tiny room piled high with packing cases, I ducked inside and tried to compose myself.

Nat and Clemence . . .

Was it really true? It would be a hasty engagement, of course. But I knew, better than anyone else, why it might have happened that way. *I think you should find someone else.* Such foolish words. Yet if Nat could act on them so quickly, then perhaps his heart had never really been mine after all.

Still, maybe matters weren't quite as advanced as Gabriel believed. Often people took months to negotiate marriage contracts. Indeed, it was even possible that Gabriel had misunderstood the Earl of Tunbridge entirely. I didn't know the earl myself, but he was said to be a hearty and optimistic man, eager to find a way into the King's inner circle. Perhaps he was merely trying to promote a match between Clemence and Nat but hadn't yet actually accomplished it.

Whatever the truth was, I needed to go out and face it. Leaving my bolt-hole, I headed for the main staircase.

I was halfway down it when I saw Nat. He was standing in front of a window just off the landing, smiling down at Clemence, who was laughing and clutching his hand.

So it's true.

Pain shot through the core of me. For a moment, I couldn't move. How could she have claimed him so fast? How could he forget me so quickly?

Clemence murmured something to Nat. As they bent toward each other, heads almost touching, I found myself suddenly gripped by fury. It enveloped me like red flame—anger with him, with her, with myself, a lashing desire to hurt others as I was hurt.

But the fury wasn't only inside me. It was outside, too. Through a gap in the window, I heard it clearly—a faint cry from the river, echoing with the terrible frenzy that had driven the waters wild.

Nat looked up and saw me. "Lucy?"

I didn't answer. I couldn't. I was already running full tilt, headed to the river. What if the Others were coming back?

† † †

Outside, the street teemed with people, most of them as jubilant as the courtiers I'd seen inside. But as I skirted around them, I heard worried voices at the edge of the crowd.

"Better safe than sorry," a frowsy woman in moth-eaten wool advised her neighbor. "There's something not right when it looks like that."

A child tugged at the woman's skirts "Where did it go, Ma? That's what I want to know. All that water. Where did it go?"

"We all prayed for it to go down, but not like this," said a sober man in plain brown garb.

I wanted to ask what they were talking about, but at best that would delay me, and at worst it might lead to trouble. Behind me, I thought I heard Nat's voice, but I didn't turn for that, either. Instead I drew my hood up tight and pressed my way through the multitudes, aiming for the river.

The crowd soon thinned out, and as I picked my way down the last lanes to the Thames, I saw not a soul. By now, I'd expected to hear the river clearly. To my consternation, however, I could not hear it at all.

The houses here had borne the brunt of the flood, and the streets were filled with the muck and wrack left by the sea. I plowed through them as best I could. High-water marks were etched on the walls around me. Broken windows revealed rooms filled with mud and pools of stinking water.

When I finally reached the Thames, the sights were even more shocking. Across from me, entire sections of Southwark had been gouged out. Gray earth yawned where solid houses had once prospered, and the remaining buildings stood in silt up to their windows.

Just as distressing was the sight of mighty London Bridge to the east. For five hundred years, it had spanned the Thames, and in that time it had survived fire and flood and rebellion alike. But no longer. Its central arch had been swept away, along with all the shops and homes that had rested upon it. Several more arches had sustained damage. How long could they remain standing?

It was a nightmare London. But what made the scene even more unreal was the river itself. The people on Cornhill had been right. There had been low tides before, but not like this. The Thames had all but vanished, leaving a wide expanse of oozing mud flats with a mere trickle of yellow water wandering through the center. It was as if someone had pulled out a plug and the river had drained away.

Small wonder people had run away in terror.

Small wonder I had not been able to hear anything.

No, the miracle was that I'd heard that faint, furious echo up on Cornhill. Had I caught it only because I'd been gripped by fury myself and open to its influence? Perhaps. Or perhaps the tune hadn't come from the river after all. Perhaps it had rung out only in my imagination.

Still, whatever I'd heard, something was very wrong here. And I was determined to find out what it was.

Hitching up my bespattered skirts and cloak, I leaped from the steps down onto the riverbed. My boots, already covered in muck, promptly sank ankle deep into it.

Ordinarily I'd have sung to the water in the mud, asking it to bear my weight, but I was leery of working Wild Magic near the Thames now, especially when it was behaving so strangely.

Keeping quiet, I pulled myself step by slurping step toward the last vestige of the river.

When I reached what was left of the Thames, I bent down to listen. A blast of pure rage hit my ear. I straightened quickly, then leaned down again to catch anything else I could. This time, I heard not just rage but anticipation.

Something was coming. But what? I couldn't begin to imagine.

My boots were sinking fast. I wrestled one foot from the mud, and when I stepped back, water filled the hole, turning it into a tiny, still pool. As I looked down at it, the water darkened, and for a dizzying moment I thought I saw snakes twisting under its surface. Startled, I wobbled, then lost my balance completely. I fell forward, obliterating both picture and pool.

On my hands and knees, splattered in mud, with my head practically on top of what remained of the Thames, I finally heard it—a wave, still in the ocean now but gathering speed.

An enormous wave.

A wave big enough to drown a city.

And it was coming this way.

CHAPTER THIRTY

A WALL OF WATER

Was there any way to stop the wave? I listened with everything I had in me, but I couldn't tell. I didn't even know how much time I had till it hit. All I knew was that fury and anticipation had tipped into action, and that the water was coming for us.

I have to warn the city.

Half-covered in oozing mud already, I got muddier still as I pushed myself back to standing. As I staggered forward, I looked up to see a woman standing at the far edge of the riverbed—Melisande's scrawny servant.

Behind her, just coming into view, was Melisande herself. Raising open palms toward the river, she began half-keening, half-crooning a song. Was she calling up the wave, or merely celebrating its existence? Either way, I had to stop her.

How, though? Wild Magic might be too risky, and yet there was nothing else.

With relief I saw men appear on the riverbank not far from

Melisande. Not my men, but at least they were wearing the King's colors. I waved to them and shouted, "Catch those women!"

As soon as I called out, Melisande and her servant bolted. Instead of chasing them, the men stared at me from the top of some river steps. Couldn't they hear what I was saying?

"Catch them!" I shouted again.

The leader of the patrol cupped his hands and bellowed at me. "You there, whoever you are! Out of the riverbed!"

"I'm the Chantress," I bellowed back, slogging through the mud toward the riverbank. "Don't let those women get away!"

Even as I pointed, however, I saw it was too late. Already Melisande and her servant were disappearing into an alleyway.

At least I'd stopped her from singing. But when I listened again, I realized that wasn't enough. I could still hear the wave coming.

All I could do now was get the King's men back before it hit. "Retreat!" I shouted at them. "Danger!"

A chorus of confusion:

"Blimey, it's the Chantress."

"Maybe it's an illusion."

"What's she saying?"

I shouted more loudly. "All of you, get back! There's a wave coming!"

More confusion in the ranks, but this time they started to retreat. The leader shouted something about finding Lord Walbrook. And then they were gone.

I lurched another yard toward land and lost my boot. As I

floundered to retrieve it, someone shouted my name. I looked up. Nat was running down the river steps toward me.

I waved him away with my muddy arms. "Go back!"

He leaped off the last step, down into the mud. "What?"

"Go *back*!" I shouted. "There's a wave coming, big enough to swallow London. Go and warn everyone!"

Behind me, I heard gurgling. The trickle of water was bubbling, quivering, widening. Giving up the boot for lost, I started to run. A second later, Nat did too. Mud hindered our every step, and frantically I wondered how much time we had left. The music from the river was growing louder by the second. By the time we reached the edge of the riverbed, it was overpowering.

Half-leaping, half-climbing, Nat pulled himself back onto the river steps and reached out for me. I gasped as his iron ring bumped up against my bracelet and our hands met, skin to skin.

As he swung me up, I caught sight of the remaining sections of London Bridge, and what looked like a hazy cloud in the distance behind them. Only it wasn't a cloud, I realized a second later. It was the white crest of a wave.

"Run!" I screamed at Nat.

We bounded up the steps together, but the wave was coming too fast. I could see it more clearly now, the water cleaving together as it barreled down the riverbed. The ground shook with a rumble like thunder.

Maybe Wild Magic would only make things worse. But it was all I had to protect the city, to protect us.

Turning toward the oncoming wave, I sought to turn its

destructive power back on itself. When the water ignored me, I turned in desperation to the wind, calling on it to blow the wave out to sea. A terrible gamble this, because I might sing up a gale by mistake. But I had to try.

As my song spun out, strong winds swooped down from all directions, singing in my ears, whipping my hair from its hood. They scattered everything before them. Debris from the flood flew through the air. I had to grab at a broken beam to stay upright, and so did Nat.

Still I sang, and in response the whole sky twisted. The winds bore down on the enormous wave, funneling around it, penning it in. The wave sang out in sudden uncertainty. Towering over London Bridge, it hovered in midair, spitting out spume.

My song was working! Now to send the water back out to the sea.

When I drew breath, I heard a strange keening sound—and in that moment, I lost control. A furious music blasted through the water, giving it new force and energy. I kept on singing, but the winds weren't strong enough to match the wave now. All I could do was beg them to protect the city as best they could from the blow that was coming.

Immense and malevolent, the wave soared still higher. The frothing gray-green wall made even the seven-story houses on London Bridge look tiny. As the wave rose, I saw terrible shapes writhing inside it—the coils of serpents, the gray tentacles of kraken . . .

Roaring with fury, the wave came crashing down. It slammed into the bridge, smashing its arches, blowing the houses to bits.

Like a vast and hungry sea monster, the wave swallowed the city—and swallowed us.

As it hit, I grabbed Nat. He wasn't the swimmer that I was, and he wasn't going to drown if I could help it. Kicking hard, I fought to keep both our heads above the surface. But brackish water rushed into my open mouth, gagging me.

Breathe. Sing.

Thrusting my head back to the surface, I gasped and spat, then sang the only song that came to me—a song I hadn't known I knew, a song that must have been buried somewhere deep inside me, a song whose meaning was plain to me.

Save us.

One phrase, and then the waters closed in again. I struck one arm out blindly, reaching for air. Beside me, Nat fought too. But it was no use. The water sucked us under, hurling us like stones into the deep.

Chest burning, I braced myself. Any second now we would hit the bottom of the river.

Instead we only sank faster, rushing down into water so black, it was like falling into a well. The otherworldly music pounded in my ears. My chest stopped burning. A second later, I realized I'd stopped breathing. Had I already drowned without knowing it?

Maybe. But then something twisted below me. I saw a faint green light even farther down and heard the song of fury coming from it.

If I'd been frantic before, it was nothing compared to this. I kicked and lunged, but moments later, I saw the flash of scales in the currents around me. Nat's hand gripped mine hard, then slackened. In the dim light, I saw a serpent coiling round him. Was it trying to kill him? I couldn't tell. I could only lash out and refuse to let go of Nat as the creature pulled him down. Moments later, something scaly snaked around my legs, binding them.

It was like the scrying, but now I wasn't the only one who was caught—and I couldn't wake up, couldn't get us away. The coiling creature dragged us down toward a circle of green light that grew larger and larger. Soon its rays illuminated everything—the shining serpent scales, the slickness of slippery tongues, Nat's slack head rolling back as if in death.

I screamed, but made no sound. All I could hear was the otherworldly singing, wild and furious and booming in my ears.

We were at the very mouth of the circle now. The light flashed in my eyes, so bright it was blinding. Then we were through, touching bottom at last.

The coils released me. I kicked out again, but my feet hit only sand. A minute later, when my eyes had recovered, the serpents were nowhere to be seen. I was in a gigantic and dimly lit cave, Nat lying flat out beside me, horribly gray-green and still. The iron ring was gone from his hand. My own wrists were bare.

As I bent over him, I became aware that I was moving through something murkier and more dense than air. Water? Maybe. Yet it didn't have water's buoyancy; I couldn't swim in it. Some kind of ether?

Whatever it was, I was breathing it. And Nat, I was relieved to see, was breathing again too—though very shallowly.

"Nat?"

He didn't respond. But maybe that was because the other-worldly singing had drowned me out. Though it no longer boomed in my ears, it had an insidious low thrum that seemed to make the ether itself vibrate. Even my stone, trapped under my sodden cape and bodice, was shaking in time with it.

I tried again, my lips almost touching his ear. "Nat?"

Still nothing. Trying not to weep, I kissed his temple, then touched my hand to his neck. His pulse was weak but steady. Surely that had to be grounds for hope. And now that I was becoming used to the ether, I could see that his color was not so terrible after all. Everything here, even my own hand, had a greenish cast; it must be a trick of the light.

But where was here? And why was no one coming? From the effort they'd made to bring us here, I'd expected to be fighting off enemies long before this.

Not that I had any idea how I would fight them, beyond using my bare hands. Listen as I might, I could hear nothing here that resembled the Wild Magic I was used to. Instead there was only the singing: low and cruel, and so controlling that my heart couldn't help but beat to its rhythm.

I rocked back on my heels and stood up. Where there was a song, there must be a singer. And perhaps it was better to go out searching than to wait to be found.

There were several mouths to this cave, but the largest was in front of me. With a quick backward glance at Nat, I crept toward it, and heard the song grow still louder. It was like a physical force, this song—like the tide of the ocean, or the pounding of a storm.

When I peered past the edge of the cave, I saw the eye of the storm—a dark-haired woman, as still as a statue, standing on a high rock at the center of a vast cavern, chanting out the furious song that was drowning the world. Her expression was remote and terrible to behold.

And the very worst shock was this: In every detail, her face was the twin of my own.

CHAPTER THIRTY-ONE
MONSTROUS LIES

My heart hammered in double time. It was like seeing my own reflection in a mirror-still sea. The singer and I had exactly the same broad forehead, the same small chin, the same wide-spaced eyes.

I blinked. No, not exactly. The singer's face was a little narrower. A little older. Framed by hair that was quite a bit straighter than mine.

I gasped. This otherworldly singer—this singer who was destroying everything I held dear—wasn't my twin. But could she be . . . my mother?

My mind whirled.

Mama is dead.

So I'd been told. So we'd all believed. But maybe we'd been wrong. Maybe she had survived. Maybe she'd been on the other side of the wall all this time.

A mad hope seized me. Without stopping to think, I ran out to her, shouting to be heard over her song.

"Mama! Mama, stop!"

I hurled myself toward her—to embrace her, to reason with her? Truly I didn't know which, but it didn't matter. When I reached for the rock she stood on, my hands flew up, burning like fire, and I was thrown back onto the sand.

"Mama, it's me. Lucy."

She didn't even look down. She kept singing her terrible song, her face as distant and serene as the sky.

I stared up at her in utter dismay. Perhaps this wasn't my mother, after all. Perhaps it was some dreadful illusion. The appearance was right, but the voice itself was all wrong—vicious and overpowering, utterly unlike my gentle mother. But—

A change in the vibration of the song warned me of another presence. I spun around and blanched.

Behind me was an enormous glowing mass, half eel, half jellyfish. Dozens more like it, only smaller, crowded behind it. In the middle of their bright horde I saw Nat, eyes closed, limbs flung out wide, completely at their mercy.

"Nat!" I charged toward him.

The largest creature lashed an undulating tentacle in my direction and hummed a soft, strange melody—a melody that had some of the same tonalities as my mother's song. My heart jolted, and I fell to the ground. For an instant I burned all over, just as I had when I'd approached my mother.

Gulping for breath, I pulled myself to my feet. Running to Nat's rescue wouldn't work. I needed a song to help me, a song to help Nat. But the only music I could hear was my mother's.

No, wait. There was something else, a dim undertow beneath my mother's melody, more cacophony than music. But I couldn't hear a note of the Wild Magic I was used to on Earth, and without it I couldn't work my own enchantments.

A few of the horde shimmered toward me, humming all the while. Wary of more jolts, I backed away. They pursued me, edging me toward a cleft in the wall. There was no way to avoid them, except by stepping into it, so I did. As they pulled away, I felt relief. The cleft was actually a small cave, and they weren't going to follow me into it. Then a bony lattice went down in front of me, and I realized I'd been trapped.

I scrabbled at the lattice, but it was thick and as hard as shell. Wherever I touched it, it burned.

Hands stinging, I screamed, "Let me out!"

"Not until you have paid," said a liquid and malevolent voice.

I looked up. It was the largest creature who had spoken, the one who had lashed out at me. And it was turning human.

Or almost human.

It hovered on the other side of the lattice, body still round and transparent but now with a woman's head in its center. Heart-stopping in its beauty, the face was fringed not with hair but with slithery tentacles. Like eels in search of a meal, they snaked through the ether, shining like blue fire in the dreary light.

Impossible to have a conversation with a being like this, and yet I had to ask. "The singer out there. Is that my mother?"

"Yes and no." The Medusa's mouth did not move, and yet the creature spoke. "She was once your mother. Now she is my voice."

"Your voice?" I repeated, dumbfounded. "And who are you?"

This time the creature did not speak, yet words cascaded into my brain: *Queen. Mother. Empress. Other.*

Pressina.

Pressina? The name was oddly familiar, but I wasn't sure why. And then I had it. "You are Melusine's mother?"

"Yes." There was a wealth of grief in the syllable—and then anger, sharp as a knife. "You took her from me. You took her, and you punished me. And so I will punish you."

"No," I said. "I didn't—"

"You did!" Fury was uppermost now—the same sort of fury I could hear in my mother's song. "She was only trying to avenge me against my husband. And you Chantresses punished her for it."

I shook my head. That wasn't the story I'd heard.

"No," I said. "You can't fool me. *You* punished her. You gave her a serpent nature because she rebelled against her father."

I ducked as Pressina howled. "A monstrous lie!" Blue-green sparks shot out from her head. "Only a human would tell it, and only a human would believe it. Here we do not punish our daughters for defending us. And looking like a serpent is no hardship for us."

This last was true enough, I supposed. And I was worried about what she might do to me or to Nat if I angered her again. Shifting farther back into the cave, I said placatingly, "Well, then, what is the truth of it?"

Pressina answered eagerly, as if savoring the chance to tell her side of the story. "The truth? Melusine always had the power to turn into a serpent. It was in her blood, as it is with all my daughters. And her father deserved punishment." Her angry voice soared higher. "He said he would love me always, but the moment he saw the scales on our girls—so light, just on their forearms—he threw us all out."

In the story I knew, it was Pressina who had left her husband. But as Pressina had just pointed out, it was a human who had written that story. Who knew what the truth was?

"So when Melusine made her father pay, I rejoiced." Pressina's jellyfish center pulsated. "Indeed, I helped her. When it was done, she should have come back to me. But she didn't. Foolish girl that she was, she repented of what she'd done, and chose to remain in your world as a Chantress and marry a man herself. And when I tried to come after her, she helped the Chantresses devise ways of forestalling me. She created Proven Magic and the cursed stones.

"But then, when her husband turned on her, as I knew he would, she decided to punish him in turn. She created new song-spells filled with fearful and powerful magic, and set them down in a grimoire."

My breath caught. Could Melusine have created Scargrave's grimoire, the grimoire that had given rise to the Shadowgrims, the grimoire I had destroyed?

Pressina continued. "And when she unleashed them on her husband, the Chantresses took the grimoire away from her and hid it."

Yes, it was that grimoire.

"She fought them, and they killed her." Pressina's voice was a howl again. "They killed my daughter. And when I tried to avenge her, they walled me in. They ignored every appeal. They wanted to keep me penned up here forever." Her face was livid green now, her serpent hair tingling with sparks. Her tentacles thrashed, and waves of raw fury and grief emanated from her, so strong, I could smell them.

Worse still, her glowing eyes were leering at me. Was it sympathy she wanted? Contrition? Right now I was willing to say almost anything that might stem her wrath.

"I—I'm sorry."

"Sorry!" The head doubled in size, and the stench of grief vanished, leaving only fury. "Oh, you'll be sorry all right, Chantress. Sorry and screaming and wishing you were dead long before I'm done. We have broken through your wall now, and we are taking back our power. And soon we will be stronger than ever, because of you."

"Me?"

"Yes, you. You and your mother both—you made the mistakes that let us wreak our vengeance."

Anguish tore at me. "What was it? What did I do?"

"You don't know?" Pressina laughed. "How delightful! Your ignorance has been your undoing—and before you die, you will give us even more of what we want. Do you doubt me?" A tentacle shot out in my mother's direction. "Look at her!"

My mother didn't turn; I saw only her back. But her singing never stopped.

"That will be your fate too," Pressina said. "But I am not without mercy." A tentacle waved toward Nat, just visible and still unconscious in the midst of the horde. "Give me your stone, and you can save him."

My hand went to my pendant, still hidden in my bodice. The stone was almost a part of me, but I would give it up in an instant if it really would save Nat's life.

Her anger faded as she watched me, and an odd expression crossed her face. "Just take the stone off and push it out through the lattice," she crooned. "That's all you have to do."

"And you'll send him back?"

"Yes."

"Unharmed?"

"If you insist."

"And you'll stop the flood?"

"NO." All her rage came rushing back. "Humans have not been kind to us, and they must pay too. The waters will rise, and we will drown them all. *You* will drown them."

"I will do no such thing."

"Oh, yes, you will. Your mother is a fine singer, but she is wasting away. I need new blood. I need a new voice. And that voice will be you. Take off that stone NOW."

A trinket, a keepsake—after my stone had cracked, that was all I'd thought it was. But if Pressina wanted it so badly, it must be something more. And since she hadn't taken it from me by force, I could only guess that the taking was beyond her powers. Even cracked, it seemed the stone offered some kind of protection here.

For the first time since I'd arrived, I pulled the red stone out of my bodice, into full view—and my jaw dropped. The cracks were gone, and there was a glow like flame deep inside it. It was a small spark, nothing like the full fire it once had possessed, but nevertheless it was undeniable. My stone had recovered at least some of its old force.

As I stared at it, mesmerized, Penebrygg's words came back to me:

Chantresses used to cross the wall to renew their powers. . . . though it was said that they had to be careful never to take their stones off while they were there, or terrible things could befall them.

I closed my hand around the stone. "The stone is mine," I told Pressina. "I won't give it to you."

Again the stench of anger. Her tentacles sizzled and flicked back at Nat. "Then we will kill the other one."

Kill Nat? I almost handed the stone over then and there. But even as my hand went to its chain, I checked myself. Once the stone was off, whatever protection it offered would be gone. And then how could I trust Pressina to live up to the bargain? What if she killed Nat anyway? At best, it seemed, I could hope that she would send him back to Earth, to be drowned with all humankind.

By my mother.

And by me.

Yet if Pressina could make threats, so could I. "If you kill him or maim him or hurt him in any way, I will never help you."

Blue lightning flashed from the tips of Pressina's hair, driving me back into the far reaches of the cave. But she did not strike at Nat.

My threat meant something, then.

"Take off that stone," Pressina hissed.

More confident now, I said, "No. Not until he is freed." *And not even then.*

But it seemed my confidence was misplaced, for Pressina's face cracked into a needle-sharp smile. "Oh, you will give it to me before then, Chantress. And believe me, you will wish with all your heart you had done it sooner."

Her tentacles flicked out, and she pulled away from me. The other creatures followed her, carrying Nat. They vanished into a dark hole, leaving me alone in my cave, my mother's endless song dimly thrumming in my ears.

CHAPTER THIRTY-TWO

FLIGHT

I had the stone, but Pressina had Nat. Where had they taken him? What were they doing to him?

It was unbearable to imagine, but I couldn't stop myself. From what I'd seen of Pressina, she was capable of almost anything. She might starve him, or torture him, or possess him as she had possessed my mother—or commit all kinds of horrors that hadn't even occurred to me. And I could put a stop to it, if I just gave her my stone. Or so Pressina had said.

Had I done right to defy her?

Racked with guilt and fear, I could think only of Nat and nothing else. But at last I pulled myself together. All the feelings in the world weren't going to free Nat, and they weren't going to save the Earth from drowning either. For that, I would have to start thinking—and doing something.

What if I took off my stone just for a moment, to see if I could hear some trace of Wild Magic? Perhaps I had a chance of defeating Pressina that way.

My hand went to my stone, then dropped back. Even when I'd been in my own world, my Wild Magic hadn't worked very well against the strange music of Pressina's realm. And Penebrygg's warning made me doubly cautious: *They had to be careful never to take their stones off while they were there, or terrible things could befall them.*

Tucking my stone back into my bodice, I tried to recall the Proven Magic that my godmother had taught me—the only kind of Chantress magic that could be worked while wearing an undamaged stone. But her dismal prediction—that if I indulged in Wild Magic, I would soon forget the techniques of Proven Magic—turned out to be true. Either that or Proven Magic didn't work in this realm. I failed with even the simplest song-spells.

After that depressing experiment, I turned to exploring every fissure and rift I could find in the cave, in search of a way out. Pressina and her kind could swim in this ether, but I wasn't able to, and even on tiptoe I couldn't reach the ceiling. Everything else, however, I went over minutely. At the back of the cave, where it was too dark to see, I groped at the walls with my fingertips, fearing at every moment that something might bite off my hand. Nothing did, but despair swamped me when I was done. Every inch of the walls had proved solid.

My only chance of escape, then, was through the latticework. Although it burned my hands, it left no marks, so I kept probing at it. I tried covering my hands with my damp cloak, but that didn't work either. I even pulled the stiff center busk out of my stays and rammed it into the lattice. The result? A broken busk—and a lattice that looked utterly untouched.

I paced round and round the cave, trying to think of something else I could do. Without Wild Magic, I not only felt powerless; I *was* powerless.

Except for my stone. Evidently it still had some value here, some power. The problem was that I didn't know exactly what it could do.

I stopped at the lattice to peer out the coin-size holes at my mother, just visible to me. How long had she been here? When had she surrendered to Pressina?

When would I?

Never. Never. Never. I marched myself around to the beat of the defiant word, determined to keep moving, if only to prevent myself from yielding to despair.

† † †

Minutes spilled into hours, but the weird green light never changed, and neither did my mother's song. Finally I halted in front of the lattice and looked out again at my mother. It still shook me to see her. For more than half my life, I'd believed she was dead, yet here she was—alive.

Even though I knew it was useless, I couldn't help myself.

"Mama!" I called.

I shouted her name and sang it, but she never turned around, and her song never faltered.

But at last someone else came.

I saw the glow first, a weird bright light on the walls. The stench came next, and I tensed. Then Pressina herself appeared, translucent and bloated, the snake hair in a frenzy around her enormous head. Her scream shook the ether:

"What have you done with him, Chantress?"

What did she mean? The only *him* I could think of was Nat. Had he somehow gotten away?

At the back of the cave, I forced my excitement down and instead made myself sound sleepy and stupid. "Done with who? What are you talking about?"

"Where is he?"

"Where is who?" I yawned and added crossly, "You woke me up."

The enormous head pursed its lips. Evidently Pressina was trying to regain some kind of control. "We're looking for the one called Nat. He's not with you?"

So he had gotten free! "No one's with me," I said. "Anyway, how would he get through the lattice?"

This appeal to reason seemed to help. She approached the lattice, stopping well short of it, and looked about. Some kind of fireworks went on in the core of her, and the cave was briefly illuminated. She could see for herself that I was the only one there.

Evidently satisfied, she swept away, ululating as she went. Other members of the horde shot by my cave, their strange cries echoing down the cavern. *Like a pack of hounds*, I thought. The hellhounds of the Wild Hunt.

Would they tear Nat apart when they found him? No, I told

myself. Not as long as he was a bargaining chip they could use with me.

I hoped I was right.

Hours passed, and still the unearthly cries came. Exhausted, my nerves stretched to the breaking point, I slumped against the cave walls, fighting to stay awake.

Mustn't let them find me asleep, I thought.

But finally, against my will, I fell into an uneasy slumber.

† † †

I thought the whisper was a dream at first. "Lucy . . ."

Nat, I thought drowsily.

"Lucy, can you hear me?"

I blinked. I was awake. The voice was real—and it was coming from the back of the cave. Incredulous, I surged to my feet. "Nat?"

From somewhere high in the shadows came the reply. "Shhh. Keep quiet, love. No one must know I'm here."

Love. Was I still dreaming? I edged toward the back of the cave but saw no sign of Nat.

"I'm up above you," he whispered. "There's a hole here."

A hole in the ceiling? It was the one place I hadn't checked, as it had been too high to reach. Even now, as I moved into the shadows, I couldn't see where it was. But when Nat spoke again, it sounded as if he were directly over me.

"It's too small for me to get through, but I think I could pull you up. My left arm's a bit sore, but it'll hold."

"What did they do to you?" I asked.

"Nothing worth worrying about." Not a real answer, but Nat never liked to make much of his injuries.

"How did you get away?" I asked.

"As soon as I was up and able to walk, a couple of the guards let me go. They hate Pressina—and I gather they're not the only ones. I could be wrong, but I think we've stepped into the middle of a civil war. Mind your head. I'm going to reach down for you now."

In the dark, I couldn't see his arms properly, but at last I touched his long, deft fingers, callused and strong.

"Here we go," he whispered, grabbing my wrists. "Keep your head down."

A second later I was shooting toward the ceiling. A scrape and a bump, and I was through to my waist, but then my hips caught on the rock. I bit back a yelp. Another tug from Nat, and a wriggle from me, and I popped through, legs and all—into rocky darkness.

"Almost there." Nat's hands slid from my wrists to my fingers. He pulled me around the corner, into a larger cavern where flickers of distant green light allowed us to see each other. His jaw was bruised and his sleeve was torn, but he was in one piece, and there was elation and heat in the look he gave me. I swallowed hard. As awful as the situation was, it was good—incredibly good—to be beside him, to feel the warmth of him, and to have him look at me that way again.

"Nat?"

He touched a finger to my lips. I felt as if I were melting.

"We have to hurry," he said softly. "The guards say they'll lead us to safety, but there's not much time."

"Where are they?"

"Close by, but it's a bit of a maze getting there. I've got it clear in my head, though."

I could believe it. As long as I'd known him, he'd had a gift for navigating labyrinthine spaces. Which was just as well, under the circumstances. Even in the faint light, I could see at least half a dozen dark holes here, all leading to who knew where.

Yet still I hesitated. "These guards—are you sure you trust them?"

"What other choice do we have?"

He was right. We had to try. I let him lead me into one of the dark holes.

A few feet in, he stopped. "I forgot."

"Forgot what?"

"The stone—Pressina can track you with it."

"Track me?"

"Yes. The guards told me. They said you should take it off as soon as you could, so she won't know where you are."

I looked up at him. Although most of him was in darkness, his eyes had caught the last glimmer from the edge of the cave. The light revealed a sly satisfaction I'd seen before. Only, it hadn't been in Nat's eyes but in Melisande's. . . .

I bolted.

Cursing, she came after me. "Give me that stone!" Her voice was more like her own now—higher and older and full of venom.

Panting, I plunged into another hole, one that showed a faint shimmer of light. A good sign, or a bad one? I didn't know, but it gave me enough light to run by. And run I did, as fast as I could. Behind me I heard more cursing and shouting. Was Melisande calling for help? I could only hope she'd been lying about Pressina tracking me with the stone, as she'd lied about everything else.

Keep quiet, love . . .

What an idiot I'd been. But there was no time to think about it now. The hole had become a tunnel, and behind me I could hear the slap of footsteps.

Run.

A few yards later, the tunnel divided. I took the right fork because it was wider.

Twenty yards later it opened out into a wide glowing cavern. Hundreds of pillars rose from the floor like giant dripping candles, but the walls were smooth and unbroken; I couldn't see a way out. Nor could I turn around. Melisande was right on my heels.

I ducked behind one of the pillars. Seconds later, Melisande raced into the room.

Her footsteps came to a stop. "I know you're here, Chantress." Her voice echoed strangely. "I saw you make the turn. You don't stand a chance. I've called for help, and the Mothers will come soon. And even if they take their time, it doesn't matter. I am more than a match for you."

I peeked out from my hiding place. She was circling the

pillars by the entrance. And—I was chilled to see—she still had something of the look of Nat about her, though the features were becoming more like her own. Without making a sound, I pulled out of sight.

"I have been a faithful servant to the Mothers," Melisande went on, "and Pressina has rewarded me. Here I have true power. And all because of your colossal stupidity."

I gritted my teeth. What did she mean?

"Yes, your stupidity," she repeated, relishing the word. "And your mother's. Pressina has told me everything. It was your mother's own Wild Magic that brought her here. When your mother sang to defend herself from the Shadowgrims, she awakened something ancient and powerful in the waters nearby—something that loves the Others as much as it loves you, something that remembers a time when you all were as one. And so the song the water offered up to your mother was one of the ancient songs, the songs of safety, the songs Chantresses used for crossing the wall between the worlds."

So that was how my mother had ended up here.

"The song cracked the wall just enough to let her through," Melisande went on. "But it wouldn't allow anyone but a Chantress in, and it wouldn't allow anyone out. The Mothers were still trapped. They took your mother prisoner, of course, and they didn't let her go. Yet as long as she had her stone, they couldn't force her to sing. And so matters stood until you came along—you and your reckless taste for Wild Magic. Little by little, your songs widened the crack your mother had made. The Mothers still couldn't get out, but finally it became wide enough that I could join them on the other side."

My stupidity, indeed. It was a mistake I hadn't even known I was making.

Melisande's voice sank low, becoming again for a moment distressingly like Nat's. "I told you already: I have my own magic, a magic that was old before Chantresses ever existed. Like all my kind, I have gone down to the water every month and offered myself to the Mothers. For centuries your wall has stood in the way, but last month I slipped through." The voice was swollen with pride. "It was Pressina herself who greeted me. She needed my help. We made a pact, and she started to teach me magic—and once I was master of illusion, I took your mother's stone."

She was moving closer. Fearful of making even the smallest stir, I held my breath.

"And how do you think I did it, Chantress?" She laughed. "Why, by turning myself into you. The Mothers couldn't do it; there's always something a little off when they try to look human, even in these realms. But I could make myself look and sound exactly like you."

Just as she'd made herself look and sound exactly like Nat.

"I went to your mother and told her I'd sung myself here by mistake," Melisande said. "I sobbed because I had no way to protect myself from Pressina, and she gave me her stone then and there. She hung it around my neck with her own fair hands. Anything to protect her daughter! And then we had her, Pressina and I."

I went cold. So that was how they had broken my mother. It

was her love for me that had betrayed her. A love she'd kept alive through so many long years.

Was that love still locked away somewhere inside her? Somewhere in pockets where Pressina couldn't reach? Or was that love something that Pressina and Melisande had taken from her too?

"Once the stone was gone, Pressina took full possession of your mother," Melisande said triumphantly. "She was Pressina's voice from that moment on—the Chantress voice that we needed to undo the old Chantresses' work. But we didn't stop there. Once the wall between the worlds was restored to its old state, Pressina had your mother sing new holes in it, so that the Mothers could pass at will. Under the guise of mermaids and sea monsters, they started to attack your world. And then Pressina taught your mother the songs that make the waters rise, and the song that calls up a great wave and sends it crashing into the land.

"Those songs come at a price, of course. Do you know what it is, Chantress?" Melisande's voice rose, taunting me. "Those who sing them waste away. Even now your mother is withering. She won't last long enough to flood the whole world and make our victory complete. That's why we went after you. The Mothers must stay in the water—their power fades quickly on land—so Pressina sent me to lure you down here. You gave us more trouble than we expected, but now we've got you."

Oh, no, you don't, I thought.

I shifted ever so slightly, trying to see if she'd left the entrance unguarded. Under my feet, pebbles at the base of the pillar crackled.

A tiny sound, but Melisande heard it.

"Ah, there you are." Her steps quickened, coming my way.

I had no magic to fight her. All I had were my wits—but that would have to do. Knowing it didn't matter how much sound I made now, I scraped up a handful of pebbles and sand. I waited till the last possible second, then flung them at Melisande's face and dashed for the entrance.

I must have gotten her right in the eyes, because it took her some moments to come after me. By then, I was shooting straight back down the tunnel again.

I took the other turn at the fork. This time, thankfully, there was no dead end, but soon the path curved, and the light dimmed. Another bend, and the light disappeared entirely. I faltered. I couldn't run full tilt into oblivion. And yet the footsteps were coming closer.

"Over here," a voice hummed on my left.

I froze. Was that Pressina?

"Over here," it insisted. "Come, or she'll get you."

Behind me I heard a shout: "I've trapped her in here!"

It was Melisande, calling out to an ally. My heart pounded.

"You must come *now,*" the voice breathed.

I followed it, touching my hand to the rock wall for guidance. There was a gap there.

"Yesssss," said the voice.

I pressed myself into the gap—and a tentacle wrapped around my wrist.

CHAPTER THIRTY-THREE

RESISTANCE

As I opened my lips to scream, another tentacle closed over my mouth—a slippery, sticky gag pressing against my lips.

Pressina.

I thrashed as wildly as a fish caught in a net. Panic drove every rational thought from my brain.

"Be still," the voice hummed. "We will not hurt you. But you must not scream, or they will find us."

There was something deeply reassuring about that hum. I stopped thrashing. Whoever this was, it wasn't Pressina.

The tentacles tugged at me, pulling me deeper into the gap. But now that my mind was calmer, I noticed that in addition to being sticky, the tentacles were velvet-soft, and their hold on me was a gentle one. My wrist wasn't sore, and I was able to breathe.

We rushed downward through the darkness. My feet didn't touch the ground. After many twists and turns, we slowed, then stopped.

"Success?" a voice murmured from above.

"Yes," my rescuer said.

The tentacles thrust me forward and released me. I fell to the ground, and something rattled behind me. I put out my arms and felt the hard and bony outlines of a latticework cage.

Panic surged again. I was a prisoner once more.

† † †

Before I could get to my feet, my captors seized the cage and whisked me down through the ether with them. I clung for dear life to the latticework, completely disoriented in the darkness. No longer caring who heard me, I shouted, "Let me go!"

"We can't," one of my captors hummed anxiously. "Sorry. Sorry."

Sorry?

"Who are you?" I demanded.

Another few darts to the left, and a shaft of malachite light gave me my answer. My cage was held by a lemon-yellow creature with twenty octopus-like arms. Nearby was a spotted starfish with a dozen eyes, all of which were fixed watchfully on me.

What on earth were these creatures?

My fear only deepened as the octopus-like one tugged me down toward the source of the light into a cavern full of beings even stranger than the ones I'd already seen: giant sea horses with fronded tails, striped fish with hundreds of fins, scaly eels with rows of jagged shark teeth. What unnerved me most of all, however, was the way they kept changing, moment by moment—shifting color, shifting size, shifting shape. Deep purple slid into black-and-white stripes and cherry-red dots. Fins stretched and compressed. Eyes widened, then disappeared—then reappeared, looking straight at me.

Pretending a calm I didn't feel, I looked right back at them. "What do you want with me?"

As one, the creatures began to babble. With a wave of its arms, the yellow octopus creature silenced them and put its single giant eye level with mine.

"We want your help," it said.

I looked at it warily. "And that's why you put me in a cage?"

A ripple like fear moved through the whole company, and they shifted even faster.

"It is necessary," the creature assured me, sounding regretful. "At least for now."

For now? "Who *are* you?" I asked again.

The octopus creature answered, seemingly for them all. "You have many names for us, I think. The fae, the faeries, the Others, the naiads, the good folk, and dozens more. You humans like names, do you not? If you must have one for me, you may call me . . . oh, shall we say . . . Odo. But do not let names get in the way of understanding. What matters is that all of us here—including you—are on the same side." To the others, Odo explained, "This is Viviane's daughter. The Chantress Lucy."

There was a collective sigh, falling away into a sound somewhere between a hiss and a drone. "Chantresssssssssssss . . ."

Fins and tails flapped, and I felt a wave of affection wafting toward me.

"I—I thought you hated Chantresses," I said.

"Pressina does," Odo replied. "And those who follow her. But most of us do not."

"But we walled you in."

"You walled *Pressina* in," Odo said. "And we know why. Most of us don't blame you."

A murmur came from some of the other creatures. The wave of affection diminished, and grief floated toward me. Was this why they'd caged me?

"But of course the magic you Chantresses worked on the wall had terrible consequences for us," Odo said.

"I—I don't understand," I said.

"When you walled Pressina in, she turned on us," Odo said. "She wanted revenge, she wanted power—and we were the only ones within reach. Oh, she made alliances, of course. She couldn't have risen in any other way, and there were always creatures who admired her cunning. But most of us hated her. We were always free and easy here in the Depths, but she'd seen the human world, and she wanted to set herself up as an empress. Many have died opposing her. Many of us"—Odo nodded at the other creatures—"have dedicated our existence to overthrowing her."

So there really was a civil war here. I'd thought that was just another one of Melisande's lies.

"Since the day she was born, she has tried to use us to feed her own appetites," a sea horse said in a voice like a dirge. "And once the Chantresses sealed us off she was insatiable. She drained most of us of what magic we had left. But it wasn't enough to destroy the wall. Nothing was, until your mother sang it down."

"But you must know all about that already," Odo said.

"I know something about it. Melisande said Pressina took my mother prisoner, but for a long while Pressina couldn't make her sing—"

"That's right," said Odo. "Pressina caged her, just as she caged you. But of course she couldn't touch her, not while Viviane had her stone."

"Why?"

Odo's eye enlarged to three times its previous size. "You mean you don't know?"

"No." My hand went to my stone.

The creatures scuttled back. "Don't tell her," one of them cried out.

"Tell me what?" I asked.

"I must," Odo said to the others. "We cannot have her help unless I do."

The creatures pulled back even farther.

Odo turned to me. "Chantress stones are made of a substance that repels our own magic." A tentacle waved, forestalling my next question. "No, no. Don't ask me what it is. No one here knows. But as long as you keep it around your neck, our magic can't destroy you, or even gravely harm you. We can cage you, we can set guards around you, but we can't do serious damage to your body or mind."

"I'm not sure mine works properly, then," I said, fingering the edges of my stone. "I've been burned by Pressina's fire."

"Burned? Chantress, a human would be incinerated by the bolts she hurls. On you, they don't even leave a scar."

Oh.

"And that's not all." Odo pulled well back from my latticework cage. "Your stone can destroy us."

"*Destroy* you?"

"Yes."

If they thought that, no wonder they'd caged me. "But when you grabbed me, you weren't hurt."

"Only because I was careful not to touch your stone."

"How could you tell, in the dark?"

"It wasn't so dark for me, Chantress. Your eyes are not like mine. And it was worth the risk."

I looked out at Odo, and at the multitude of sea creatures ringed around us. "And now you're keeping me in this cage because you're worried that I might kill you?"

"Err . . . yes," Odo said. "We'd much prefer it if you killed Pressina."

"I should think so." I tucked the stone far down inside my bodice and eyed them all through the latticework holes. "Look, it's safe to let me out now. We're on the same side. And I'll keep the stone well away from you, I promise."

The sea creatures murmured uneasily.

"If we're going to accomplish anything, we have to trust her," Odo said to them. "She is our ally, not our enemy—and she cannot help us if she is caged."

A sighing sound of acceptance came from some of the creatures, but others continued to show signs of agitation.

"You can hide from her if you feel the need to," Odo said patiently.

Here and there, creatures scuttled for safety, holing up in cracks and fissures or leaving the cave entirely. Most, however, held their ground.

"All right, then. I'm going to let her out now." Odo probed at the cage with delicate, fingerlike tentacles until an opening appeared.

I stepped through it, taking care not to move too hastily, lest I alarm anyone. "Thank you."

Odo's giant eye surveyed me with satisfaction. "Now we can make plans."

"Yes." As a few of the hidden creatures peered out at me, dozens of questions crowded my mind. "But before we start, I think you'd better tell me more about how my stone works here. It used to be cracked, before I came here. Why isn't it now?"

"Whenever you Chantresses come to our world, your magic grows stronger," Odo said. "It has always been like that. Some say it is our blood thickening and renewing in you. And since the stones are part of your magic, they grow more powerful too. It has been so long since Chantresses came here that we were surprised that there were any left with power. The wall weakened all of us, including you."

"If I took off my stone, would I hear Wild Magic?"

"Yes, but not as you know it," Odo said, waving several arms to emphasize the point. "Do not be hasty. Our Wild Magic is far richer and stronger than anything you can hear on Earth—so powerful that even when your stone is on, you can't help but hear the thrum of it. Sometimes you even can discern the outlines of a tune, if the singer is close enough. You can heard something of the song your mother is singing, can't you? And a deep humming in the ether, like an undertow beneath everything?"

I nodded.

"That is only a faint echo of the Wild Magic you would hear if your stone were not protecting you," Odo told me. "Your Chantress songs are merely the tiniest part of it. The ether here allows every bit of Wild Magic to reach us, while your own world blocks most of it. That is part of what undid your mother when she took off her stone. It was as if she had lived all her life in the murky depths of the sea, only to find herself suddenly on the surface, in the full glare of the blinding sun. And in that moment, Pressina attacked and took possession of her."

"I see." I swallowed hard. "And if I took off my stone, I would be blinded too?"

"You would. After the first shock, you might find that you could start to work with the Wild Magic here. You have our blood, so it ought to be possible. But in practice, you would be unlikely to get the opportunity. And even if you did, as a novice you would be very vulnerable. If I were you, I would not take the risk; I would keep the stone on. My best advice is to ambush

Pressina and attack her with the stone while you are still wearing it."

I shuddered. That would mean getting very close indeed to that horrible eel-haired head and the gelatinous mass beneath and around it. But I didn't want to end up like my mother either, becoming nothing more than Pressina's voice.

"I wish I had attacked her when I first saw her," I said. "Or that my mother had."

"You didn't know. And I doubt your mother did either. In any case, she never had a chance," Odo said sadly. "She was so weak when she arrived, almost drained of power. Pressina took her prisoner right away. Your mother was desperate to get back to you, but Pressina told her she would never see you again unless she sang the wall down. Viviane refused to do that, so Pressina kept her locked away for years."

"Did you try to help her?"

Odo looked down at my feet, as if abashed. "Not for a very long time, I'm sorry to say. We were afraid of that stone, you see. But the longer your mother held out against Pressina, the more some of us began to wonder if we might be able to make an alliance with her. So we started to try to devise a plan to put ourselves in touch with her, which was itself a great challenge. For years we struggled to find our way to her. And then Melisande came, and everything became much more urgent."

"Did Pressina take possession of her?"

"Not in the way she took your mother, no. She needed two things from Melisande, and both required that Melisande stay alive and intact. One was her ability to impersonate other humans in a convincing manner."

That I already knew about. "And the other?"

"Her magic. Once a Chantress surrenders her stone, Melisande knows how to destroy it—something we ourselves cannot do, since contact with it kills us." The great eye rose and fixed on me. "At the time, we didn't know exactly what bargain Pressina and Melisande were making, but we could see they were hatching a plan. The one benefit was that Pressina was distracted, and that gave us the chance to reach Viviane. I was the one chosen to approach her. She was doubtful at first, but she didn't try to kill me. She listened. And then she chose to trust me. We talked about you. It was how she endured everything, she said—by thinking about you."

My throat tightened.

"We made plans then," Odo said. "And we almost got her out. But we were too late. Melisande came to her and tricked her—"

"I know," I said. "She told me." I burned, remembering her glee in the telling: *She hung it around my neck with her own fair hands. Anything to protect her daughter!*

The great head shook sadly from side to side. "We felt Pressina's power grow as she took possession of your mother. And we saw the stone destroyed with our own eyes, in a pool of blue fire."

My mother's stone, gone forever. I wanted to touch my own stone for reassurance, but I checked myself. I mustn't strike fear into the creatures around me.

"We despaired," Odo said. "But now we have you, and you have your own stone. You have the power to kill Pressina."

"And I will," I said. "So help me, I will. And then I will take my mother home."

There was a flurry of consternation from the creatures. Odo's eye dropped down again.

"What is it?" I asked. "What's wrong?"

The starfish said something I couldn't quite catch.

"No, we have to tell her," Odo said in reply. "It wouldn't be right if we didn't." It wriggled and raised a sorrowful eye. "I'm afraid it won't happen like that, Chantress."

"What do you mean?" I asked.

"Your mother and Pressina are bound by enchantment now." The great eye held mine. "If you kill Pressina, you will kill your mother, too."

CHAPTER THIRTY-FOUR
BLOOD MAGIC

I stared at Odo in shock, feeling as if I'd been hollowed out. "Are you sure?"

"Yes. If Pressina dies, so does your mother. That is the nature of their bond."

The hollow feeling was still there, but there was resistance now too. "Then I can't do it," I said. "I can't kill Pressina."

"You must," said the starfish who had helped cage me.

"Not if it means killing my own mother. No."

The starfish shot out an extra arm. "She would want you to."

"No," I said again.

The creatures shape-shifted around me, eyes multiplying, till I felt as if thousands were judging me.

At last Odo said, "Then we must find a way to break the bond first."

A tremor passed through the creatures. They didn't have to speak for me to perceive their unhappiness. Many of them turned white. Others deflated to half their size.

A flash of anger went through me. Was it so much to ask, that I should be allowed to rescue my mother?

"You needn't be involved," I said. "I'll do it myself."

"You can't," said the starfish. "You have to get past the spell of protection to reach her, and you need our help for that."

"The spell of protection?" My anger dwindled, and so did my confidence. There was so much in this world that I didn't understand. I turned to Odo. "Is that what threw me back when I tried to reach my mother before?"

"Yes," Odo said. "Pressina has set that spell around your mother to guard her. But do not fear. I know how to get you through. And I myself will go with you."

A tremulous hum came from the crowd of sea creatures.

I looked at Odo doubtfully. "Are you sure it will work?"

"Quite sure." And Odo did sound certain, though I sensed a deep sadness in him that I didn't understand. But perhaps the source of the sadness was somewhere else.

"Once I'm through, is that all?" I asked.

"No, Chantress," Odo said. "That is not all. It is not that easy to possess a person, not even for Pressina. It requires blood magic—songs that can be sung only if the magic-worker draws blood from the captive. In the case of your mother, it was especially strong blood magic, for she comes from Pressina by a direct line of descent. As do you."

I shivered. I didn't want to be related to Pressina in any way. "Pressina is my ancestor? Are you sure?"

"Yes," Odo said. "The precise shape of your mark proves it."

I looked down at my Chantress mark, seeing for the first time how much it resembled a tiny coiled serpent.

Odo wasn't done instructing me. "You must not attempt to take your mother away from her rock until the link is broken, or else her mind will shatter."

A shattered mind? I could hardly bear to think of it.

"How do I free her?" I asked.

"It is simple. You must get her to recognize you. You must bring her back to herself."

Simple, yes—but was it possible? My heart fell. Already I had called to her so many times, and she hadn't even blinked. "And how do I do that?"

"We do not know." Odo wriggled in what might have been frustration or apology. "I can only tell you this: Blood magic can always be undone. And with Chantresses, the undoing usually has nothing to do with magic and everything to do with being human. Once you pass through that spell of protection, even saying her name might be enough to break the spell. Failing that, you could touch her, or perhaps anoint her with a drop of your own blood—"

"But you don't know if any of that will work?"

"Not for certain," Odo conceded. "But we can give you time. At least we can if we create a disturbance beforehand to draw Pressina and her creatures away. Her chamber is very close to your mother's, you see."

The creatures' reluctance was more understandable now. "But if you do that, you might die. And if I fail, you will have given up your lives for nothing."

A shiver went through the creatures.

I bent my head. Perhaps it *was* too much to ask.

"She is our enemy as well as yours," Odo said. "We have a right to risk our lives for this—if we chose to." It swept its tentacles in a wide arc, as if appealing to the whole company. "Take courage, all of you. Remember that Pressina is drawing no small part of her power from Viviane. If Chantress Lucy can sever the link, then Pressina will be easier to defeat. It is worth the risk."

The creatures seemed to find strength in that. Their colors came back, pale at first but brightening.

"And if we succeed, there will be two Chantresses to fight Pressina," a small silver fish peeped. "Mother and daughter."

Vivid colors rippled through the crowd in response.

Odo's color was deepening too, from gold to orange-red to crimson. "Tell me now, all of you, shall we help the Chantress rescue her mother?"

"YES." The low vibrating hum filled the cave.

"Then let us go now," Odo called. "They are already in disarray, searching for the Chantress. There is no better time than the present."

So soon? I needed time to prepare.

"NOW," the company sang. They were trembling again, but this time with purpose and resolve. All around me, creatures were inflating to twice their size, popping out spikes, growing mouths full of teeth. When I turned back to look, Odo had thirty legs that glowed like coals.

"How do you do that?" I asked.

Bubbles of laughter came from it. "Better to ask, how could we not?" More soberly Odo added, "In your world, as I understand it, you try to keep magic and emotion separate. But here we use our emotions to power our magic. And as our moods and desires change, we change our outward forms. For change is in the music all around us, Chantress. It's the strongest magic there is—the magic of transformation." The great eye swiveled. "Indeed, to us the wonder isn't that we shift; it's that you stay the same."

Odo turned to the others, murmuring too fast for me to understand. But as I stood there, another worry came to the fore. Events had moved so quickly that I hadn't had time to address it, but I had to speak up now.

"Odo?" I put a hand on one of its tentacles.

Odo turned back to me. "Yes?"

"Do you know anything about Nat, the human who came here with me?" I said. "He is missing—"

"Ah, yes," said Odo. "That is one of the matters we were discussing. It is something that worries us, for no one knows where he is or what side he is on. Two of his guards disappeared with him, and we do not know what has become of them. Do you know him well? Is he a friend?"

"Yes." I was anxious that they understand he was not an enemy, that they not attack him. "He is here only because he was with me. He means you no harm, believe me. He is thoughtful and loyal and kind."

"And you love him." Odo spoke as if it were plain as day.

Maybe it was. I bit my lip. "Yes."

"He may yet be safe, Chantress," Odo said gently. "There are many kinds of resistance here, and it may be that someone, somewhere is protecting him."

Please may it be true, I prayed silently.

"But for now you must put him out of your mind," Odo said. "We must give everything to what we do next, or we cannot succeed." Again he spoke to the others. When he finished, different parties split off in various directions.

"Come!" Odo curved a glowing tentacle around my hand. "There is one thing more I must ask of you."

"Yes?"

"You must step inside the cage again, so that I may transport you."

I turned doubtful eyes on first the cage, then Odo.

"Trust me," Odo said. "Please."

Hoping I was making the right choice, I stepped inside.

"There." Odo shut the door. "I will take you to your mother."

CHAPTER THIRTY-FIVE
BREAKING THE BOND

Up and up we traveled, mostly through darkness. Odo's arms no longer glowed, although several of them continued to be wrapped tightly around my cage. In occasional rays of emerald light, I caught sight of some of the other creatures who were accompanying us: four giant eels, a band of many-legged starfish, two creatures with teeth that gleamed like a shark's, and a school of spotted silver fish.

After a while, I began to hear singing—the raw and terrible voice of my mother.

At last Odo halted, setting me down on a ledge. All but the very end of one arm dropped away from me. "We must wait here," it whispered.

I stood still. The fins of the silver fish fluttered outside my cage.

The singing was coming from just above us—above and to the left. In the slight space between beats I could hear faint sounds on my right, too. Laughter? Moaning? I wasn't sure what I was listening to, but Odo's arms were guiding me to look toward it. When I did, my heart skipped a beat. My eyes were level with a tiny aperture in the stone, and through it I could see down into another chamber. Within it, Pressina was holding court. Twice as large as everyone else, her snake-hair head coming and going, she screamed at the hordes around her.

"Do not fail me again! You must find her. You must find them both!"

My stomach lurched at the hatred in her voice. But she had said "both." Did that mean that Nat was still free?

"Find them NOW!"

Before the horde could obey, a reverberation like a gong came from deep below. Cries of alarm went up from both Pressina and the horde. Shouting orders, Pressina led the charge out of the chamber, down to the regions where the alarm was sounding.

"Now!" Odo grabbed my cage and shot up into the great cavern where my mother stood on her rock, singing. Odo charged toward her headfirst, tentacles wrapped tightly around my cage. The eels and fish darted beside us, flashing green in the pale light.

I braced myself for the impact.

Just before we touched the rock, the shock hit. Eels and fish went spinning back, bright as lightning bolts. An instant later Odo convulsed around me. But it seemed the eels and fish had drawn away some of the magic's power, because instead of bouncing back, we kept going.

A great heart-walloping jolt made my fingers shoot sparks. And then we were through, falling against the rock on which my mother stood. Odo's tentacles went limp, and the cage came down hard, smashing into pieces. My palms scraped against the rock, stinging as the blood came. But that was nothing compared to what Odo had suffered. The long limbs sprawled around me, burnt and unmoving.

I know how to get you through, Odo had said—and yet had looked so sad. Was this why?

I cried out, and the great eye half-opened. "Go," Odo whispered. "Go to your mother."

The eye rolled up and shut, like a light going out.

Odo was gone.

Appalled, I glanced up at my mother, her face uncannily serene as she sang down destruction on us all. For a second I almost hated her. How many deaths could be laid at her door—including Odo's?

But of course the spell of protection hadn't been her idea, just as it hadn't been her choice to sing. She was merely Pressina's pawn. As I would be, if Pressina got hold of me.

And she was so tired, my mother. Despite her seeming serenity, I could see the hollows under her eyes from here, at the foot of her rock. She seemed to be aging even as I watched, her skin growing dull and tight, as if it were shrinking. Under it you could see the shape of her bones.

She is wasting away, Pressina had said.

Could I make her recognize me? Could I bring her back to her true self?

I started climbing the rock. "Mama!" Odo had said my voice

might be enough, once I was inside whatever bubble it was that protected her. "Mama, it's Lucy."

Nothing. I climbed the rock, touched her feet, then her hand. Her fingers remained as still and cold as stone. I might as well have been touching a statue.

Blood, Odo had said. It might take blood to get her to recognize me.

I bent and swiped my hands against the rock again, opening the grazes on my palms. Scarlet drops seeped through the scored skin. Again I touched my mother's hand, then touched my bloody palm to her face, her lips.

Nothing made her recognize me. Nothing stopped the song. Even when my hand was right up against her mouth, the singing poured out from her. She was unshaken, unbroken, unmoved.

"Mama?" I tried again. And then, "Viviane?"

I was standing right in front of her—eye to eye, as I had never been tall enough to stand when I was a child. Yet she gave no sign that she even saw me.

Out of the corner of my eye, I saw a few silver fish shaking frantically. A warning sign? Was Pressina coming? How much time did I have?

If only I could work magic here! But no, that was all wrong. It wasn't magic that would break this spell, Odo had said. It was something human. But what?

Not my voice, not my touch, not my blood. And I couldn't think of anything else.

I squeezed my mother's stiff hand. "Mama, you have to listen. You have to come back."

But no matter what I did, she wouldn't, she couldn't. And Pressina was coming and I was about to be caught and Odo had died for nothing . . .

With my bloody palm, I rubbed at my brimming eyes. What good would crying do? I needed something that would break the spell, something human, something that could reach inside the walls that Pressina had built around my mother and send them crashing down. But I couldn't come up with anything. My mind was blank. And—

Tears.

I touched my hand to my wet lashes, then seized her hand again. "Mama, can you hear me? It's Lucy."

Unbelievably, her fingers twitched, then curved around mine. The singing broke off.

"Lucy?"

I looked up to find my mother's eyes—aware, alert—pinned on me.

"It's really you?" The hoarse voice spoke with the sweet intonation I remembered. "It isn't a trick?"

When I spoke, my voice was hoarse too. "It's me, Mama. I promise you. This time it's for real."

A moment later she had her arms around me, and both of us were laughing and crying. Ten years we'd lost, and yet now I'd found her. I was shaking with grief and joy.

I thought she would ask about Pressina right away, but she

didn't. She just stroked my hair and held me to her, and when she finally did speak, it was about something else entirely.

"You're so tall," she said in wonder. "You're all grown up. I knew you must be, but . . ."

With a shake of her head, she pulled back from me. I tensed. Did she doubt I really was her daughter?

But it seemed she just wanted to see me properly. "You still have your father's curls," she said with delight. "And the tilt of your head—that's his too." She pulled me back into an embrace. "Oh, if only he'd lived to see you! He would have loved you so much."

I said hesitantly, "Did he . . . know about me?"

"Oh, yes. He was so happy he was going to be a father. We were both so happy. . . ."

A tight coil inside me released. After all the lies and gossip, I'd finally learned the truth. My father had loved her to the last. He had loved *us*.

But already my mother's mind was racing on. "The Shadow-grims, Scargrave—they haven't hurt you? I've been so afraid."

Oh, there was so much she didn't know! "They're gone. I destroyed them."

"You did? Oh, Lucy, how wonderful." There was relief in her voice—and a touch of maternal pride. But as she went on, I heard regret and pain, too. "I meant to do that myself. That's why I brought you to the island, to keep you safe while I fought. But they caught me, you know. Or do you?"

"Yes."

"And the Wild Magic that saved me brought me here. And I've been here ever since."

Her voice shook, and so did her hands. Looking at her, my heart filled with concern—and fear. In the first rush of joy, I hadn't seen the truth, but now it was all too plain. The mother I'd found wasn't the strong mother I remembered, the one who had protected me from all comers. When she touched my face, her fingers were as brittle and light as dried leaves. Her arms were stick-thin and trembling. In every way, she was dangerously weak.

Had I found my mother only to lose her?

No. A fierce determination swept through me. I would protect my mother just as she once had protected me. I would defeat everyone who stood against us, and I would bring her home.

I put my arm more securely around her. "Come with me."

Raising her up, I guided her down from the rock. She trembled when she saw Odo's still body. "Is that—"

"Odo. Yes."

"Did Pressina use me to kill him?"

The look on her face was painful to see. "No," I said quickly. The magic had been Pressina's.

My mother still looked grief-stricken. "Did I kill anyone else? I don't remember what she made me sing, but I know it wasn't good."

This wasn't the time to tell her what her singing had done. "You meant no harm, Mama." When she started to shake her head, I pulled her firmly forward. "Please, Mama. We can talk about it later. You must come now."

Murmuring a silent blessing to Odo as we passed by the still figure, I braced myself for a struggle as we left the rock. But whatever had guarded the place before was now gone. Was that because my mother was no longer bound to Pressina? Or because Pressina's power was waning now that she didn't have my mother's power to bolster it? Either way, it was a good sign.

But we weren't out of the woods yet. Silver fish rushed toward us, enveloping us in a cloud. Their voices rang out like tiny bells:

"Beware Pressina!"

"She's coming!"

"Run!"

My mother blanched and stumbled against me. Running was not an option, not for her, and neither was attacking.

"We need a place to hide," I told the fish. "A place where I can ambush Pressina."

"Follow us!" They darted away.

I looped my arm around Mama and tried to keep up with them. But after a few brave steps, she faltered and covered her ears.

"The music," she mumbled, wincing as if in pain. "The music . . ."

My stone shielded me, but she had nothing. And she was so weak.

The silver fish circled around us again, fins beating faster than ever. "Hurry, hurry! She comes."

"Go," my mother whispered. "Leave me here. Make yourself safe."

"No." I wasn't going to stir from her side. "We'll go together."

We were within a few feet of the cavern walls when the stench rolled over me—a wave of rage and rot and triumph.

Recognizing it before I did, my mother shrieked and sank toward the ground. As I grabbed for her, Pressina shot into the cave, her head ringed with blue flame.

CHAPTER THIRTY-SIX
MONSTER

Pressina wasn't alone. There were fewer of her followers than before, but the ones that were left were ferocious. No longer translucent, they'd sprouted barbed tentacles and sharp fangs.

Shrieking, Pressina ordered the horde to attack. "Separate them!"

As they swooped toward us, I stepped in front of my mother and held out my stone. At the sight of it, the horde's line broke. Their confusion was all the greater when a detachment of spiked starfish and shark-toothed dolphins barreled into them.

"We'll hold them off," a starfish shouted to me. "You see to Pressina."

They did more than merely hold the horde off. Trilling a strange high melody, they beat Pressina's followers back the way they had come, then gave chase. In moments, friend and foe alike disappeared out of sight.

I thought Pressina would go to her followers' defense. Instead she swung back toward us. "I'll deal with you myself, then."

I thrust out my stone as far as the chain would allow. "Touch us, and you die."

"Touch you?" Pressina cackled. "There's no need for that."

Hovering well out of my reach, she sang a low and guttural melody. Her vast body blazed up and shot out bolts of blue lightning.

"Keep behind me!" I shouted to my mother. Odo had said that as long as I had the stone, Pressina's magic couldn't kill me. But it could kill my mother—and it was my mother that Pressina was aiming at.

Soon the bolts came so thick and fast that my whole body burned, and I could not catch a breath, but I always, always stayed between Pressina and my mother. And I drew courage from the fact that every bolt was costing Pressina precious strength—strength she could not afford to waste, now that she no longer had my mother's magic to draw on.

The trouble was that my own strength was being tested too. The bolts couldn't kill me, but as Pressina circled around us, I was finding it harder and harder to move quickly enough to intercept them. And I had an even bigger problem: While I was guarding my mother, I couldn't attack Pressina. The closer Pressina came, the stronger her bolts were, but she was always careful to stay just out of reach.

Did I dare take off my stone and sling it at her? If my aim were true, I would be in danger for only a moment before the stone hit. I fumbled at the chain.

Behind my back, my mother saw what I was doing. "No," she

whispered, putting her hand over mine. "You mustn't. It's too great a risk."

"I have to do something." Letting my hand fall, I jumped to catch the next bolt. When it slammed into me, my whole body burned again.

Behind me, my mother whispered, "I can't bear this."

I didn't look back, just concentrated on Pressina. "It's all right, Mama. Just look out for yourself."

"I won't hold you back." There was a sound like a gulp, and she started to sing something—nothing a Chantress would recognize, but a weird otherworldly song.

My heart turned over. What was she up to? Was she giving up and going back to Pressina? "Mama, no!"

Still watching Pressina, I reached back for my mother—and touched something thin and slimy. An instant later, the song stopped, and I felt nothing at all.

If I was shocked, so was Pressina. I saw her eyes spin. "NO!" She darted to my left, taking aim at a tiny green sea snake gliding for a hole in the cave wall.

I gaped. Was that my mother?

I leaped in front of it, cutting off Pressina's water bolt, and the sea snake vanished into the rock.

Pressina let out a cry of fury. Remembering my mother's advice, I didn't try to throw the stone. There was no need. Pressina's attack on the sea snake had brought her closer than ever before. And now that my mother was safe, I had nothing to lose. I charged straight for Pressina, stone outstretched.

She saw me coming. With another cry, she flew up and away, and I was left alone in the cave.

Where had she gone? What would she do next?

I glanced up and around the vast cavern, my head darting this way and that, every muscle tense. There were so many cave openings and clefts and tunnels that I couldn't possibly keep watch on them all—and yet Pressina might emerge from any one of them. Indeed, she might even be here already, hiding just inside the mouth of one of the farther caves. . . .

Glancing around again, I saw something that made my heart stop—Nat peering out from one of the upper caves. He put his finger to his lips, warning me to keep quiet, then vanished back into the cave.

Was it really Nat?

Or was it Melisande?

SLAM!

A bolt rammed into me from behind. Reeling, I spun around and saw Pressina in the entrance of a cave above me. She had a tiny green sea snake in her tentacles.

"Now we shall have some fun," she crooned. To my horror, she gave the snake a squeeze. It gasped like a human. Another squeeze, and I heard my mother's moan.

Pressina looked from the snake to me and laughed. She knew I was too far away to touch her. Bending her eel-haired head over the sea snake, she started to squeeze again.

In one swift motion, I pulled off my stone and flung it at her.

As a roar of music enveloped me, I saw the stone hit her square in the stomach. A perfect throw. Pressina dropped the snake and grabbed the stone . . .

. . . and turned into Melisande.

I screamed.

Melisande had my stone, and she was too far away for me to get it back.

But even worse was to come. The little sea snake was now singing a tune that rose sinuously above the din around me—a song like the one I'd heard from my mother and other creatures as they'd transformed. Only it sounded immeasurably louder and stronger now that I didn't have my stone.

It was a song for shifting, but the singer wasn't my mother. It was Pressina.

The tiny snake snout reared up and shifted, and Pressina's eel-haired face laughed at me. Below it, the slender green body started to lengthen and swell and ripple with sharp claws.

Behind me, my mother's voice shrieked, "Don't let her take your blood, Lucy! Don't let her possess you. Shift!"

Shift. It was my mother's command. It was the song in the ether around me. Now that my head was no longer reeling from the first assault of unbridled Wild Magic, I heard it plainly. Odo was right—it was everywhere, the dominant tune of this place, spiraling out in never-ending tendrils and twists. But how did I find the start of the song? How did I choose what I became?

A tiny green sea snake shot out of a cave and dashed toward me, singing with brave ferocity. It was my mother, giving me a way into the music—not just the right notes but the emotional key to them. *Here we use our emotions to power our magic*, Odo had said, but I hadn't understood what that meant till now. Following my mother's lead, I tapped into my own fierceness and fury, taking up her song like a battle cry. As anger swelled inside me, I started to shift. My arms shortened, and my nails lengthened. My legs cleaved together, and my body twisted.

But even as I changed, my mother changed too. She was becoming larger and larger, impossible to miss. With a roar, Pressina went after her, slinging a bolt straight at her.

My mother burned just as Odo had. Her snake body fell to the floor, unmoving, a charred and lifeless coil.

She was dead. As Pressina rounded on me, I let out a cry of grief and fury. *Mama!*

But the cry echoed strangely, for already my mother's song had changed me completely. Like Pressina herself, I was full grown, sinuous, and green. My scaly hands had lethal talons. I was a serpent, a sea dragon, a monster.

Pressina shot toward me, claws outstretched. Despite my grief, my new body seemed to know just what to do. Indeed, my grief—and the rage that came with it—seemed to make me stronger. Although I was slightly smaller than Pressina, I was faster. I dived low and careened past her, unscathed.

Only a few breaths to recover, and then she launched herself at me again. This time I sprang upward, narrowly avoiding those long sharp nails. As I skimmed past the walls, I saw Melisande below me, hugging my stone to herself as she watched the battle from the mouth of the high cave where she and Pressina had tricked me.

Could I get the stone away from her? I reached out as I passed her, but she saw me coming and pulled back into the cleft. Was she about to work the magic that would destroy my stone forever?

I tried to double back to see, but Pressina headed straight for me. I escaped her by inches—and now the advantage was hers.

Up and down and all around the cavern she chased me. Yet as the minutes passed, I realized that either I was becoming more skilled or she was tiring. The distance between us was increasing. Still, I couldn't see how to win without the stone. On my next dive away from Pressina, I twisted past Melisande's small cave and tried to see if she still had it in her hands.

What I saw shocked me. Nat was tackling Melisande beside a pool of blue fire.

Was it the real Nat? It must be. There was no reason for anyone else to take that form to attack Melisande.

Hope jolted through me, then fear. Pressina must not see him. Determined to distract her, I flung myself to the other side of the cave. This time when Pressina dove for me, I didn't evade her. I swiped at her side and drew blood.

My claws were sharper than I'd realized. Pressina howled and tumbled down to the cavern floor. The gash I'd opened up in her scales was enormous, and it pulsated with blood. For a moment I thought I'd finished her off.

But no, when I darted closer to check, there was still fire in her eyes, and she snapped at me. It seemed she was only nursing her injury.

Keeping well away from her teeth and claws, I soared up

again—and saw Nat grappling with Melisande, trying to get my stone. Though he was bigger and stronger by nature, there was a pallor about him that frightened me. They were right by the edge of Melisande's high cave. I was afraid Nat would fall, but as I hurtled toward him, he jerked and rolled, and it was Melisande who went tumbling down, bumping against the cave walls until she hit the rocky ground headfirst.

"You fool!" Pressina screamed. Melisande was past replying. She lay still, her limbs distorted.

My stone was in Nat's hands now. He stood at the edge of the cave and held out the necklace, opening the chain wide.

My claws were dexterous as well as sharp, but there was no room for error. Banking abruptly, I wheeled toward Nat—and saw the dread in his eyes. Although he was helping me, he was horrified at the sight of me. Clearer than words, the look on his face said, *You are a monster*.

Sliding the tip of my smallest claw into the chain, I snatched the necklace away. Anger coursed through me, and bitterness and pain. I had the stone, but at what cost? Now I was a monster not only in the world's eyes but in Nat's.

Below me, Pressina snarled. I clamped down on my pain. Nothing mattered now except winning this battle. Landing well out of her reach, I twisted my neck down and worked the chain over the top of my head. That was enough. Seconds later, the stone was sliding against my skin, protecting me and deafening me. Within moments, I dwindled and became human again.

Small though I was, I still felt dragon-fierce as I looked in triumph at Pressina. She couldn't possess me anymore, not while I had my stone. Her bolts couldn't kill me. She couldn't fly; she was still on the cave floor, bleeding. Victory was almost mine.

But there I was wrong.

With a roar, Pressina launched herself upward—not at me but at Nat. With a snatch of her claw, she caught him and sank to the floor some twenty feet away from me.

"Strike me with that stone, and he dies with me," Pressina hissed.

In her coils Nat struggled, but he could not free himself. Aghast, I stood rooted to the floor, one hand cupped around my stone.

"Do you doubt me?" She tightened her grip on Nat. "Killing comes naturally to me, I promise you. And I myself am not so easily killed as you think." Humming the shifting song, she lengthened and thinned and changed color, until she was almost impossible to see against the cave walls. The only parts of her that were clearly visible were her yellow-green eyes, her serpent tongue, and the coils still wrapped tightly around Nat. "You can throw that stone, but will you hit me?"

I stared at her, afraid to move a muscle. How could I be sure of hitting such a target? And what would happen to Nat if I did?

Breathing heavily, Pressina fixed serpent eyes on me. "What, so silent? Is your tongue still forked?" She laughed. "Let me make a suggestion: You shall bargain for his life."

Nat twisted his head free and tried to speak. She lashed the tip of her tail against his mouth, silencing him.

"Yes, a bargain," Pressina said. "If you will sing for me for just a short while, your friend goes free. We will send him back up to the world unharmed."

We had been down this road before. "If I say yes, you will use me to drown the world. So he would die anyway."

Pressina looked put out, then gave a sly laugh. "Yes, I'm afraid those would be the terms. But if they do not please you, I can suggest others. For this friend is more than a friend, is he not?"

My heart began to race.

Her pupils flicked from Nat to me, narrowing to tiny crescents. "You love him, but he does not love you. He doesn't like your magic; he fears you are a monster. So they say in your world; so Melisande told me."

My cheeks went hot.

"Do you think I do not know what that is like?" Pressina said softly. "I, too, was called a monster by the man I loved. But here, in my own world, I have the power to change things. I have the power to make this man love you."

Don't listen, I told myself. *Don't listen.*

But her silky voice was mesmerizing. "Sing for me, Chantress, and I will keep him here just for you. You have my word on it. I need only a little of your power to finish my work, and after that I promise to give you what you want. He will forget the world above; he will care only for you. And together you will be happy—far happier than you ever could be on Earth."

I tried to close my ears, but the pull of the voice was too strong. I couldn't help imagining it—Nat in love with me, the two of us together always. . . .

"What is the Earth to you, anyway?" Pressina whispered. "Humans don't trust you. They hate and fear you. You don't belong there. It's only here that you can be truly happy. Only here that he can truly love you."

I found myself nodding. But then I saw Nat's eyes above Pressina's scales, wide open and angry. I froze, horrified. Even if Pressina was telling the truth, how could I sacrifice everything—Nat's free will, his sanity, the lives of everyone on Earth—to gain love? No, not even love. Just some cheap imitation of it.

Pressina had seen only the nod. "Yesssssssss. That's right, Chantress. Take off your stone and sing for me, and I will make you happy."

I nodded again. My fingers found their way to the chain and started to pull. It was a terrible choice, but I'd made my decision.

"Yessssssssss." The serpent tongue flicked, and the coils started to relax.

Yanking the necklace up, I screamed, "Jump, Nat!" As the Wild Magic of the place rushed in on me, I sang the shifting song at the top of my lungs, and I flung the stone at Pressina.

CHAPTER THIRTY-SEVEN
LEAVING

As Pressina twisted and Nat leaped, I sang a variation on the shifting song—changing not myself but the stone. I poured all my anger and all my fury and all my love for Nat into the singing, and in an instant the stone expanded to hold them all. When it careened into Pressina, it was as big as a boulder, impossible to evade.

With a screech that rivaled the cacophony of the Wild Magic, she blew apart. The blast shook the whole cave. Still half-caught in her spirals when the stone hit, Nat flew up in a whirlwind of green scales.

As loose rocks cascaded from the rumbling walls, I screamed Nat's name. Had I killed him, too?

The whirlwind let him go, and he fell to the cave floor. Dodging the rocks, I ran toward him, but my foot caught on something and I tripped. Reaching out, I found my stone, small and dull and more cracked than ever, but still in one piece on its chain.

When I flung it on, it did nothing to deafen me, but at least I was becoming more used to the music. Even if I couldn't understand much of it, it no longer made my head swim.

Rising to my feet, I rushed over to Nat. He was unconscious, burned, and bruised, and his limbs were sticking out at odd angles. I started to weep. He was still breathing, but for how long?

Looking around for something that would help him, I caught sight of another body, that of the sea snake that had been my mother. And there was Melisande, half-buried under rocks, and Odo, at the foot of the rock where my mother had stood . . .

Death. Death everywhere.

And then singing.

The music poured out of the small caves and rifts and tunnels. I couldn't understand the phrases, but it was entirely different in mood and tempo from what I'd heard from Pressina's horde.

Moments later, starfish and sharks and squids shot into the cave, dancing around me in a dazzling rainbow of colors. Soon the whole place shimmered with vibrant creatures and their ever-changing speckles and stripes and spots.

"You did it!" a school of fish shouted.

"You killed Pressina!"

"You freed us!"

"And we helped," a small shark-toothed creature said proudly. "We beat back the others."

"The last ones gave up when Pressina died," a squid told me. "Without her magic directing them, they seemed to forget why they were fighting us."

A school of fish cheered.

"But you do not rejoice," a starfish said to me. "You are sad?"

"My friend is dying." I gestured at Nat, choking on the words. "And my mother is gone, and Odo—"

"Take heart," the starfish said. It glided around to everyone who had fallen, even Melisande, then returned to me. "The one under the rocks has no life in her, and neither does Odo. And neither, I am afraid, does your mother."

My heart clenched.

"But your friend is not dead yet, not quite," said the starfish. "We must see what we can do for him."

"You can do something?" I asked.

"We can try," it told me. And it began to sing.

The song passed like lightning from creature to creature. Soon the whole cave was echoing with it. The hopeful melody twisted my heart, and so too did the sight of them, crowded around Nat, as if by their mere presence they could lend their strength to him.

Was there still a chance he could be saved? On Earth, there would be none. But perhaps here it was possible.

I started to sing with them.

As the music circled the room, the shifting started—not in the singers this time but in the ones who lay still. Nat's bruises and burns faded. His bent limbs straightened. But before he moved or spoke, the music faded.

"Don't stop," I begged.

The starfish waved one of its arms. "We have done all we can, Chantress. But simply being here in the Depths is a strain on him.

The guards who helped him escape say that he was struggling with the ether even then, and now he is badly injured. If you wish him to heal more fully, you must take him back to your own world."

A golden fish murmured to me, "There is no guarantee that he will heal, even in your world. He is very weak. But he will do better there than he will here."

"How do I bring him there?"

"We will help you through the wall between the worlds," the starfish said. "The rest is up to you. But you must go quickly. Now that your mother's song is no longer there to hold the gaps in the wall wide open, they are narrowing. Soon we may not be able to get you both through. Come!"

As the starfish spoke to me, two eels, singing tenderly, were popping out huge fins to scoop up Nat and bear him away.

I turned. "But my mother—"

"We will sing her into peace, and the others, too," the starfish said gently. And indeed, some of the creatures were already singing a melody so strange and sweet that my eyes brimmed again. My mother was returning to her human form, and if her body was mangled, her face was serene. Nearby lay Odo, whose terrible burn marks were fading; indeed, all of Odo was fading. And now my mother too was vanishing . . .

"Wait." I ran to her. I could barely see her cheek as I knelt to kiss her, but I could feel it, cool and soft beneath my lips. For a moment we were together again. Then the music twined around us, and she was gone from me forever.

My eyes were streaming, but the starfish was calling, and Nat needed me. At the starfish's bidding, I took hold of one of its arms, and we started down a tunnel, the finned eels carrying Nat behind us. The pale green light of the ether grew darker: grass-green, fir-green, forest-black. When we stopped, the starfish pointed to the still darker path in front of us. "We are at the thinnest part of the wall, the oldest hole. Will you take him through?"

"How do I carry him?" I asked.

"You simply need to keep hold of his hand," the starfish said. "For the journey you are making, that will be enough."

I grasped Nat's hand, which lay unresponsive in mine.

"Are you ready?" the starfish asked.

I hesitated. "After this, everything depends on me?"

"Yes," the starfish said. "But take courage. Listen!"

I closed my eyes. From the darkness came the very faint sound of a familiar Wild Magic. It was a song calling me home.

"Thank you," I said to the starfish. "Thank you, everyone. I'm ready to go now."

I started to sing. Suddenly the last vestige of green light was gone, and we were in the chilly, salty sea.

Up and up and up we went, and I thought of nothing but Nat's hand in mine and the Wild Magic on my lips. Although we were underwater, my lungs seemed inexhaustible, and I felt as if I could sing forever. Yet as we continued to climb, Nat grew heavier and heavier. Soon I was struggling to keep hold of his hand.

What if I wasn't strong enough to bring him all the way back? What if he was already dead?

Keep singing. Don't let go.

We kept moving upward, but the journey became harder and harder. And just as I thought it couldn't get any worse, Nat's hand slipped.

I caught hold of his fingertips. I didn't lose him. But the effort of holding on to him was excruciating. I couldn't concentrate on my singing anymore. I was hardly making a sound, and we were barely moving.

I had almost given up when Nat squeezed my fingers.

He was alive!

With new heart, I poured myself into my song. Moments later, we shot up into the shallows. Light was coming through the water. Our heads popped above the waves.

I saw sky.

And sand.

I couldn't find the strength to sing another note, but it didn't matter. The waves themselves were washing us in. I gulped in a sweet breath of air and let the tide take us.

CHAPTER THIRTY-EIGHT

AFTERMATH

Later I was told that Nat and I landed on a Thames sandbank, where fisherfolk rescued us. I was so weak, I had to be carried to safety along with him.

By the next day, I was well on my way to recovery. Not so, Nat. In a makeshift infirmary, he lay motionless, hardly breathing at all.

The infirmary was in St. James's Palace in London, where the King had moved his Court, now that the danger of flooding was over. Though not as high as the property on Cornhill, it was much bigger—and since it was well away from the Thames, it had sustained less damage than Whitehall and the Tower.

That night Norrie, Penebrygg, and I stood vigil together, with others coming and going at intervals. We burned candle after candle, determined not to miss a single movement or twitch—anything that would give us hope.

Earlier that day, from my bedside, I'd relayed the essentials of the battle against Pressina to the King. I'd wanted him to know that the floods were over, that it was safe to rebuild. Now, as the other watchers withdrew and the flames crept down the candles, I told Norrie and Penebrygg more about what I'd seen in the Depths.

They, in turn, told me how our world had fared while I'd been gone. Judging from the reports that were rolling in, London was the only place to have been struck by a great wave. I'd feared the whole city would be drowned, but the evacuation and my wind magic had muted the wave's impact. The death toll was in the hundreds, not thousands, and most of the city's buildings were still standing.

Nevertheless, the wave had devastated many Londoners. Although the Thames now meandered harmlessly within its banks, people's houses were half-buried in muck. Their belongings were ruined or washed away. Docks and entire shipping yards had vanished, so all supplies now had to be carried in by cart.

Already, however, Londoners had begun rebuilding.

"It's all most of them can talk about at the encampment," Norrie said. "Some are still in mourning, but the rest want to get on with their lives."

"Everywhere you go, you see people busy reclaiming their ground," Penebrygg said. "And sometimes the damage isn't as bad as it first looks. When I went out to my house yesterday, the lower floors were in a terrible state, but everything in the attic was intact—books and tools and clocks. I even found a spare pair of spectacles there, and I do believe they're every bit as good as the old ones." Putting his hand up to them, he yawned.

"You've been up too long, Dr. Penebrygg," Norrie said. "You should get some sleep."

"I can't leave the boy," Penebrygg said, but even as he spoke, he yawned again.

"There's a bed in the room next to this one," Norrie said. "You take it for now, and Lucy and I will sleep later. Nat's going to need round-the-clock care for a while, so it's best we sit up with him in shifts."

After some urging, Penebrygg finally agreed to this. After he left, Norrie said, "That man has been driving himself much too hard."

I nodded but never took my eyes off Nat. A few minutes later, I said, "Was that a blink?"

Norrie leaned in. "Maybe."

For hours I'd been holding Nat's hand. Now I squeezed it. "Nat, can you hear us?"

There was no response.

I tried again and again, until Norrie stopped me. "You can't bring him back by force of will alone, lamb. Now, if you had some magic for him, that would be different—"

"I don't." Healing had never been in my gift. I released his hand and turned away, choked with anxiety. "There is nothing I can do for him."

Norrie laid her hand on mine. "Child, you mustn't give up hope. And whatever happens, you mustn't blame yourself either."

"But I failed him, Norrie. I didn't bring us back fast enough. And I didn't protect him from Pressina." My nails dug into my palms. "I failed Mama, too. If I had been quicker—"

"Hush, child." Norrie put her arms around me. "You did your best. That's all you could do."

"But I failed her. I failed them both. If he dies too—"

"Don't say it!" Norrie hugged me tighter. "He's held on this long, Lucy. That must mean something. As for your mother, I see no failure of yours there. You rescued her from a terrible captivity."

"But she died." Tears stung my eyes.

"Yes." Norrie pulled back and smoothed my hair from my forehead. She'd always been far too matter-of-fact for tears, but in the faint orange glow of the banked fire, I saw that she was crying now. "And we all wish she hadn't. But I'll tell you this, child: What your mother wanted more than anything else in this life was to know she'd kept you safe, and to see you face-to-face again. And you gave her that." She hugged me again. "You gave her that."

It was the merest flicker of a flame against the black despair I felt. But it was all I had to hold on to—that and the hope that Nat would somehow survive.

† † †

Another day passed, and Nat still did not wake. Hour after hour, I stayed by his side. To my surprise and relief, there was no summons from the King—or anyone else—to take me away.

Left to myself, I would have kept watching him, but Norrie and Penebrygg were worried that I was still not completely recovered myself. Insisting that I take a break, they sent me to rest in the rooms that had been allocated to Norrie, just across the courtyard from the temporary infirmary. And there Sybil came to see me.

Dressed in soft woolens rather than silks, she gave me a ferocious hug and a look of deepest sympathy. "I'm so sorry, Lucy. About your mother, about Nat . . ."

When I winced, she changed the subject. "When did you last eat?"

"I can't remember—"

"Then I'll see that you're fed now. We must get you strong again." She rummaged through the food cupboard, then sat me down in front of a cold meat pie that Norrie had squirreled away earlier that day, after I'd left it untouched. "Now eat."

"I can't." I was too worried about Nat.

Sybil looked at me with her warmhearted eyes. "While there's life, there's hope, Lucy. At the encampments, I've seen people make astounding recoveries this week. But you really must eat. I'm going to stay here until you do."

As I picked at the pastry, she told me more about some of the recoveries she'd seen among the refugees. Modest though she was about her own part in this, I could read between the lines. She was working miracles. With Joan as her redoubtable second-in-command, and a score of volunteers at her disposal, she had requisitioned several noble houses and grounds in the higher parts of London and had found shelter for everyone who'd asked for it.

"Sometimes the rooms are very crowded," she admitted, "but it's something. And they're all getting soup every day, and bread and ale, too, when I can find them."

"They are lucky to have you on their side," I said, thinking I was lucky to have her on mine.

Sybil blushed. "I don't know about that, but it *is* awfully nice to be useful. I've told Henry that, even when this is over, I'm not going back to my old life. I know the kind of queen I want to be now." She looked at me with resolve in her eyes. "And I won't let anything stop me."

I smiled for the first time since I'd returned from the Depths. "Good."

"And what about you?' Sybil said more hesitantly. "I've told Henry he must give you time to recover—and I gather Norrie and Dr. Penebrygg have said much the same. He's given orders that you're not to be disturbed."

So that was why no one had summoned me.

Sybil went on. "What you've been through must have drained your powers, and I'm sure it will take a while for your magic to reach full strength again. But the city needs you, Lucy. As soon as there's anything you can give . . ."

I looked down at the table and the half-eaten pie. The truth was that my powers, though not fully restored, were recovering rapidly. If pressed, I could do some magic. But I didn't want to be pressed; I couldn't bear to leave Nat. Yet how could I say so? I was a Chantress—and that didn't leave much room for being human, even with a friend like Sybil.

The silence stretched out, and then Sybil put her hand on mine. "Come when you can, that's all I ask," she said with a compassion that made me wonder how much she guessed at. "And now, I'm afraid I must go. I need to see Henry."

"And I need to see Nat," I said.

Once we were out on the landing, Sybil gave me another swift hug. "I know you've been through a lot, Lucy—and Nat, too. But it's good to see that these terrible misfortunes have brought you two together again."

I looked at her, dismayed. Was that what she thought my vigil meant? Did other people think that too? Painful as it was, I'd have to set the record straight. "We're not together, Sybil. Nat's engaged to Lady Clemence."

Her gloved hand went to her lips. "To Clemence? Are you sure?"

"Yes." My heart twisted, remembering the two of them together on the stairs. "It happened just before the great wave hit. Gabriel told me."

"And Nat confirmed it?"

"I couldn't ask him. In the Depths, we . . . couldn't speak."

"Then maybe it's not true."

"Even if it isn't, I don't think there's any hope for us," I said steadily. "Some things just aren't meant to be."

You are a monster.

Sybil looked as if she wanted to ask questions but didn't quite dare.

"Lady Clemence hasn't been to see him, as far as I know," I went on. "But—"

"She isn't here," Sybil said quietly. "Her sister was injured by the wave, and Clemence is nursing her at her father's estate in Sussex."

So that was why Clemence hadn't come. Perhaps even now she was hoping to return to London and make her way to Nat's side.

"Did she say anything to you about Nat before she left?" I asked.

"No, but I saw her for only a moment that day, after the wave hit. She came to beg permission to leave my service and look after her sister. We didn't speak of anything else. Everything was in chaos." Sybil shook her head. "Half my ladies-in-waiting left me that day, though that may be for the best. Now I know who I can truly rely on."

In the distance a bell tolled the hour.

"Oh, Lucy, I'm so sorry, but I can't stay. Henry will be waiting—"

"It's all right." I started for the stairs. "We both have places we need to be."

And while I was in mine, looking after Nat, I wasn't going to allow myself to think about Clemence at all.

† † †

When I knocked on the infirmary door, it took some time for Penebrygg to open it.

"Ah." He stepped back, steadying his floppy cap over his tired face. "Come in, my dear. Come in. Norrie's gone off to badger the Royal Physician and see what else can be done for the boy. But I think it's just possible he's finally on the mend."

There was a note of good cheer in his voice that I hadn't heard for some time. "Has something happened?" I asked as he shut the door behind me.

"Nat's responding when I speak to him," Penebrygg said with suppressed excitement. "Just for the last half hour, mind you, and only in the barest way. He turns his head toward me. Nothing more. But that's an encouraging sign, don't you think?

"Oh, yes. May I see him?"

"Of course." He led me around a screen to the bed where Nat lay. "I'm wondering now if I should perhaps try to exercise his limbs for him—flex his fingers and such. Sir Barnaby was here earlier and suggested the idea to me. He's seen cases where the muscles withered away from lack of use, and we can't have that, can we?"

"No, no," I said, but I was only half-listening. From what Penebrygg had said, I'd hoped to find Nat looking stronger and more himself. But he looked just as he had when I'd been with him earlier that day—his long legs motionless under the counterpane, his skin pale over the strong bones of his face.

"Speak to him," Penebrygg urged me. "Talk to him just as you usually do, and see if he responds."

I curled the beloved fingers around mine. "Nat? It's Lucy."

He jerked his hand away.

Penebrygg looked startled. "He's not done that before. Try it again."

I slipped my hand into his, more gingerly this time. "Can you hear me, Nat?"

This time he not only yanked his hand away but his whole body started to shake.

"Nat, it's all right. It's just me."

The shaking became more violent. Though his eyes remained closed, his face was etched with panic.

"Come away, my dear." Penebrygg shepherded me back from the bed. "Come away now."

When we were on the other side of the screen, he said, "I must say, I didn't expect that to happen."

Neither did I. My own hands were shaking.

Penebrygg peered past the edge of the screen. "He seems all right now, but I shouldn't like to test him again. Very distressing for you both, I think. For all of us."

"I understand," I said. "I'll come back another time."

Penebrygg hesitated. "I think it might be best if you left it for a while, my dear. It may be that your voice reminds him of all he suffered down in Pressina's realm. And I think we can all agree that it's best he not be disturbed in any way just now."

I won't say a word, I wanted to tell him. *I'll sit in a corner, quiet as a mouse. Just let me stay near him.*

Yet perhaps even that would distress Nat. Perhaps the only thing I could do for him was stay away.

"Yes," I managed to say to Penebrygg. "Quite right. If he calls for me, then I'll come. But not until then."

I went out into the hall and pressed my palms against my burning eyes.

You are a monster.

CHAPTER THIRTY-NINE
REBUILDING

After that, I could not sleep. I could not eat. I was lost. All that night and into the next day, I didn't move from the rooms that Norrie and I shared. I refused to see people. I could not bear to show my face to anyone. I felt as if I no longer wanted to live.

You are a monster.

Norrie wasn't worried about me at first. She had heard about Nat's reaction from Penebrygg, and she thought it was just as well that I was taking a break from nursing. She wanted me to rest. But when she saw from the circles under my eyes that I wasn't sleeping, she became concerned.

"You mustn't take it so hard, lamb," she said as I stared blindly out the window. "Patients take all kinds of fancies when they're ill, and it means nothing at all. You should try speaking to him again tomorrow."

"Penebrygg thought I should stay away." My voice sounded leaden even to me.

"Well, if not tomorrow, then perhaps the day after. I'll have a word with Penebrygg myself, shall I?"

"No. He's right." It was almost too much effort to speak. "Just leave it—please."

Norrie was quiet for a moment, then laid a hand on my shoulder. "I'll leave it, if that's what you want. But in exchange, you need to do something for me. You need to put on your boots and your cloak, and you need to go out in the fresh air. Only for a little while, mind. But you need to do it right now."

I'd heard that tone of voice from Norrie before but not for a very long time. Back when I was a little girl and I was grieving for the loss of my mother, she'd spoken to me with just that mixture of kindness and absolute firmness. And I had always obeyed—as I found myself obeying now, despite everything.

Five minutes later I was walking through the courtyards of St. James. And once I was walking, I kept going, like a clockwork figure that dumbly marches on the path set for it, without seeing or feeling anything.

But I was hardly clear of the palace walls when someone rushed up to me.

"You're the Chantress, an't you?" It was a child—ragged and small but bold as a sparrow.

I forced myself to nod.

"There, what did I tell you?" she said to another child, even smaller and more ragged, standing behind her. She turned back to me in satisfaction. "I knew you'd come. I knew you'd help us with the house."

My sight sharpened. Beneath the satisfaction, there was something that looked a lot like desperation—a desperation even deeper than my own.

"House?" I repeated.

"Ma and Pa say they can't save it." There was a tremble in her voice; I'd been right about the desperation. "The mud's higher than I am, and when they tried to slop it out, the side wall gave way. And we've nowhere else to live."

A wall. A side wall that needed fixing. And a child who needed a home.

I could do something about that.

"Chantress?"

I took a deep breath and forced myself to stand tall. Maybe Nat didn't need me, but there were others who did.

"Show me," I said to the child, and I offered her my hand.

† † †

A week later, I stood on the northern section of London Bridge, looking out over its broken edge. Far below me, the Thames sparkled in the late afternoon sunlight, alive with small skiffs and rowboats that people had salvaged from the flood.

It was hard to believe that this was the same wild river that had smashed the bridge down. But then, it wasn't the river that had been to blame.

"So you see the difficulty, Chantress." The King rested his hand on a wooden rail that had been hastily affixed to prevent people from falling. "The cracks in the remaining parts of the bridge can be mended easily enough, but in order to join the two parts of the bridge together, we'll need to sink in new supports. And we'd want to get them in quickly, before winter sets in. Do you think you could hold back the water while we do that?"

I listened to the Thames for a moment before answering. There were so many strains in its music. It could be demanding, haughty, peaceful, and mischievous all at the same time. But ever since my return I had not heard a single note that truly worried me.

"Yes," I said to the King. "Of course I can hold the water back for you."

Beside us, Sir Christopher Linnet looked up from the wide book where he was sketching out plans. Ever since the King had put him in charge of the rebuilding effort, that book went with him everywhere. "Now that I have you both here, I wonder if we might discuss some other projects—"

"We need to focus on the essentials, Kit," the King cautioned him.

"Yes, yes," Sir Christopher nodded. "The bridge, the exchange, a place for Parliament to assemble—I have that down here. But it would be foolish to ignore all the other possibilities that present themselves . . ."

I looked out across the river to low-lying Southwark and down to the curve of the river at Whitehall and Westminster. So much devastation—and yet it was true that there were great possibilities as well. We'd had to put off the opening of Parliament by three months, but the flood had given us an excuse to rebuild and enlarge the traditional chambers at Westminster. All of us were determined to build a city that was stronger and more resilient than ever.

Even Gabriel, now recovered from his head injury, was working around the clock, to the great admiration of the remaining ladies-in-waiting. Although he was brusque with me, I'd heard him bantering with a few of them the other day. It was a relief to know that my refusal hadn't destroyed his buoyant nature.

As for me, I was a long way from banter, but at least I was keeping one foot in front of the other. There were times when it tore me apart to think of how Nat had pulled away from me—and how even now, a full week later, he still hadn't recovered. But London needed me, and that kept me from sinking into despair again. Day by day, I could see that I was helping to bring London back to life.

And Londoners appreciated what I was doing. Instead of holding up iron crosses, they cheered me for even the smallest acts of magic—drying a cellar, shoring up a wall, retrieving a carriage wheel from the riverbed. Their goodwill helped keep me going.

"We have done a great deal already, of course," Sir Christopher said, flipping through his book of plans. "But rather than merely rebuild this city, I propose that we *redesign* it. We must seize the moment we have been given. Take this bridge, for instance." He held up one of his sketches. "We could simply replace what is missing, of course. But how much better if we were to build an entirely new bridge, a bridge along Italian lines, with a much more graceful structure—"

"We will discuss it later in Council," the King said firmly. "But I'm not at all certain it could be considered essential work, Kit."

"It depends on how you define 'essential,'" Sir Christopher argued. "This bridge would be a thing of beauty. A beacon for the ages. Speaking of which, Your Majesty, we might think about rebuilding St. Paul's, too. It was a rather decrepit structure to begin with, and I strongly suspect the floods have weakened the foundations. I have some drawings here . . ."

"And I should like to see them sometime," the King said. "But just at the moment there is something more critical I must discuss with the Chantress."

As Sir Christopher wrestled with his sketchbook, the King motioned for me to accompany him back down the bridge. "You have done magnificent work for us here in London, Chantress. But there are other parts of the kingdom that were hard hit by flooding too. Of course the damage was worst here, but now that the situation is improving, I should like to send you on a quick tour of the coastline—"

"All of it?"

"As much as possible, yes. Repair whatever you can. Of course we'll need you to come back to London to fix the bridge and help us prepare for the opening of Parliament. Once that's done, you can go back out again. This crisis has revealed all kinds of weaknesses in our sea defenses, and I expect there will be enough work to keep you occupied all winter and well into the spring. Perhaps even for a full year."

So he was sending me back on the road. I would be continually on the move again, continually lonely. My heart fell at the thought. But perhaps a life of loneliness was the only one open to me. Perhaps it was all I could hope for.

Yet something in me rebelled.

"Your Majesty," I said quietly, "I think that is more than I can take on."

He looked at me, eyes startled and very blue beneath his copper hair. "What's that?"

"I can't do it," I said more firmly. "I pledged myself to serve this kingdom, and I will. I want to. But I can't do everything you want me to do."

In the Depths, emotions were a source of power. And perhaps they could be in this world too—if I stopped damping them down, if I approached them with honesty. I wasn't shifting; I wasn't changing my form. But with every word I spoke, I could feel that I was becoming more truly myself.

"I've been on the road for the past year and a half, and I'm weary," I said. "Norrie is growing older, and I see too little of her. I miss Sybil, too. And I want to make some kind of home out of Audelin House before it falls apart. I'll go to the places that most need me, I promise you. But I can't go everywhere, and I can't travel all year long. Not anymore. I'm sorry, but that's how it is. I'm a Chantress, but I'm human, too."

The King didn't flare up in anger, or crumple in despair. Instead he looked resigned, almost as if he'd been expecting me to say this for some time.

"I'm sorry to hear it, Chantress. I won't lie. But I can't say I wasn't warned. Walbrook used to say I took too much advantage of your magic, that it would be better for everyone if it were employed less often. Penebrygg's said much the same. And Sybil has been worried that I'm working you to death." He sighed, then gave me a rueful smile. "I can't promise to leave you alone; we need you too much. But from now on, I promise to think more carefully before I call on you. A bit more self-reliance will do us no harm."

I felt as if a heavy burden had been lifted from my shoulders—and now that it was gone, it was much easier to give what I could.

"I still do want to help," I said to the King. "I meant it when I said that I would go to the places that most need me. Tell me what towns have been hardest hit, and let me see what I can do."

"There's Gravesend in Kent, down the Thames from us," the King said immediately. "Their docks and their ferries were swept away by the backwash of the great wave, and they've been begging me to send you. And there's Tilbury Fort, too. You know how critical it is to our defenses—and we've been told half the cannon are gone, and all the gunpowder is soaked through."

I'd been reluctant to leave London while Nat was still unconscious, but these places weren't very far away. And—as long as I was being honest with myself—I had to admit it wasn't as if Nat needed or wanted me here.

"I'll go today," I said. "With some of my men, if they can be spared." They had been working hard on the rebuilding effort.

"Of course," the King said. "And when you get back, you must take whatever rest you need."

† † †

As we left the bridge, a twisted piece of illustrated paper fluttered in the brisk wind and landed by my feet. Glancing down, I saw the word "monster" and froze. Was this a new broadside about me? Despite all I'd done, did people still see me as a horror, a freak?

With dread, I picked up the sheet.

The King had turned away to have a word with Sir Christopher, who had caught up with us. "About those sketches . . ."

Flattening out the paper, I saw the title plainly: OUR ANGEL SLAYS THE MONSTER. Beneath it was a woodcut of a singing woman with wings, slaying a fearsome beast. A scan of the lyrics revealed that the woman with wings was meant to be me.

I stared at the title again. Angel? Monster? Whatever they called me, it had nothing to do with reality. The truth was far more complicated.

Shaking my head, I crumpled the paper. Maybe I couldn't stop other people from judging me, but I could stop looking to them for approval. Maybe most people would never be able to accept me for who I really was—not the broadside makers, not the Court gossips, not even Nat—but I didn't have to follow suit.

I could still decide to accept myself.

I held up the crumpled paper and let the brisk November wind take it from me. As I watched the paper fly away, I felt lighter than I had for a long time.

† † †

It took me five full days to set things to rights in Gravesend and Tilbury. I couldn't resent the time I spent there—the people were too grateful, and they were in desperate need—but I was glad to get back to London.

My men and I came into the city in the small hours of the night, on the incoming tide. When we reached St. James's Palace, only the guards were up, and even the torches were giving up the ghost.

"I think we'll wait till the morning to make our report to the King," I said to Captain Knollys after we passed through the gatehouse. "You and the men should try to get a little rest before then."

Knollys raised a graying eyebrow. "And you?"

Just behind us, Barrington piped up, "Chantress, would you like an escort to your rooms?"

I had to smile. He was ready to drop, I knew, but he was loyal to the core. They all were.

"Thank you, Barrington, but it's not far. I'll be fine on my own." I held up my hand as they started to protest. "All of you, get some sleep!"

After parting from them, I made my way toward the rooms I shared with Norrie. When I reached our courtyard, I hesitated.

I couldn't see Norrie's windows from here—they were on the other side of the building—but the infirmary window was in plain sight. And Norrie and Penebrygg had kept a light burning there even in the darkest hours.

There was no light there now. Did its absence mean Nat was—

Not letting myself even think the word, I ran up the stairs and knocked on Norrie's door, softly at first, and then louder.

At last I heard footsteps coming. Norrie pulled back the door. "Who—" she began, and then she saw my face. "Oh, child, you're back at last!"

She dragged me over the threshold and steered me through the darkened room. "We've been waiting and waiting. The most wonderful news—"

She opened the inner door. There was Nat, standing by the window, wide awake.

CHAPTER FORTY
MANY WATERS

"Lucy." Nat came forward, with a note in his voice that made me tremble.

Norrie backed into the outer room, murmuring something about mending. The door closed, and Nat and I were shut in together. I stared at him, hardly able to believe my eyes.

He stopped well short of me. "Is something wrong?"

"No," I said quickly. "It's just . . . you're awake."

He smiled. "Yes."

"For how long?"

"Almost three days now."

"And you're well? You're not feverish or injured or—"

"I'm fit as can be," he assured me. "The only trouble is that I've been waking very early. I suppose it's because I'm all caught up on sleep."

There were merely a few feet between us now. I wanted to close the gap, but I didn't have the right to. Looking for something to say, I seized on the first thing that came to mind. "Have you seen many people yet?"

"A few. Sybil, for one." There was an odd look in his eyes. "She came to see me the day before yesterday—and we had a very interesting conversation."

I felt a prickle of apprehension. "You did?"

"She wanted to know if I was betrothed to Lady Clemence. She said Gabriel had told you I was." He looked at me with exasperation. "You believed him?"

Was he saying it wasn't true? My heart began to race. "You said you were going to find someone else. I saw you together, and Gabriel said that he'd talked with her father, and the earl was drawing up a marriage contract—"

"Then the earl was getting rather ahead of himself," Nat said. "He's been angling for a way into the King's inner circle for some time now, and he thinks an alliance with me will get him what he wants. And perhaps he finds it difficult to believe I would refuse an earl's daughter."

"But—you have?"

"I came close to saying yes," Nat admitted. "He caught me just after you and I had quarreled, you see, and instead of giving him a point-blank refusal, I asked for time to consider the idea. I thought of what you'd said, that I ought to choose someone else, someone who could give me a normal life. By that light, Clemence would be a very suitable match. She's kind; she's fun to sing with; she agrees with everything I say. So, yes, I was tempted to propose to her and be done with you."

My heart contracted.

"But then I saw Clemence herself the next day," Nat said, "and I realized that proposing wouldn't be fair to her, or to me, or to you. My heart wasn't in it." His steady eyes held mine as he came closer. "I've told you before, and I'll tell you again: The one I want is you."

I felt as if someone had handed me the sun—dazzled but disbelieving.

"I know you think it will never work between us," Nat said. "But you're wrong. Of course we'll argue sometimes; we're only human. But I don't want to be with someone who always agrees with me. I'm a scientist; honest arguments don't scare me. And I don't care tuppence what the broadsides say about us, or what the Court gossips think."

I didn't either. Not anymore. That wasn't what was holding me back.

"All that matters to me," Nat said, "is that you're Lucy—and I love you." When I didn't speak, he looked at me, suddenly uncertain. "But maybe you don't feel the same way?"

There was a knot in my throat. "It's just that . . . I'm not sure that's how you really do feel, deep down. When you were asleep, you wanted me to go away."

He looked at me in dismay. "I did?"

"When I spoke, you pulled away from me in terror." It was hard to speak; I had to force the words out. "That's why I stopped visiting. Penebrygg thought it best."

"He was wrong." Nat drew me down onto the high-backed bench by the fire. "Lucy, if I looked terrified, it was because I was afraid for you. When I was asleep, I had nightmares that Pressina had trapped you, that I couldn't get the stone to you quickly enough, that you were calling out to me in agony—"

I must have looked unsure, because he said, "It's true, Lucy. But even if it weren't, you can't hold a man responsible for what he does in his sleep. And an enchanted sleep, at that."

"But I saw the same expression on your face when you were awake," I said softly.

He frowned. "When?"

"When I turned into a serpent. The look you gave me," I said. "The horror . . ."

"No!" He cupped my face. Under his dark brows, his eyes were clear and direct and loving. "I won't lie. When you changed form, I was stunned. I didn't know you could do that. But I was grateful, too, because I'd thought everything was lost, that Pressina was going to kill you, and then you turned the tables on her."

"And when I swooped up to you?"

"I was horrified, yes—but not by you. It was the situation that was so dreadful. I was afraid I wouldn't be able to get the stone to you, that Pressina would attack you first."

"You weren't thinking that I was a monster?"

"No." He looked genuinely surprised. "Why should I?"

"I was a serpent, Nat. I had scales. And claws. And teeth."

He smiled. "It was amazing to see, you know. You twisted in the air. You *flew*. And yet somehow you were still Lucy all the time. How did you do that?"

There was not a trace of repugnance or fear on his face, only curiosity and wonder.

And now there was wonder inside me as well. I'd always known that Nat was a born scientist, that he tried to keep an open mind about everything. But I hadn't realized, until now, quite how open his heart was too.

"Do you know what's truly amazing?" I asked him.

"What?"

"You."

Still smiling slightly, he raised an eyebrow. "Because I don't think you're a monster?"

"Among other things." I touched my hand to his rough chin. "There is no one else like you in all the world, Nat. And I love you for it."

Outside, a gust of wind rattled the window, and a distant bell chimed. Nat traced the back of my hand with his fingertips. "Then will you marry me?"

Again I stood at the top of a precipice, where everything depended on what I said next. And as before, there were so many reasons to say no. We both had a lot to lose, and there would be many challenges ahead of us. No magic on Earth could guarantee that everything would turn out well for us. No magic could make our life an easy one.

But this time I wasn't going to make my decision out of fear. I was going to make it out of hope. I was going to make it out of love.

"Yes," I said.

I reached for Nat, and he reached for me. And when our lips met, I heard music—the music of joy.

HISTORICAL NOTE

This book is steeped in both magic and history. Which bits are real?

If you were to go back to the real London of 1670, you would see many of the same sights I describe here. Westminster really was a low-lying place built on marshy ground, the Tower was prison as well as palace, and Cornhill was and is one of London's highest points. Although the gargantuan Whitehall Palace sounds like fiction, it was real too. A true "city within a city," it did indeed have more than fifteen hundred rooms, as well as a Great Hall and tiltyards and courtyards galore. It burned to the ground in 1698, but if you go to London today, you can visit the Banqueting House, which survived.

A few caveats: Even though the story takes place in 1670, the overall geography of *Chantress* London is roughly that of the real-world London of 1665, before the reshaping of the city by Sir Christopher Wren and others. Lucy's London also has more embankments than actually existed at the time—but there were some real-life seventeenth-century plans for more.

I wrote much of this book during the winter of 2013–2014, when we had record rainfall here in England, with terrible winter storms. At times I felt as though I had only to watch the news to see how flooding could affect the country. To get the details right, however, I also read many articles and studied many maps of London, past and present. My account of the rebuilding of London owes a great deal to accounts of the actual rebuilding of the city after the Great Fire 1666.

While Charlton Park is a figment of my imagination, it's modeled on genuine enclosures of the 1600s. The enclosure process—which began centuries earlier—was hugely controversial, and it really did cause great hardship for ordinary people. Despite riots against it, eventually enclosure became the rule, changing the British landscape forever.

Other "real bits": The term "elemental" was used by the real Paracelsus more or less the way I've used it here. Actual British monarchs almost never married commoners, and when they did, they courted trouble. Broadsides really were the "gutter press" of their day, with catchy lyrics, gaudy woodcut illustrations, and enormous popular appeal. Posted in pubs and plastered on walls, they had a huge circulation.

While not strictly speaking real, the legend of Melusine is a very old one. Its roots run especially deep in France and the Low Countries, but the story was popular in many parts of medieval and Renaissance Europe, and many versions exist.

ACKNOWLEDGMENTS

Warmest thanks to Kit Sturtevant, Nancy Werlin, Jo Wyton, Paula Harrison, Kristina Cliff-Evans, and Teri Terry, who read the whole book in draft and gave me such helpful comments. You are a fabulous team of readers.

Many thanks to my editor, Karen Wojtyla, for her patience and insight, and to assistant editor Annie Nybo for helping in myriad ways. My thanks also go to publicist Siena Koncsol and associate art director Michael McCartney, and to Bridget Madsen, Bara MacNeill, and Chrissy Noh.

I appreciated Julie Just's support as I started this book, and I'm grateful to everyone at Pippin Properties for seeing me through. Special thanks to Holly McGhee, whose kindness and good sense are invaluable.

Much as I love spending time in the *Chantress* world, writing a trilogy on deadline has been no easy task. Loving thanks to my dear family and friends for their encouragement and good cheer. I'd be lost without you.

Cheers to my choir, who helped me find the magic in music even on difficult days. I'm also grateful to all the readers, reviewers, and bloggers who have taken these books into their hearts. I also appreciated the collective wisdom of the Mid-Career Writer's Gathering at WisCon37.

Deepest thanks to my daughter, who graces my days with her stories and songs, and to my husband, brilliant reader and best friend. Life with you is the best music I know.